By Trevor Douglas

The Bridgette Cash Mystery Thriller Series

Cold Comfort

Cold Trail

Cold Hard Cash

The Cold Light of Day

Out In The Cold

Hot And Cold

I finished this book during the height of the COVID-19 pandemic and will never forget the actions of the first responders and healthcare workers who risked it all to save untold lives. This book is dedicated to their untold stories of sacrifice and dedication.

Vinci Books

vinci-books.com

Published by Vinci Books Ltd in 2025

1

Copyright © Trevor Douglas 2020

The author has asserted their moral right to be identified as the author of this work in accordance with the Copyright, Designs and Patents Act 1988. This work is a work of fiction. Names, characters, places and incidents are the product of the author's imagination or are used fictitiously. Any resemblance to actual persons, living or dead, places and incidents is entirely coincidental.

All rights reserved. No part of this publication may be copied, reproduced, distributed, stored in any retrieval system, or transmitted in any form or by any means, including photocopying, recording, or other electronic or mechanical methods, nor used as a source for any form of machine learning including AI datasets, without the prior written permission of the publisher.

The publisher and the author have made every effort to obtain permissions for any third party material used in this book and to comply with copyright law. Any queries in this respect should be brought to the attention of the publisher and any omissions will be corrected in future editions.

A CIP catalogue record for this book is available from the British Library.

Paperback ISBN: 9781036702021

Printed and bound in Great Britain by Clays Ltd, Elcograf S.p.A.

Monday 3:40 PM

Bridgette paused at the top of the rise to take in the scene below. Despite her tall athletic build, she was slightly out of breath from her walk up the steep incline from where she'd parked her car. Breathing in deeply, she studied the paradox before her.

The serenity of the fir trees swaying gently on a light breeze at the edge of Lake Barnett was in stark contrast to the flurry of activity she observed below. Shielding her eyes from the late afternoon sun, she recognized one man instantly as the group of four worked together near the water's edge. She'd worked with him before and knew him to be a consummate professional. The other three people she'd never met, but she figured they were just as capable. Although she was out in the open and less than a hundred feet away, nobody looked in her direction. Their focus was entirely on a fifth man who was floating face down about fifteen feet from the water's edge. Partially obscured by a tall cluster of reeds, it was impossible for her to see anything more than a vague outline of the man's body from her current position.

Her boss, Chief Inspector Felix Delray, had told her the man had probably been dead for a week when he'd assigned her the case, but had conceded that was mostly a guess based on the sketchy details phoned in by the witness who had discovered the body.

Bridgette wasn't afraid of death. She had seen her fair share of dead bodies in her short career as a homicide detective. However, the smell of putrefying human flesh always made her nauseous. She'd come close to vomiting several times during her first murder case when she had watched the forensic team exhume the body of a young woman from a shallow grave. It had taken all her resolve to hold herself together and she knew today would be no different. She marveled at the stoic determination of the forensic team as the smell of the decaying corpse assaulted her nostrils as it wafted up on the gentle breeze. Bracing herself for what lay ahead, Bridgette withdrew a small tube of Vicks VapoRub from her jacket pocket and rubbed a liberal amount on her top lip. She waited a couple of seconds until the vapor was all she could smell before making her way down the slope through knee-high grass that was still wet from overnight rain. When she was about twenty feet from the water's edge, the four turned as one to acknowledge her presence as she passed under the police tape. Three of the team gave her a subtle nod. With their faces mostly hidden behind surgical masks, it was impossible to tell if their nods were accompanied by a friendly smile or not, but under the circumstances, she didn't think so.

The fourth member of the group, Doctor Ray Warner, was the Vancouver city coroner. Bridgette had worked with

Warner on previous cases and had enormous respect for his abilities.

Warner bent down and removed a surgical mask from a large plastic medical box he seemed to carry everywhere and handed it to Bridgette. His voice was clear enough as he said through his mask, "You have any trouble finding us, Bridgette?"

"No, Ray. The chief's instructions were good enough."

"Where did you park?"

Despite the Vicks, Bridgette found the smell of the body overpowering and waited until she had her mask fitted before she responded, "Back on the road behind your van."

Warner nodded once and then turned back to face the lake. They watched for a moment as the three forensic technicians fitted what looked like fishing waders over their white overalls before heading to the water's edge. One of the two women in the group carried a digital camera which prompted Warner to say, "We've been here about an hour and have searched and photographed the surrounding area but have found nothing significant. We'll take photos as a record of each step of the recovery, so this could take a while."

"Any idea of the cause of death?"

"Not yet. It looks like a drowning, but the reeds are making it all but impossible to get a good look at him. All we can tell so far is that he's a big guy, maybe six two or three. The uniformed officers here with us are searching around the lake's edge for any sign of a boat or canoe that he might have fallen from."

Warner pointed to a walkie-talkie he carried on his utility belt and added, "They'll contact me if they find anything, but I haven't heard from them yet."

They watched in silence as the technicians waded into

the water before Bridgette said, "The witness who called this in? Have you spoken to him yet?"

"Yeah, *she* met us at the road and then brought us down to the body but didn't want to stay, which I can understand."

Bridgette fought the urge to vomit. After regaining her composure, she responded, "She lives around here?"

Warner dragged his gaze away from the technicians who were carefully making their way through the reeds in about three feet of water and pointed south. "The woman's name is Julie Playfair. She brought her dog down here for a walk. That's when she discovered the body. She lives about half a mile further up the road. There are only a few houses on this road, and she lives in the last one on the left. You won't have any trouble finding it, so I told her to go home and wait for you."

Bridgette turned her gaze back to the lake and watched for a moment as the technicians continued their work. Their progress was slow. She estimated the dense clump of reeds at the water's edge was close to twenty-five feet in diameter. They were approaching the body from two sides, wading a single step at a time before stopping to search for evidence and take more photographs.

She said, "This recovery isn't going to be quick, is it?"

Warner shook his head. "We're going to be here awhile."

Bridgette closed her eyes for a moment. When she felt confident she could speak without heaving, she said, "This might be a good time to interview the witness."

"I expect it will be another hour at least before we get the body out of the water, so unless you see value in watching us work, go see her now."

Bridgette needed no more encouragement and said a

brief goodbye to Warner before heading back up the hill again. She kept her mask on until she reached the top of the rise. After removing it, she turned and looked back at the scene below, and zipped up her jacket to keep out the cold. Shielding her eyes from the glare of the sunlight that reflected off the lake, she watched the technicians progress through the reeds. She estimated they were now less than ten feet from the body but were still patiently stopping after each step to photograph and carefully search for evidence before moving forward again. Bridgette frowned. Already there was something about the scene she didn't like. She would talk to Warner about it when she returned, but for now it was time to interview Julie Playfair.

Julie Playfair lived in a two-storey white colonial at the end of Barnett Road. The house was set back from the road and partially hidden by mature trees in the front garden. After turning left onto the driveway, Bridgette noticed a late-model, gray two-door Mercedes coupe parked out front at an odd angle, almost as if the driver had been in a rush to get inside. As she drove up the driveway Bridgette presumed the car belonged to Playfair. The front door of the house was opened by a woman in her mid-fifties with a stylish bob haircut. Dressed in designer jeans, boots and jacket, the ashen look on the woman's face belied her professional image.

She made no move to leave her house watching Bridgette warily as she got out of her car and made her way across the gravel driveway to the front door.

When Bridgette was about ten feet from the front door, she said, "Good afternoon, I'm looking for Julie Playfair."

In a cultured voice, the woman responded, "You've found her. And you are?"

"Detective Bridgette Cash from Vancouver Metro Police," said Bridgette as she held out her business card. Playfair took it and said, "Let's go inside, it's much warmer there."

Bridgette followed Playfair down a short hallway into a sitting room on the right. Playfair motioned her to sit on a leather sofa and then said, "Can I get you a cup of coffee before we start?"

Bridgette politely declined and waited for Playfair to be seated in a chair opposite. "This must have been a big shock for you."

Playfair let out a lengthy breath. "It sure was..."

"Perhaps you could tell me in your own words what happened?"

Playfair nodded several times, almost as if collecting her thoughts before she answered, "I travel regularly for work and have spent the last three weeks at our head office."

"What you do for a living?"

"I'm a contracts lawyer. One of my firm's principal clients is acquiring another company which required my presence in Rochford. I normally don't like to be away that long, but sometimes you have to do what you have to do."

"And when did you get back?"

"Yesterday afternoon. I picked up Bonnie on my way home from the airport and then took her for a long walk as soon as we got home."

"Bonnie?"

"She's my German Shorthaired Pointer. She's actually the one who discovered the body. We were walking down by the lake when she started to bark frantically at something in the reeds. I thought it may have been a sick or injured bird at first, but when I got closer and smelled that smell, I knew it wasn't a bird…"

Playfair closed her eyes for a moment and then continued, "I didn't get too close. As soon as I realized what it was, I put Bonnie on her lead and came home and called the police. I went back and waited on the road and then led them down to the spot where he'd drowned. But I didn't want to hang around, so I came back here to wait for you."

Bridgette made a note to check Playfair's travel movements later. She could see by the distressed look on Playfair's face that she was probably telling the truth and gently asked, "Can I call you Julie?"

Playfair nodded.

"Julie, do you live here alone?"

"Yes, it's just Bonnie and me now. My husband and I divorced three years ago and he now lives on the other side of the country."

"You didn't notice anything suspicious before you left?"

"No, nothing out of the ordinary. Barnett Road is very quiet. We all look out for each other."

"How many people live on this road?"

"There are five houses on the road, but only four of them are occupied. Long ago they were all working farms, but over time the farmland got consolidated and the houses on this road got sold to city people like me who were looking for a quieter life in the country."

"So all your neighbors work in the city?"

"Mostly. Jerry and Nancy who lived next door are retired now, but they've been in Europe for the past two months."

Bridgette made another note to get a list of all Playfair's neighbors before she left.

Playfair commented, "Nothing like this ever happens here. It's one of the reasons I moved here."

Bridgette nodded politely and then changed tack. "Do you get much traffic on this road other than your neighbors?"

"No. As you can see out front, the road ends at my property."

"What about tourists or fishermen interested in the lake?"

Playfair shifted in her seat. "It's not a big lake and I'm told with all the reeds and silt, there aren't too many places to fish on this side. I've seen the occasional boat out in the middle when I've been walking Bonnie, but boats close to this side of the lake are rare."

"You haven't had any flooding in the lake recently?"

"No."

"What about currents?"

Playfair frowned. "Not that I know of. The lake is normally very still, so much so that at times the water around the edge gets quite stagnant. Why do you ask?"

"The water is only three feet deep where the body was found."

Playfair looked slightly confused as she replied, "I'm not sure what you're getting at?"

"When bodies are found in a lake, the normal assumption is the person has drowned. But this man's body was found in the middle of a thicket of reeds. It's highly unlikely the body managed to drift that far into the reeds, and it would also seem unlikely that a grown man would accidentally drown in just three feet of water so close to the lake's edge."

Playfair nodded. "I see what you're getting at. So you think he was murdered?"

Monday 4:48 PM

Bridgette spent another forty minutes interviewing Julie Playfair. Her suggestion that the man might have been murdered had shocked Playfair but had hardly surprised Bridgette. The rest of the interview had been as much about evaluating Playfair's honesty as it was about discovering additional information.

After studying Playfair's body language as she answered each question, Bridgette concluded the witness was unlikely to have been involved in the man's death, but she would still make the necessary checks on her story. After making her way back to the crime scene, she was glad she'd kept her mask as she descended the slope again. Stopping about halfway down, she studied the forensic team at work while she applied a fresh batch of VapoRub to her top lip.

The man's body had now been removed from the water and was currently resting face up on a flat piece of land about ten feet from the water's edge. As part of her criminology degree, Bridgette had taken several subjects in human anatomy and knew the bloated corpse was in an advanced stage of decomposition. She was reluctant to proceed any further. The swollen features and greenish-black color of the man's skin made visual identification all but impossible and while that made the man difficult to look at, it was the smell that was causing Bridgette to balk. She recalled some facts she'd learned about decomposition of bodies in water and how it was a perfect breeding ground for bacteria. And these microorganisms were now well on their way to dissolving the man's internal organs.

She descended the rest of the slope and stopped a few feet short of the team who were crowded around the body.

Warner looked up as she approached and said, "Good timing, Bridgette."

"What have I missed?"

The forensic photographer continued taking photographs while Warner moved away from the body. "White male, around thirty years of age, but I'll have a better idea after I've done a full examination. There's no ID on him and I'd say he's been in the water about a week."

"Cause of death?"

"Almost certainly gunshot wounds."

"He was shot?"

"He's got a bullet hole in his back."

"Did that happen here or elsewhere?"

"Hard to say. He was floating high in the water, which is usually a fair indication he didn't drown, but I won't know for sure until I've done a full examination."

Bridgette took a couple of steps towards the lake. "When I saw the location of the body in the middle of the reeds, I did wonder. It seemed hard to imagine a body floating that far on a current into such a dense thicket."

Warner stood alongside her. "Give me forty-eight hours and I'll have a lot more information for you."

The Cold Light of Day

"There were no signs of any drag marks around here?"

"No, but I wouldn't expect to find any anyway. They've had two overnight rainstorms in the last week and any trace would be long gone."

Bridgette turned and looked up at the rise she had just come down.

"It's a remote area. It's possible he was shot here, perhaps even as he hid in the reeds, but I think it's more likely he was killed somewhere else."

"I agree. This is as good a place as any to dump a body."

"What's the plan from here, Ray?"

"We'll be here for a while yet completing our initial investigation. If the uniforms don't uncover anything else, we'll bag the body and head back to town."

"How long until we can get a DNA sample?"

"I'll make it a priority. There's a good chance…"

Warner was interrupted by his forensic photographer. "Doc, come take a look at this."

Warner walked back to the huddle of technicians to see what they'd discovered. Bridgette reluctantly followed but stopped about eight feet away and watched as the photographer pointed to the man's short-sleeved shirt and said, "He's got a tattoo."

Warner moved in closer and said, "Where?"

Using a pointer that resembled a knitting needle, the photographer pointed at the man's right arm and said, "On his upper bicep."

Warner produced a tiny flashlight from his pocket and knelt down. After gently lifting the man's sleeve, he studied the marking for about thirty seconds. "This could help with identification."

Bridgette hadn't been standing close enough to see what Warner saw. "What did you find, Ray?"

"He's got what looks like a dragon tattoo. It's hard to make out because of the decay and mud that's covering his body, but we'll clean it up and photograph it again when we get back to the lab."

Warner stood up and then added, "With a little digital enhancement, I'm sure we'll get something we can use."

Bridgette studied the man's body for a moment. Now getting somewhat used to the smell, she noticed for the first time he was wearing a short-sleeved shirt, steel cap boots and work pants.

She noted, "He could have come straight off a construction site."

Warner nodded. "We'll have to trawl through Missing Persons records. Hopefully the clothing might help narrow down the search."

"I'll make a start on it when I get back to the office. It's not a lot to go on, but you never know."

"If I come up with anything else significant, I'll call you."

Bridgette took this as her cue and said, "I'm going to call in on each of the other residents before I head back into town."

She said her goodbyes to the forensic team and then headed back up the rise. Pausing at the top, she looked back at the setting sun which was beginning to cast an eerie orange shadow across the lake. Thankful that she could breathe fresh air again, Bridgette stood for a moment watching the forensic team setup lighting equipment to help them continue their work. The silence was interrupted by her phone vibrating in her pocket.

Bridgette retrieved it and checked caller ID hoping she

could let it go through to voicemail, but when she saw the number, she knew it was a call she needed to take.

"Hi, Chief."

"Hey, Bridgette. Just called to see how it's going out there?"

"Ray's team has just recovered the body."

"A drowning?"

"No. He's been shot in the back."

There was a pause before Delray replied, "Well, it looks like you just got your next murder case."

Bridgette filled Delray in on the sketchy details she had so far and then gave him a brief summary of her interview with Julie Playfair. Delray listened without interrupting and then said, "So what's your next move?"

"I'm just heading back to my car. I'll do initial interviews with the other residents who live on the road if they're home before I head back to the office."

"You could be hours."

"I guess."

More silence before Delray said, "I can't stay late tonight, I promised my wife I'd take her to the ballet ... but I did want to talk to you before tomorrow."

Bridgette had a fair idea where the conversation was heading but asked anyway, "What about?"

"Your new partner. He starts tomorrow."

Bridgette wasn't sure how she felt about having a new partner. Her first partner had been killed in a shootout while she was still on her first murder case. Since then, another officer had lost his life while working a case with her. She'd heard rumblings in the Homicide room that she was bad luck and trouble, and while she tried not to take it to heart, it played on her mind.

"You still there, Bridgette?"

"Yeah."

"I know what you're thinking, and like I've said to you before, homicide work can be dangerous and sometimes things happen that are out of our control."

Bridgette wasn't sure how to respond. As she watched the uniformed officers return to the crime scene below, pangs of guilt wracked her body as she thought about her two colleagues who were now dead.

Delray continued, "I know you start early, so let's meet first thing tomorrow morning. There are a few things I want to go over with you before we do the introductions."

Bridgette didn't know a lot about her new partner, only a few sketchy details that her boss had provided in a previous meeting. She knew his name and that he had worked most of his ten-year career as an undercover cop in narcotics. When she had asked why he wanted to join Homicide, Delray had been vague in his answer. She'd pushed for more information and had learned he was returning to police work after an extended sabbatical. When she'd asked why a relatively young officer needed a sabbatical, Delray had waved her off with a we'll-talk-about-that-later answer.

Bridgette was tempted to ask again now but knew this wasn't the time or place and made a mental note to bring up the subject when they met in the morning. Keen to get on with her interviews, she responded, "I'll be in around seven thirty, Chief. Do you want me to come straight to your office?"

"Yeah, do that. We'll discuss your new partner and then you can fill me in on the case."

Delray disconnected leaving Bridgette alone with her thoughts. She checked her watch. Now well after five PM, she hoped at least some Barnett Road residents would be home from work and available for an interview. As she thought about how she would approach them, she realized this might be the last time she got to work on her own.

With just over twelve months' experience as a police detective, she realized her new and more experienced partner would be the senior officer and would get to call the shots. She had no trouble taking orders and while she respected authority, many of the senior detectives within Homicide dismissed her because of her age and gender. Delray was the notable exception. He continued to encourage her with each case she solved. She hoped her new partner was more like Delray than her other male colleagues but wasn't counting on it.

She sighed, thinking, *You'll know soon enough*, as she turned and headed back to her car.

Tuesday 7:31 AM

Bridgette paused at the door to Chief Inspector Felix Delray's office and knocked. Even though Delray had an open-door policy, Bridgette had never felt comfortable barging in. She waited for him to look up from a file he was studying on his desk. "Come on in, Bridgette."

"Thanks, Chief." Delray's twelve by twelve office was spartan and chaotic. After settling into a chair, she looked over the mountain of case files that seemed to permanently cover her boss' desk. She watched him lean back and massage his neck. "Are you okay?"

"I'm fine. I've spent the last hour reading an autopsy report and have barely moved." Delray gave her a wry smile before adding, "You wouldn't understand, but when you're over fifty, you can't sit in one position for too long before you seize up."

Bridgette nodded. "I'll keep that in mind."

Delray removed his thick, black-rimmed glasses. "I want to hear about your case, but first things first, we need to talk about your potential new partner."

"Potential?"

Delray pursed his lips as if debating where to start. "What do you know about Levi Frost?"

"Not much more than what you've told me. Early thirties, been on the force for around ten years, most of that time as an undercover narcotics cop."

"Anything else?"

Bridgette paused for a moment. "Rumors mostly."

"Such as?"

"He was good at his job and well-respected, but…"

"But?"

"He had some sort of mental breakdown. Most cops are surprised he's coming back."

Delray nodded. "I was one of them."

Bridgette frowned. "Sorry, I'm not following?"

Delray leaned forward. "This is what I wanted to talk to you about. Frost is a good cop. He started in uniform and then joined narcotics and pretty soon got hooked on undercover work. He was part of a team that was having a lot of success, particularly with organized crime gangs…"

"But something happened?"

"About fourteen months ago, Frost's Undercover team were involved in a stakeout at a warehouse on the west side of the city. They were trying to take down a major cocaine ring, but things didn't go to plan and several of the dealers made a run for it when the team moved in to make the arrests. Frost found himself chasing one of dealers who was trying to escape."

"I think I remember reading about it?"

"You probably did, although the identities of the police officers involved were never disclosed."

"If memory serves, there was a high-speed car chase and a young boy was killed?"

Delray grimaced. "The dealer made it to his car before Frost could stop him. Frost pursued him in a squad car and was about a block back when the dealer deliberately swerved to hit a boy on a pedestrian crossing."

"I can't imagine how hard that would have been to witness…"

"Tell me about it. Anyway, Frost stopped the chase immediately and called an ambulance, but the boy died in his arms before the ambulance arrived."

"So that's why he's been on leave?"

"Pretty much. Apparently, he felt personally responsible for the boy's death and was diagnosed with post-traumatic stress disorder which is understandable given what happened. No one expected he would ever come back, but he's passed all his psychiatric assessments and was cleared to work again."

"So why Homicide?"

"He didn't want to go back to undercover work, and I can't say I blame him. The Commissioner has taken a personal interest in his case and thinks he might be a good fit for Homicide."

"And what do you think?"

Delray ran his fingers through his short curly hair. "I've had a few conversations with him over the past two months, including the formal interview. The Commissioner didn't put any pressure on me — he told me to only offer him a job if I thought he would fit in."

Bridgette nodded, unsure what to say.

Delray continued, "I got to thinking, what if it had been me in that situation? It didn't take me long to realize I'd want a second chance. He deserves no less."

A million thoughts flashed through Bridgette's mind.

Delray often said working Homicide was a dangerous job. She didn't see how someone with questionable mental health would cope with the challenges but was careful with her response. "Well, if you think he'll fit in that's all I need to know."

Delray leaned back in his chair. "There are no guarantees with this Bridgette. This could be a mistake. But after thirty years on the force, I've gotten pretty good at reading people and he seems solid. But only time will tell."

"So, can I ask why me?"

"Fair question. In theory, I should have placed him with one of my senior detectives — someone with a lot more experience. If I was going by the book, that's what I would have done."

"But you're not going by the book?"

"Not this time. He's on a three-month trial and I need someone with good people and observation skills to work with him. Someone who can read between the lines to figure out if he's going to be okay or not. A psychological assessment can only tell you so much. I've worked with guys who have been falling apart on the inside but have somehow convinced a doctor they're okay."

Delray paused a moment to study Bridgette before adding, "Even though you're not much more than a rookie, you read people better than anyone else I know."

Bridgette felt flattered by Delray's confidence, but also out of her depth.

As if reading her mind, he added, "I appreciate this is a lot to take in. I haven't told him who his partner is — in fact, I've suggested we may place him with several detectives during his probation. If you don't want to do this, I fully understand, but what I'm asking is, work with him for a week and see how it goes. If that works out, we try it for another week. If you don't think it will work at any point, we'll try him with someone else."

Bridgette stared back across the desk at her boss. At just over six foot one and with the build of an aging wrestler, Delray was quite intimidating to look at, but Bridgette didn't intimidate easily. She had built up a strong working relationship with her boss and had earned his trust and respect through the number of cases she had solved in her short career.

She knew he was expecting a truthful answer so that's what she gave him. "I have two concerns."

"Okay. What's the first?"

"Does he know about my reputation?"

"I've told him about your three murder investigations and how you've had a one-hundred percent success rate. He was very impressed."

"With all due respect, Chief, that wasn't what I was referring to."

Delray pursed his lips and leaned back in his chair. "I know this isn't easy, Bridgette, but we've had this conversation before. You gotta let it go. It wasn't your fault."

Delray's body language told her he didn't want to talk about her record. Even though she'd closed out three murder cases in her first twelve months it had come at a cost. On her first case, her senior partner and mentor had been shot and killed when they tried to arrest a serial killer. On her third case, another detective had failed to follow procedure and had been killed in a shootout. While neither death was her fault, it still weighed heavily on her mind.

She decided to push the point. "Two cops died on my first three cases ... that gets talked about. I hear them and I can't say that I blame them for thinking the way they do. I just want to make sure that he…"

"He's aware," said Delray firmly. "I've been very upfront with him."

"And he still said yes?"

Delray held her gaze. "It didn't faze him at all. If memory serves, his response to me was, 'Being a cop is not for the faint hearted.'"

Bridgette wasn't sure how to respond. While she was thinking, Delray asked, "What's the second concern?"

Deciding it was wise to move on, she answered, "The new case. The next couple of days will be critical, but if you think he'll fit in and won't slow us down then I'm happy to give it a try."

Delray mused, "Let's give it a week and see how you go. Deal?"

"Deal."

Delray put his glasses back on and said, "Okay, bring me up to speed on the case. What happened yesterday?"

Bridgette relaxed a little and started by giving Delray a recap of the murder scene, then mentioned she was expecting an update from Ray Warner later that morning.

Delray frowned as he replied, "He'll have the autopsy completed this morning?"

"No. But he found a tattoo on the man's bicep. It was hard to see it in any great detail because of the decomposition and mud from the lake, but Ray promised to get it cleaned up and photographed for me as soon as he could to help identify the victim."

"So, no ID on the victim as yet?"

"No."

"And he was shot in the back?"

"Correct."

"And nobody saw or heard anything?"

"Not so far. I interviewed the woman who found the

body and one other local resident, but neither of them saw or heard anything."

"When are you interviewing the others?"

"I've set up appointments for later today, but I'm not hopeful we'll learn much."

"Why not?"

"The body was found in a patch of reeds on an isolated dead-end road where only a handful of people live. There are no streetlights and when I left to drive back last night, it was almost pitch black. If someone drove up there late at night, they could have spent hours there without being noticed … it's almost the perfect spot to dump a body."

Delray pulled his glasses off again and chewed on one of the arm tips. "No witnesses and no identity will make this tough."

"I'm going to see Missing Persons this morning to see if they can shed any light on the man's identity. The fact that we know the victim has some kind of dragon tattoo on his right bicep may help."

Delray drummed his fingers on his desk. "If we don't get a breakthrough by tomorrow on his identity, we're going to have to put a team on this."

Bridgette didn't like the idea of her case being farmed out to a team of detectives, but knew Delray was right. She hoped the tattoo would provide the breakthrough on the man's identity. Keen to move on from any more discussion on turning her case into a team investigation, she said, "Speaking of team, what's the plan for the meeting with Levi Frost?"

"I've set up an introductory meet and greet here in my office for nine o'clock. He did an orientation day yesterday, so today he starts the real police work."

Bridgette looked at her watch. "I should get going. I've got a lot to do."

As she headed for the door, Delray said, "There's one thing that bothers me about this case already."

She turned. "And what's that."

Delray chewed on his glasses again for a moment. "This reminds me of a case I worked almost twenty years ago. They found a body floating in a creek behind an industrial park. The victim had been shot in the back and then dumped. It turned out the victim was a missing business owner from the park and was found less than a hundred yards from his office. He ran a furniture removal business and had been feuding with a fellow business owner in the park on and off for years, mostly about where he parked his trucks. The two owners had come to blows on more than one occasion and things had gotten so bad that the victim had taken out a restraining order just two days before he was murdered. We never found the murder weapon and didn't have a witness. We were pretty sure we knew who the killer was but could never prove it. We brought the business owner in for questioning seven times but couldn't get him to crack. I remember after one interview he gave me a wink on the way out and said, 'you're going to have to do better than that.'"

Delray shook his head then added, "The prosecutors told us we didn't have enough evidence for a conviction. Even though we'd put up large rewards for information, we never got any further. I've never felt more frustrated in my life."

Delray held Bridgette's gaze. "Sometimes it's easy enough to figure out who did it, but proving it can be an entirely different matter."

Tuesday 8:58 AM

It was almost nine when Bridgette got the call from Delray. She had desperately wanted to use the time before meeting her new partner to work with Missing Persons on the identity of the John Doe murder victim, but taking on a new partner meant there were other things she needed to attend to. She had compiled a file, albeit brief, of everything she knew so far about the case, which included notes on the crime scene, a witness list and some of her own musings on lines of enquiry she thought worthy of pursuit. Although not fully prepared when the phone call came, she was satisfied it was close enough when she picked up the phone. "Hi, Chief."

Delray was brief and said, "Frost is here in my office. Come on in and we'll get the introductions started."

Bridgette got up from her desk and walked through the Homicide room to Delray's office. She could see Levi Frost already seated and in deep discussion with Delray when she knocked on the door. She tried not to stare overtly at her new partner. "Come on in, Bridgette."

She gave a polite nod to Levi Frost as she walked into the room. Frost had a close-cropped haircut and neatly trimmed stubble beard, both of which were flecked with gray. She figured he was about thirty-five, although the gray made him look older. Even though he stayed seated as she walked in, she could see by his long lean frame he was well over six feet tall.

Before she had a chance to sit down, Delray said, "Detective Cash, I'd like you to meet Detective Frost, our newest addition to the homicide team."

Frost stood and extended a hand. "Nice to meet you," he said in a deep, warm voice.

Bridgette offered a brief smile. "Likewise," before sitting in Delray's second visitors' chair.

Never one for awkward silences, Delray kept the meeting moving. "I don't have a lot of time to spend with you both this morning, so I'll keep this brief."

Turning to face Frost, Delray said, "As I explained to you, Levi, you'll be working with Detective Cash this week helping her with a murder case that came in yesterday. It may turn into a team event if we can't identify the John Doe quickly, so we'll see how that pans out in the coming days. Whatever happens, I'll be looking to find you a permanent partner in the next two weeks. Any questions?"

Bridgette could see from the puzzled look on Frost's face that he probably had a hundred questions, but he simply responded, "I think I'm good for now."

Delray nodded and then looked at Bridgette. "As I explained to you earlier, if we don't make a breakthrough with the man's identity today, we'll need to put together a task force on this. We're starting to field media calls already and I don't want this turning into a circus."

"That's fine by me, Chief." Bridgette went to add that

she was looking forward to working with Frost but was interrupted by Delray's desk phone.

He looked down at the screen and held up a finger. "Ray Warner. I think it might be worthwhile all of us hearing what he's got to say."

After pressing the answer button, Delray continued, "Hi, Ray, you're on speakerphone. I've got Detective Cash and her partner for this week, Detective Levi Frost in the room with me. I assume you're ringing about the body you found at the lake?"

Warner's voice came back through the tinny speaker. "I tried Bridgette's desk phone just now and when I got no answer, I thought I would ring your number — I'm glad I've got you all together."

Delray said, "What have you got for us, Ray?"

"Good news and bad news. The good news first — I'm ninety-nine percent sure we've identified the body. We believe the man's name is Paul Ringwood."

Delray observed, "That was quick."

"The deceased has a large mole on his right bicep just below the dragon tattoo, and that's how we got a match. The odds of two bodies turning up with those physical attributes are in the millions." There was a long pause. "But we have a problem."

Delray frowned. "What's the problem?"

"This is bizarre, and I can't explain it. Missing Persons couldn't find a match for anybody currently reported missing. I asked them to widen their search for anyone in the system with a dragon tattoo and a mole on their right bicep. They got a match in criminal records for a guy named Paul Ringwood."

"Okay."

"It would seem this Paul Ringwood was a small-time

drug dealer about ten years ago. Two minor convictions. Known to the Stanwyck police."

"Stanwyck as in the town forty minutes north of here? So that's where he was living?"

"That's the last address we have on file, but that was ten years ago."

"So what happened? Did he drop off the grid?"

"You could say that."

Bridgette could see the frustration growing on Delray's face. He scowled. "I'm not following."

"Paul Ringwood was murdered ten years ago."

Delray sat up straight in his chair. "Murdered? How can that be? I thought you said he'd only been dead a week?"

"And I stand by that assessment. The body of the man I have lying here in the morgue has been dead for less than ten days. I'd stake my professional reputation on it."

Bridgette couldn't hold back any longer and asked, "So is there a mistake with the police records, Ray?"

Warner responded, "I'm not sure. All I can tell you is Missing Persons looked up Ringwood's murder case file and according to what we have on record, this man was murdered ten years ago."

Delray shook his head. "This is bizarre."

"I'm just about to start the autopsy. I'll make it a priority to get the bullet out. I figure you're going to need it as soon as possible."

"Thanks Ray, we'll get someone over there later to pick it up."

"Also, there's one other thing you need to know."

Delray's eyes widened. "There's more?"

"According to the police file, they convicted somebody of Ringwood's murder. He's been in prison for almost ten years."

After completing the call with Ray Warner, the office was silent for a moment while they processed the news. Finally, Delray said, "This just doesn't make sense. How can someone be dead for ten years and their corpse only be a week old?"

Bridgette responded, "We should start with the old case file now that we know his name. Maybe we can learn something from that?"

"Good idea," said Delray turning to his computer screen. "Let's see what NatTrack has to say…" and began typing furiously on his keyboard.

NatTrack was a recent addition to the Vancouver Metropolitan Police service. It enabled police officers to search a national grid of police databases for information on criminals and cases. After a few teething problems, they could now access information from across the entire country in seconds.

Delray muttered, "Paul Ringwood," and pressed enter. While the computer trawled its databases for matches, Delray swung his flat screen monitor around so that Bridgette and Frost could see the search results.

Bridgette felt a tingle of excitement as she watched the screen refresh a few seconds later. With his reading glasses perched on the tip of his nose, Delray pointed at the top result and said, "Bingo," before using his mouse to open the record.

Unable to see the screen properly, Frost moved his chair closer to Bridgette's. Delray said, "Sorry, Levi, I can't swing the screen around anymore, but what I have here is the case file for Ringwood's murder."

Bridgette moved her chair about a foot to the left to

allow Frost to move over even further. After he had repositioned his chair, she said to her new partner, "Better?"

Frost nodded. "Thanks."

They all read in silence for a moment before Delray said, "He was murdered ten years ago just like Ray said, but do you notice what's interesting?"

Bridgette replied, "His body was never recovered."

Frost said, "How do you convict someone of murder without a body?"

Bridgette said, "I remember studying a case as part of my criminology degree where a man who lived in Florida was convicted of murdering his wife, even though her body was never found."

Frost raised an eyebrow. "How does that work?"

"According to the case file, the husband had a long history of domestic violence and the police had to intervene regularly to protect his wife. The husband repeatedly threatened to kill her, even in front of police. One day the woman disappeared, never to be seen again. She had no friends or family outside the local community and no reason to travel. Her bank accounts and credit cards were untouched. After an extensive search, which found no trace of her, the police concluded that she'd been murdered and her body dumped somewhere in the Everglades; and the jury agreed. Although it's rare, there are cases where someone is convicted of murder without a body, murder weapon or eyewitness."

Frost said, "So let me get this straight. This guy disappears ten years ago, and everyone presumes he's dead — murdered in fact, but he's been alive the whole time?"

Delray nodded. "It would appear that way."

Frost shook his head. "And then he turns up here dead, murdered after all?"

Bridgette answered, "We probably shouldn't jump to conclusions, but as bizarre as it may sound, it's the best explanation we have right now."

Delray looked from Bridgette to Frost. "This is getting complicated. What are your first thoughts, Bridgette?"

Bridgette pulled at what remained of her left earlobe; a habit she found hard to break while she was thinking. "Right now, I'm thinking about Alex Hellyer."

Frost said, "Alex Hellyer? Who's he?"

Bridgette pointed halfway down Delray's screen. "He's the guy currently sitting in prison for Ringwood's murder."

Tuesday 11:05 AM

Bridgette pulled the dark gray, police-issue Ford sedan to a halt in the car park in front of a two-storey brown and yellow brick building. As she switched off the engine she glanced at the stone letters embedded in the front wall which read City Morgue.

"Have you ever been here before?" she said.

Frost said, "A couple of times," as he studied the flat-roofed building with narrow windows. He added, "Undercover work doesn't normally require you to come here much, but I assume working Homicide you're here regularly?"

Bridgette nodded. "I seem to spend a lot more time here than I ever imagined."

After their meeting with Delray, they had returned to Bridgette's work pod in the Homicide room to study the Ringwood case in detail. They had learned little else about the victim other than he had disappeared ten years earlier and had been presumed murdered. Apart from two minor drug possession charges dating back twelve years, there were no other records in the system for Paul Ringwood or any alias. Bridgette and Frost had both agreed this wasn't surprising given every police system across the country now had him listed as deceased.

Bridgette found Levi Frost to be insightful while they discussed the case. They both agreed if the dead man was in fact Paul Ringwood, he must have been living under a false identity for the previous ten years, which didn't help their case. Knowing who he was ten years ago didn't help them solve a crime committed a week ago. They had agreed it was almost like starting a murder investigation with a John Doe. Frost had readily agreed with Bridgette's proposal that they drive over to the morgue as soon as possible to pick up the bullet that had killed Ringwood and start the process of getting a ballistics match. The drive had been relatively quiet. The getting to know you 'small talk' hadn't been appropriate under the circumstances and she had used the time to think through as many investigation angles as possible.

Bridgette opened the door to get out of the Ford. "I assume you've seen a few autopsies in your time?"

"Not many."

As they walked toward the building Brigitte said, "I'm okay with autopsies, but not great with bodies that have been dead for a week or more."

Frost frowned. "You're not alone there." He pushed open one of the heavy double wooden doors that led into the morgue's sparsely furnished reception area.

Bridgette crossed the tiled floor to a reception counter that looked as though it was as old as the building itself. She pressed a buzzer that was screwed to the desktop. She could hear a muffled ring somewhere in the back of the building. "Somebody will be here to get us shortly."

Frost said nothing. They stood awkwardly in the middle of the foyer until a woman in her early twenties wearing a surgical gown appeared in the hallway. "Detectives Cash and Frost, I assume?"

"Yes, we're here to see Doctor Warner."

The woman replied, "Doctor Warner is currently performing the autopsy on the body that was brought in last night. If you're okay to join him, I'll get you both fitted up with a mask and gown and then take you to the examination room."

Bridgette and Frost followed the woman down the hallway and into a small room on the right. The woman pulled two blue surgical gowns down from a pile on a shelf. "Here, put these on."

After they had donned their gowns, the woman handed them each a surgical mask and said, "I'll get you to fit these now and then we'll head straight to the examination room."

Bridgette cursed under her breath as she realized she'd forgotten her Vicks VapoRub. She wondered how she would cope with the smell of the decomposing body in the confined space of an examination room. She hoped she would hold it together. Having to dash to the bathroom to vomit would be embarrassing in front of her new partner. She glanced across at Frost as she fitted her mask. He seemed relaxed enough which she took to be a good sign.

They followed the woman to the end of the hallway. She stopped and opened a steel door on the left that was signed Examination Room 2. The overpowering smell of decomposing flesh almost knocked Bridgette off her feet. She covered her mouth then nodded to the woman before stepping into the room. As the door closed behind them, Warner, who was standing on the opposite side of a stainless-steel examination table in the middle of the room, said through his mask, "Come and join me, Detectives, we've got a lot to talk about."

Bridgette found herself unable to move for several seconds as she studied the body of Paul Ringwood. Now fully naked, the blackened and bloated corpse looked even less human than it had done when he had been pulled from the lake. Warner had already begun the autopsy by making a Y incision that started at the victim's collar bones and finished just above the pelvis. A thick layer of skin, muscle and fatty tissue had been pulled back to reveal the victim's internal organs. Normally, organs were pink or red, but Ringwood's organs were gray — almost black — another sign that decomposition was well advanced.

Bridgette stole a sideways glance at Frost who also seemed to be bracing himself for what was ahead. Stopping two feet short of the examination table, she hoped her inner turmoil wasn't too noticeable.

Seemingly unaware of her predicament, Warner said, "You've come at a good time."

"What can you tell us, Ray?"

Using the fingers of his gloved left hand for guidance, Warner pushed what looked like a pair of forceps gently into the man's chest area. As they disappeared into blackened watery tissue that Bridgette presumed was one of the victim's lungs, he said in an almost conversational voice, "I've got one of my lab technicians currently analyzing the victim's clothes. I don't think we're likely to get much in the way of trace evidence given he's been in the water so long, but you never know. I've also finished my external examination. Not much to report really. He's got a couple of scars on his arm that look they might have come from a knife fight, but apart from that… "

They watched in silence as Warner waggled the forceps

around before he added, "The condition of the victim's organs is pretty much as I expected. Decomposition is well advanced and a lot of the tests that I would normally run are a waste of time as they'll be inconclusive."

Warner stopped talking for a moment while he pushed the fingers of his left hand deeper into the man's chest until they almost disappeared. Bridgette felt her forehead beginning to bead up even in the refrigerated air.

As if he was talking to himself, Warner said, "Just a little deeper… " A moment later he exclaimed, "I think we have it," as he withdrew the surgical instrument.

Taking half a step back from the table, he held the forceps up to an overhead light and studied the small blackened object he had removed from the victim's body. Turning the forceps to the left and right he said, "It looks like a .38. It's damaged, as you would expect, but it's in good enough shape to get some useful data."

The bullet made a clunking sound as Warner dropped it into a stainless-steel tray. Turning to his assistant he said, "Jane, can you get this cleaned up and bagged for the detectives, please."

Warner looked across the table at Bridgette and Frost. Bridgette could almost see the grin behind the mask as he asked, "How are you guys doing?"

Bridgette managed to choke out, "I'm coping."

Frost said, "Me too," but there didn't appear to be much conviction in his voice.

Warner responded, "This will take a couple of hours. I'm just about to remove the internal organs. Do you guys want to stay or…"

Bridgette blurted out, "Unless Detective Frost thinks there's merit in staying, I think we should get the bullet back to ballistics as soon as possible."

Frost mumbled, "I concur."

Bridgette took this as her cue and headed for the door.

Warner said, "Jane will need about ten minutes to clean up the bullet and take a few photographs. She'll then fill in the chain of command documentation. Then you'll be good to go."

Bridgette turned at the door, "Is there anything else we need to know for now, Ray?"

"Not really. Like I said, I'll have a full report to you this evening. If I find anything else significant, I'll call you right away."

Bridgette and Frost both thanked Warner and left.

Looking forward to breathing fresh air again as they got outside, Bridgette felt the familiar urge to vomit stronger than ever. "I'm going to need a minute," she said, and headed for the bathroom.

Tuesday 12:45 PM

The drive back to the office started out as a quiet affair. No one spoke for almost ten minutes with both detectives lost in their own thoughts. Frost had his side window down a fraction to let in fresh air — something he hadn't done on the way to the morgue. Even though it was winter, Bridgette didn't mind as the fresh cool air was settling her nausea.

It was Frost who finally broke the silence when he said, "Cutting up dead bodies. I couldn't do *that* for a living."

"Ray seems to find the work satisfying and he contributes a lot to solving cases."

"I think I'd rather stick to catching bad guys."

Bridgette smiled for the first time in hours and said, "Me too."

"Tell me I've been thrown in the deep end."

Bridgette frowned and asked, "What do you mean?"

"Tell me it doesn't get any harder than what we just did back there."

In the twelve months Bridgette had been a detective, she'd been shot at — losing the tip of her left earlobe in the process — stabbed in the thigh and involved in several other scuffles while trying to make arrests. But she played down her answer. "Some days are better than others."

Still feeling nauseous and not wanting to talk about the case for a moment, Bridgette changed the subject. "What made you choose Homicide?"

"When I told them I wanted to come back, they offered me a desk job, but I couldn't do it. I thought if I'm going to be stuck behind a desk, I may as well retrain as an accountant."

Bridgette gave a wry smile. "A lot of us aren't cut out to be accountants."

Frost stared out the window. "I couldn't go back to undercover, but I still wanted something challenging."

"I heard about what happened to you. I'm sorry."

"Thanks. I'm trying to put it behind me."

"If you don't mind me saying, I'm surprised you came back."

There was a prolonged silence, which made Bridgette think she'd overstepped the mark. To her relief, Frost eventually replied, "At first I wanted to quit, but I like being a cop. Once I'd recovered, I thought I'd give it another shot."

More silence followed. Bridgette didn't think it appropriate to push any further so she changed the subject. "I had an early morning meeting with the chief today. We talked about how you and I would work together."

When Frost didn't respond, Bridgette added, "When I asked Delray about who would be lead detective on this case, he said he'd leave it up to us to work out."

"I've not worked Homicide before, and from what I've heard of your record, you're pretty good at your job."

Bridgette was surprised by Frost's answer. She knew most cops would jump at the chance to take the lead role and wasn't sure if Frost had another agenda. "I guess we can work it out as we go along."

Frost twisted in his seat to look directly at her. "Delray mentioned I would be working with you for the rest of this week and then maybe transfer to someone else next week. I figure that's code for I'm on trial with you too, not just Homicide?"

Bridgette decided a blunt question needed a blunt answer. "I think that's a fair way to put it. The chief is very keen to see this work for you. In time, I'm sure he'll figure out who's going to be the best match."

They were silent again as Bridgette navigated the heavy afternoon traffic. She wasn't sure what to make of her new partner yet but appreciated his candor. As they drove across the Iron Bridge over the river, Frost said, "What's the plan for the rest of the day?"

"We'll lodge the bullet with the Ballistics team for analysis, and then I've got interviews lined up with the residents of Barnett Road who I couldn't interview yesterday." She added as an afterthought, "But I'm not sure they're going to be much help."

"Why's that?"

Bridgette gave the same summary she'd given Delray earlier that morning. "A lonely road, forty minutes out of town. If Paul Ringwood was either murdered or dumped out there in the dead of night, I think it's a long shot that anyone would've seen or heard anything we can use."

Bridgette turned off the motorway to start the last part of their journey back to the Metro South building.

Frost said, "So if the interviews don't yield anything, what's the plan from there?"

"I've been giving that some thought. I think we need to go back ten years and start at the beginning. We need to find out everything we can about Paul Ringwood's former life and why he disappeared."

"It might be hard to track down witnesses ten years on, don't you think?"

"Maybe, but I know exactly where the first witness we need to interview lives."

"And where is that?"

"Maximum security at the Vancouver Penitentiary."

"Alex Hellyer?"

Bridgette nodded. "If he's about to be exonerated for a murder he didn't commit, I'm hoping he'll be cooperative and have a lot to tell us."

Tuesday 5:55 PM

Bridgette pushed back from her computer screen and stared up at the clock on the wall in the Homicide room. They had been back in the office about forty minutes and had little to show for their day. She sighed as she recalled the interviews with the remaining two couples on Barnett Road. They had yielded no additional information, just as Bridgette suspected. Neither couple had seen nor heard anything out of the ordinary in recent weeks and both neighbors were horrified that the murdered remains of someone had been found so close to their homes.

On the way back into the city, they'd discussed what they would focus on next. Frost had agreed going back to the Ringwood's disappearance ten years earlier was a good starting point. Mindful that Delray would turn the murder investigation into a team event if they didn't make a breakthrough shortly, they spent the rest of the day searching NatTrack to learn as much as they could about Ringwood's criminal background, with Bridgette focusing on the original murder case and Frost on Ringwood's criminal record. Frost stood up and peered over the petition that separated the two work spaces. "Have you found anything?"

Stifling a yawn, she said, "Not really. He was living in Stanwyck and working as a stonemason at the time of his disappearance. When he didn't show up for work, one of his colleagues went to his home after work to check on him. He found the garage door open and a pool of blood inside. He called the police immediately and while nobody was sure what had happened, they listed him as a missing person and opened an investigation. An intensive search was made of the local area and a reward posted for information, but nothing came of it. That went on for weeks. They even trawled sections of the local river looking for his body but found nothing. It was as if Ringwood had disappeared off the face of the earth."

Frost nodded. "Which he did for almost ten years."

"I've now started reading the case file for Alex Hellyer. It would appear he lived in Stanwyck at the same time as Ringwood — only two streets away, in fact."

"That's interesting."

Bridgette said, "They found a partially burned knife in an incinerator at the back of Hellyer's house. The blood on it was a match for the blood they found in Ringwood's garage."

Frost frowned. "So, let me get this straight — he tried to burn the knife, but they found enough blood on it to get a DNA result?"

"That's what the report says."

"How did they make the connection between Hellyer and Ringwood?"

"According to the Stanwyck detective in charge of the

case, Ringwood and Hellyer had been seen arguing in public about a week earlier. He was a person of interest."

Frost leaned his elbows on the petition and mused, "It sounds like a set up."

Bridgette glanced back at her computer screen. "There's a lot more here that we need to look at. After we interview Hellyer, I think we'll need to take a trip out to Stanwyck. I'm sure we can learn a lot from the detective who was in charge of the case."

"What I want to know is, how does Ringwood live off the grid for ten years without being found?"

Bridgette continued to stare at her computer screen. Her own father had lived off the grid for almost twice that time as both a fugitive of an organized crime gang and the police force he had served. Even though he had been posthumously exonerated, his murder was still raw. She preferred not to talk about it. She realized Frost probably wasn't aware of this and simply replied, "He must have been very smart and very careful."

Keen to change the subject, she asked, "Have you discovered anything interesting?"

Frost had been checking into Ringwood's criminal background. "Nothing that stands out. Ringwood had two convictions for selling small quantities of marijuana, but that's all. It looks like he led a reasonably quiet life. No history of violence and no pattern of behavior that would suggest he was heading towards being a career criminal."

Bridgette looked up at Frost. "A lot can change in ten years, particularly if you're trying to protect your real identity."

"You might be right, but I've dealt with a lot of drug dealers, and this guy's history — at least what we know of it — doesn't fit." Frost was about to elaborate when his cell phone rang. After checking the screen, he mumbled, "This is my wife. I've gotta take this."

Bridgette returned to the case file but found it hard to concentrate as she heard Frost's voice waft over the petition as he talked to his wife. "Yeah, I'm still here."

Bridgette felt like she was intruding into his privacy as they were the last two detectives in the Homicide room.

Bridgette debated going to the bathroom, but when Frost raised his voice, shouting, "I don't always get to decide," Bridgette fixed her eyes on her computer screen again. Slightly embarrassed that she had overheard what was clearly a heated personal conversation, she decided to act as if she hadn't heard the exchange. A moment later, Frost informed her that he had to go and apologized he couldn't stay longer. It was clear from his clenched jaw that the call had upset him.

Bridgette responded, "Thanks for all your help today, Levi. We haven't made as much progress as I'd like, but that's the way it goes sometimes."

Frost pulled on a coat promising to be back in the office by eight the following day. After they'd said their goodbyes, Bridgette watched him as he headed for the elevator. She couldn't help but wonder what his home life was like. The trauma of what he'd been through would have surely put strain on his marriage. She wondered if his wife was anxious about him returning to police work. That would be understandable. She decided it wasn't something she should dwell on but would keep in the back of her mind. Conversations about Frost's private life, particularly his marriage, would be a no-go zone.

Turning back to her computer, she clicked on a link that took her to Alex Hellyer's record. She frowned as she read the details and then almost jumped out of her chair as a voice behind her said, "How did it go today?" Delray let out a short laugh. "Sorry, I didn't mean to startle you," as Bridgette turned around to face him.

Bridgette put a hand to her chest. "I thought I was alone."

"You are," said Delray, pulling up a chair. "Everyone's gone home. It's only you out here and me in my office. So how did Frost go today?"

"Better than I expected," she said.

"And what does that mean?"

"I was sure he would try and pull rank on me given he's been a cop for ten years."

"But he didn't?"

"No. He was quite open about not having any experience in Homicide and was happy for me to take the lead."

Delray nodded. "Well, that's refreshing."

Amused, she said, "I've discovered one thing we have in common."

"What's that?"

"He doesn't like autopsies either."

Bridgette gave Delray a rundown of what they'd done that day. He sympathized when she told him none of the residents of Barnett Road had seen or heard anything out of the ordinary. Then they talked tactics and to her relief, her boss didn't mention anything about turning the case into a team investigation.

As they wrapped up their conversation, Bridgette told him, "I'm going to add the Stanwyck detective to our interview list. Based on what we know now, Ringwood's murder ten years ago was almost certainly staged."

"That could be tricky. Cops don't take kindly to other cops investigating their work."

Bridgette sighed. "I thought my key witness would be Alex Hellyer, but I'm not sure he will be very helpful now."

Delray raised an eyebrow. "Why not?"

"I've just been reading more on his case file. Alex Hellyer was attacked in prison just after he began his life sentence. He didn't recover very well. He has the mental capacity of a five year old."

Tuesday 7:06 PM

Bridgette paused in the foyer of the Coach Bar and Grill to scan the room for her dinner date. The restaurant could seat two hundred, but tonight there were fewer than half that number of patrons. The dark timber walls and mood lighting made it difficult for her to see clearly. After scanning those who were sitting at a long bar to her left, Bridgette finally spotted a slim woman with shoulder-length blonde hair in a rear booth who was waving at her. Bridgette gave a subtle nod then threaded her way between the tables and chairs towards the rear. Coach wasn't her favorite place to eat, particularly on the weekend when live jazz music made it all but impossible to have a decent conversation, but the food was good, and it was only a five-minute walk from her work.

As she approached the table, the blonde woman said with a pretend frown, "You're late!"

"Sorry. I got talking to my boss."

The woman rolled her eyes and said, "You've gotta be more original than that, Bridgette."

Bridgette laughed and sat down. "It's the truth."

Renée Filipucci was, like Bridgette, a self-confessed gym junkie. They trained together most nights and had been friends for almost a year. Once a week, they took a night off from training to share a meal together and talk about things other than exercise.

Bridgette enjoyed their friendship but was always on guard when the discussion turned to topics beyond training and exercise. Filipucci was a sub-editor for the Vancouver Advocate, the city's main daily newspaper and she would unashamedly pump her friend for information on active cases. Bridgette didn't mind the banter but often ended such discussions with the line, 'You'll need to contact media liaison for a comment.'

While Filipucci always took the hint and backed off the work conversations, she wasn't so keen on backing away from Bridgette's other pet hate; talking about her love life. Bridgette knew Renée meant well and wondered if either topic would come up tonight. "How was your day?" asked Filipucci,

Keen to stay away from the new case itself, Bridgette replied, "I got my new partner today."

With a sly smile, Filipucci shot back, "Is he cute? How old is he?"

Bridgette gave a knowing smile. "About thirty-five and very married!"

Filipucci pouted. "He doesn't sound like fun."

Bridgette shook her head pretending to be disgusted. "You never change Renée; it's not supposed to be fun."

Filipucci laughed.

Keen to change the subject, Bridgette asked, "And how about your day?"

"Same old, same old, really. Overworked and underpaid, but a girl can dream."

Bridgette picked up the menu and asked, "Have you decided what you're eating yet?"

"I'm not sure. I think it's a toss-up between the lamb salad and a T-Bone steak." Filipucci giggled adding, "Not that you'll be entertaining either of those two options."

Bridgette ignored the subtle jibe. Although not a vegetarian, she avoided red meat in favor of fish and chicken. It was a hangover from a diet she'd adopted in her early twenties when she had competed regularly in martial arts tournaments. She glanced down the menu options and said, "I think I'll go with the sheet-pan Italian chicken. That looks healthy."

Filipucci said, "Yeah, that sounds good. I think I'll have one of those as well."

After ordering their meals and drinks, the conversation quickly turned to gym workouts. Bridgette's goal in training four or five nights a week was to maintain her physical condition and keep in shape for the grueling demands she was often confronted with as a detective. Filipucci, on the other hand, used the gym as a means of therapy after a messy divorce and a year that saw her weight balloon by twenty pounds. Bridgette was proud of the change she had seen in her friend in the last six months and was pleased to see her getting her life back together.

Once their drinks had arrived, Filipucci said, "Been on any good dates lately?"

In truth, Bridgette hadn't dated anyone for a long while. Still reeling from her father's death, the thought of trying to resurrect her love life was something she wasn't ready to contemplate. Filipucci knew this, but that never seemed to stop her asking the question. Bridgette raised her eyebrows and said, "And when do I have time to go on a date?"

"What are you doing Saturday night?"

Bridgette laughed. "Are you asking me out on a date? I didn't know you'd become a lesbian?"

Both women laughed before Filipucci replied, "One of the journalists I hang with at work has four tickets to the basketball. He's already promised a ticket to another guy he works with but wondered if I knew anyone so that we could go as a foursome. What do you think?"

This wasn't the first time Filipucci had tried to set her up on a blind date. Bridgette liked basketball, and not ruling out the option entirely, gave a wry smile and said, "I've never had good experiences with blind dates. What makes you think this would be any different?"

Before Filipucci could reply, Bridgette's smartphone buzzed. Normally she would have let it go through to voicemail, but when the screen flashed Ray Warner's phone number, she knew this was a call she should take.

She grimaced and said, "Sorry. Do you mind?"

Filipucci seemed to understand and said, "Just make sure I get the scoop and not some other low-life journalist if it's going to make the news."

Bridgette got up from the table and pressed answer as she walked towards the door. "Hi, Ray."

"Hi, Bridgette, sorry to call so late. Do you have a moment to talk?"

While weaving her way toward the front door, Bridgette said, "Can you hold on a moment? I'm in a restaurant and need to step outside where it's not so noisy."

"No problem. Let me know when you're ready to talk."

Bridgette walked through the foyer and out onto the street. She moved a few feet away from the entrance to make sure she wasn't overheard then said, "I hope the background noise isn't too bad for you, Ray."

"I can hear you loud and clear and I won't keep you long."

"So, how did the autopsy go?"

"You'll have the full report in your inbox when you get to work in the morning, but I thought you'd like a quick summary anyway."

"I'm all ears."

"Good. Well, as I suspected, the victim had no water in his lungs, so he didn't drown."

"So he definitely died of gunshot wounds?"

"There's been a lot of decomposition with his internal organs but still enough evidence to clearly prove he died from a gunshot wound. Also, we dragged the reed area in the lake where we found the body, just to be certain it wasn't a suicide."

"Did you find anything?"

"Three tin cans and a horseshoe, but no gun."

"It begs the question, was he murdered there or somewhere else?"

"I'm sure you'll figure that out. Either way, that lake is a good place to dump a body."

Warner then spent another two minutes giving Bridgette a summary of the rest of his findings. She learned little else other than he'd revised his initial estimate of how long the body had been in the water from a week to closer to ten days. Before he disconnected, Warner encouraged Bridgette to call him at any time if she had questions. Bridgette thank the coroner for his call and stood for a moment silently replaying their conversation over in her mind before she returned to the restaurant.

Warner had been right, of course — the lake was a

perfect spot to commit a murder or dump a body. She looked towards the restaurant, feeling guilty. She knew she should get back inside to join Filipucci, but instead thought, *this won't take a minute*, and quickly opened up Google Maps on her smartphone. She keyed in the location for Barnett Lake while she pondered whether the murderer had chosen the location by chance or if it had been planned? As the screen refreshed, she thought it more than likely that the murderer had local knowledge. After locating Barnett Lake on the map, she placed her thumb and forefinger on the screen and splayed her fingers wide to zoom the map out. Barnett Lake was a forty-minute drive from the city, but only ten minutes from Stanwyck.

Bridgette didn't believe in coincidences. "What are the odds?"

Satisfied she had a new plan of attack for tomorrow's investigation, she walked back to the restaurant. She thought about Levi Frost as she pushed open the front door. Under normal circumstances, the information Warner had shared with her would be something she would pass on to a partner straight away. But these weren't normal circumstances. She shivered slightly as she made her way back to her table as she recalled Frost's angry words, 'I don't always get to decide.'

Wednesday 2:27 AM

Bridgette sat bolt upright in bed gasping, her heart hammering in her chest. She glanced at the digital clock next to her bed as she swept damp hair off her face. She breathed in and out deeply until her heart rate returned to normal, a routine she practiced after every nightmare. There were two nightmares she had regularly. The first was the feeling of the ground opening up beneath her sucking her into a black hole, and the second was a day at school when she was seven. The nightmare about the ground opening up and swallowing her was always intense. She would thrash in bed, desperate to wake up to make the dream stop. But once settled, she could usually go back to sleep. The school dream was a different matter entirely. She was always in the same place; waiting out front of her school for her mother to pick her up, but she never came. The dream left her feeling sad and empty.

She had talked to her psychologist about it on more than one occasion. Her therapist said it was an ongoing anxiety response to her mother's murder twenty years earlier. She had been prescribed medication to help her sleep, but little in the way of practical help.

Bridgette sighed as she slipped out of bed. Sleep would now elude her. The nightmare had ended tonight as it always did with her realizing her mother was gone forever. She padded through her living room into the tiny kitchen of her apartment. After pouring herself a glass of water she sat on a stool and thought about the dream again. Truth be told she had never gotten over her mother's murder and twenty years on she was still struggling. She wondered again if she would have coped better if her father had been around. Accused of her mother's murder, he had gone into hiding the day after the death. While her aunt had done her best, she drank too much and suffered from a lack of self-confidence after a messy divorce. As Bridgette sipped her water, she wondered how much of an influence her aunt had been on her development.

Bridgette allowed herself to think back to her school days. She had been picked on by the girls following her mother's death. She learned that children could be incredibly cruel and vicious, but as a seven year old grieving the loss of her mother, her aunt's advice to simply 'stay away from them' left her confused and bewildered.

Despite doing well academically in school, she always doubted herself. Even though she tried to keep a low profile, the bullying by her female classmates continued into junior high and became worse as her athletic build and good looks started attracting the attention of the boys in her class. Eventually she found acceptance after getting into martial arts. She found solace in mastering the discipline, partly for escape and partly to protect herself. She remembered mounting the dais in her first year of senior high to accept a trophy as school champion thinking this would be her turning point as the crowd cheered for her. But almost as soon as she left the stage, the doubts returned.

She continued to excel in everything she did. She knew no way other than to overachieve. Despite now having two degrees, an IQ of 151, and three solved murder cases under her belt, she still doubted herself as a detective. Do I really belong? Am I good enough? She'd been asking herself these questions since she was seven. She'd hoped after twelve months as a detective she would have settled into her role and overcome her self-doubt.

She shook her head in frustration. Enough time and money had been spent on psychologists to expunge the demons. But try as she might to escape them, they always seemed to find her, especially in her sleep. She could build walls in her mind to compartmentalize the things in her life. She could create mental rooms for things she didn't want to think about, and for the most part she never entered them. She could carry on a normal life, seemingly confident and well adjusted. But sleep invariably brought it all undone. The doors in her mind were flung open when she drifted off to sleep. In her dreams the demons would taunt her, 'we're back and there's not a damn thing you can do about it.'

She sighed as she thought about her father again. At first she had been angry with him for abandoning her. She recalled the phone call out of the blue shortly before his death. She instantly recognized his voice even though she hadn't heard it in twenty years. So many questions yet little in the way of answers in just one single phone conversation that she still treasured to this day. She was glad he had finally been acquitted of her mother's murder even if it hadn't been until after his death. This brought her some closure and a sense of peace that she desperately craved.

Bridgette sat still for a moment and put all her memories back into their rightful rooms and then eyed the box of sleeping tablets on her kitchen bench. At times she felt pathetic — almost as if she was constantly hiding behind a mask. She hated taking the pills because they made her groggy the next day but right now she couldn't afford to bring anything less than her A game to her job.

The loss of two cops during cases she had worked on still played on her mind. While no one blamed her, their faces would appear in her mind almost immediately when she woke up. She found it hard to escape the guilt even after she had squeezed them back into rooms she preferred to avoid.

She resigned herself that she needed more help, but it wouldn't be pills. That was no way to live. Maybe she needed a new psychologist? Someone who understood her dreams and who could help her conquer her demons once and for all. Bridgette let out a long sigh and stood up. She finished the glass of water in one gulp then padded back to her bedroom.

Wednesday 7:04 AM

Eager to read Warner's autopsy report, Bridgette arrived at the South Metro precinct early. But her plans for the day were derailed as soon as she logged on to her computer. A message in her inbox from the Missing Persons Unit alerted her to a new case in the national database that might interest her. The man's name was Paul Johnson, and although he was a white male in the right age range, it was the distinguishing body feature of a dragon tattoo on his right bicep that piqued her interest.

Bridgette was almost positive they had a match for Paul Ringwood, and thirty minutes later made a phone call to the missing man's distraught partner to arrange an interview.

Even though the partner lived three hours north in the city of Bolton, Bridgette felt it required a face to face. By the time Levi Frost arrived at 8 o'clock, she had already booked out a pool car in readiness for the trip. She gave Frost the option of staying behind to read the autopsy report and prepare for more local interviews, but he insisted on going with her.

The journey itself was quiet. Frost appeared moody and conversation was almost non-existent, which suited Bridgette as it gave her time to think through the questions she wanted to ask. With only one stop for gas, a bathroom break, and a take-out coffee, they reached the outskirts of Bolton at just after eleven AM. Although not as big as Vancouver's population of three million, Bolton was still a reasonable-size city and suffered from traffic congestion.

Bridgette checked the car's GPS. "Only ten minutes to go now."

Frost studied the traffic ahead and said, "It's good that she lives on the south side. If she lived on the north side, we could easily add another hour with this traffic."

Moments later, the GPS told them to turn left off the freeway and they quickly found themselves driving through a hilly area, more densely populated with trees than houses.

Frost remarked, "She lives in a rural area."

Bridgette had also noticed the further they drove, the fewer houses there were. She glanced at the GPS again. "It appears so. Less than five minutes now."

They continued until the GPS instructed them to turn left onto a road barely wide enough for one car.

Frost said, "It's like being in a forest."

"I keyed the house number in as part of the address. The GPS should tell us exactly where we need to stop."

On descending a small hill, a neatly maintained white clapboard house came into view. It was set back from the road amongst a cluster of trees.

"This is it," she said, turning into the driveway.

Frost said, "I'm going to let you do all the talking, if that's okay? I think we're more likely to get useful information from her if she's interviewed by a woman rather than a man."

Although a little surprised by Frost's suggestion, Bridgette wasn't about to argue. As she brought the car to a halt, she said, "I've been thinking about what we should tell her. Until we get a positive DNA match, we can't jump to conclusions."

"I agree."

Bridgette took a deep breath before opening her door. Delivering bad news was the worst part of her job. After walking up onto a small front porch, Bridgette knocked. The door was opened almost immediately by a petite woman with long brown hair in her early thirties. The woman's swollen belly suggested she was at least seven months pregnant and Bridgette's heart sank. The woman's eyes were red from crying. She sniffed and wiped her nose with her hand then asked, "Yes?"

Bridgette said, "We're here to see Carrie Singleton?"

The woman nodded. "That's me."

"I'm Detective Cash and this is Detective Frost from Vancouver Metro police. I phoned earlier about your Missing Person's report."

Singleton's bottom lip quivered, more tears welling in her eyes. "Come in."

She led them into a small sitting room with a sofa and two matching floral chairs. Singleton offered them coffee, but Bridgette declined for them both.

After Singleton had settled in her chair, Bridgette said, "I'm sure this must be a very anxious time for you, Carrie — is it all right for me to call you Carrie?"

The woman nodded.

"I'll try to make this as easy as possible."

Singleton stared but didn't respond. Bridgette took a breath.

"You reported your husband missing late yesterday?"

"He's my partner, not my husband. Paul and I never married."

"How long has he been missing?"

Tears streamed down Singleton's face again. She brushed them away with her sleeve and said, "Nine days. He's dead, isn't he?"

Bridgette responded cautiously, "We don't know for sure."

Silence descended on the room as Singleton put her head in her hands and wept. After almost a minute, she lifted her head and said, "Sorry."

Bridgette told Singleton her reaction was understandable, then asked her to tell them about the day Paul disappeared.

"It was an ordinary day. Just like any other day really. Paul works as a stonemason and left for work about six-thirty, just like normal. I work as an orderly at the local hospital and had the late shift, so I didn't get home until after eleven. His truck was parked out back like it normally was, but there were no lights on inside the house. I assumed he'd already gone to bed. There was no sign of any disturbance and apart from the back patio being wet everything looked normal. But, when I came inside, there was no sign of him. He wasn't asleep in bed like I expected."

Singleton broke down and wept again. "I didn't know what to do. I went outside and checked the barn and then checked all around the yard but couldn't find any sign of him anywhere. His truck was here, so I figured he couldn't be far away. It was so unlike him; he doesn't go anywhere."

Singleton sat back and sucked in a deep breath. "I knew

something was really wrong but didn't know what to do. I called his work first thing in the morning and they said he'd left work the day before at four PM just like he always did."

"And his truck is it still parked outside?"

"Yes."

"Did Paul have any typical routines after work? For example, did he go to a bar or stop at a supermarket?"

"No. He left the shopping to me and rarely went out."

"Had he been his normal self recently? Did he appear anxious, or was there anything out of the ordinary that you noticed?"

"Not that he told me about." Singleton looked down at her belly and said, "He was as happy as I've ever seen him and really excited about the baby."

Frost broke into the conversation and said, "Why did you leave it nine days to report him missing?"

The question appeared aggressive, more aggressive than Bridgette thought Frost meant, and Singleton recoiled.

Bridgette said soothingly, "Carrie, you're not in trouble. We're just here to help you find Paul."

Although Bridgette also wanted an answer to Frost's question, she decided to come back to it later and asked, "How long have you known Paul?"

Singleton sat up straighter. "I met him eight years ago. He told me right at the start that he had a past that he didn't want to talk about. I didn't care. I knew he was a good man."

Bridgette nodded to encourage her to keep talking. "Did he ever give any details?"

"He told me he had two minor drug convictions but had learned from his mistakes. Coming to Bolton was a chance to start a new life."

"And where did he work?"

"He worked as a contractor for a local stone masonry company."

"Did he ever talk about being in trouble with anyone?"

"No."

"No signs that anyone was following him?"

"No. Not that he ever mentioned. But I always knew he was hiding from something. He admitted as much, and it was pretty obvious when he insisted on being paid in cash for his work."

"Did he go out much?"

"Hardly ever. Like I said, he mostly kept to himself. He was very careful about keeping his friendship circle small. He never used social media and didn't like his picture being taken. Even so, we were very happy."

Frost asked, "Did he have a driver's license?"

Singleton shook her head. "He didn't like leaving a paper trail of any kind. The deeds for the house are in my name ... in fact every legal document is in my name."

This heightened Bridgette's suspicion that Ringwood was living off the grid. She would explore the theme later, but for now, she glanced at Frost, and said, "Is Paul's truck still parked out back?"

"Yes, do you want to see it?"

"Yes, please."

They followed Singleton through the kitchen and a door that led onto a concrete patio. Bridgette could see a white Toyota truck parked less than thirty feet from the back door on a gravel driveway. The truck had wide tires and looked clean and well maintained.

As she walked around the vehicle she said, "So is this is where he always parked?"

Singleton nodded. "I backed it up the following morning just to check the ground where it was parked. I don't know what I was looking for; blood, some kind of clue, I don't know…"

"You didn't find anything.?"

"Nothing, so I moved it back to where it is now, and it hasn't been moved since."

Bridgette scanned the area at the back of the house. Apart from the barn that had a heavy padlock on the door, there were no other buildings. The entire area was open. Through the trees, Bridgette could see two houses about seventy yards away. She said, "How do you get on with your neighbors?"

"We get on fine. We don't have much to do with them, although we usually get together for drinks at Christmas."

Bridgette nodded and made a mental note to interview all the neighbors later in the day. As they went to walk back inside, Bridgette said, "You mentioned the patio was wet when you came home that night?"

"Yes."

Bridgette peered up at the patio's fiberglass roof which looked to be in good condition and unlikely to leak, even in heavy rain. She turned to Singleton and said, "Had it been raining that night?"

Singleton frowned. "No. It hadn't rained at all that week as I recall. I remember as I came in that night, I was going to ask Paul why the patio was wet, but I never…"

Singleton's eyes welled with tears again. Bridgette opened the back door and said, "I think we've seen enough out here for now, let's go back inside."

After they were seated in the sitting room again, Singleton said, "Why would anybody want to hurt Paul? He's a good man."

"We're not sure anything has happened to him yet, Carrie, but hopefully we can find out." Trying to steer the conversation away from awkward questions she couldn't answer, Bridgette asked, "Did Paul ever mention Vancouver or Stanwyck? Like maybe he knew people there?"

"No. As I said, he never talked about his old life. I have no idea where he came from before he moved to Bolton."

Bridgette nodded and was about to ask another question, but Singleton got in first. "If you're from Vancouver, why are you here?"

"We currently have an open investigation that could be connected, Carrie," said Bridgette.

"You wouldn't have come all this way to talk to me unless you'd found someone."

Bridgette took a breath and held the woman's gaze. "I'd be being less than honest with you if I said no."

Singleton got up from the sofa and walked over to a side cabinet. After opening a drawer, she pulled out two folded pieces of paper and brought them over to Bridgette. The first was a newspaper clipping. "Paul was a good man. Earlier this year, he volunteered every Saturday for close to three months to help rebuild part of the old school that burnt down. Only a good person does that."

Bridgette went to reply, but Singleton cut her off by handing her the second piece of paper. "Paul had a dragon tattoo on his right arm. I never wanted him to get one, but eventually I found one that I really liked. So I paid for it as a birthday present."

Bridgette stared at the picture of a Japanese dragon motif that looked to be identical to the tattoo on Ringwood's arm. Then Carrie grabbed the picture.

"I want to see the body."

Wednesday 4:48 PM

Bridgette and Frost spent a further hour with Carrie Singleton but they learned little in the way of new information. It was clear Singleton was emotionally and mentally exhausted. Bridgette promised to stay in touch. Now certain that Paul Ringwood and Paul Johnson were the same person, she convinced Carrie to give her a hairbrush belonging to Johnson to do a DNA comparison.

They spent the rest of the day interviewing some of Johnson's neighbors and work colleagues but learned nothing of significance. It was now close to five PM and they had just started the three-hour drive back to Vancouver. Frost insisted on taking his turn at driving which was okay with Bridgette. After settling into a cruising speed on the freeway, Bridgette said, "We need to call the chief and give him an update."

"Fine by me," said Frost, his eyes on the road.

Bridgette hit speed dial and placed her smartphone on speaker so that Frost could hear the conversation.

Delray answered on the fifth ring. "I was hoping to hear from you. I've got Cunningham climbing all over me for an update. Apparently, this case is grabbing media attention and they're not letting go."

Bridgette said, "Levi and I are on our way back to Vancouver now, Chief. We just got on the freeway after a reasonably successful day."

Delray shot back with one of his trademark lines, "Okay, let me have it."

Bridgette gave her boss a rundown of the interview with Carrie Singleton. Delray listened without interrupting as Bridgette summarized the key points. She told Delray about the picture of the dragon that Singleton had shown her and how it was an almost perfect match for the tattoo on Ringwood's arm.

Delray was quiet for a moment before he said, "Well, that's about as clear cut as it gets, but it's wise you're bringing back a DNA sample. Given the condition of the body, it would be nice to spare her the task of having to formally identify her partner."

Bridgette thought back to the last image she had seen of the bloated and putrefying remains of Paul Ringwood in the morgue. "I couldn't agree more."

"So we are certain this Paul Johnson was living off the grid?"

"Everything points to it. He has no credit cards and apparently no driver's license and he'd even convinced the boss of his company to pay him in cash, even though that's illegal."

Delray replied, "He must have been damn good at his job," and then paused a beat. "His partner knew nothing about his background, even though they've been together for eight years?"

"She knew about his two drug convictions, but that's all." Bridgette explained how they had interviewed some of Ringwood's neighbors and work colleagues before concluding, "From all reports, he was a quiet, likeable guy who kept to himself."

"So, one thing that puzzles me — why did she wait nine days to report him missing?"

"I asked her that exact question," said Frost.

"And what did she say?"

"She said Paul had made her promise that if he ever got into trouble or disappeared, she wasn't to call the police."

Bridgette could hear Delray let out a grunt before he replied, "By the sounds of things, it wouldn't have made any difference."

After a small silence, Delray added, "Well, this is good work guys. This is a solid lead. So what's the plan for tomorrow?"

"That's why we called. There's still another two or three days of interview work up here. It would be good to see if we can get hold of any CCTV footage from the area. It might help us figure out his last movements."

"That sounds like a plan, but I'm not sure Vancouver Metro will be doing that work. I had to pull a few strings with Bolton Police to allow you to interview Singleton on your own today, but that will have to change if it's an ongoing investigation. I'll make some calls and see what comes of it. I've got Lee and Grundy coming off a case, so I can offer them as backup to Bolton Police, but that may take a day or two organize. So what else are you planning?"

"We're keen to explore the Stanwyck angle. We want to understand why Ringwood's body would turn up three hours away from where he lives and so close to his hometown. Levi and I don't believe that's a coincidence."

"I couldn't agree more."

Bridgette looked across at Frost and replied, "We think we should start by visiting the prison tomorrow on the way out to Stanwyck to learn what we can about Alex Hellyer, given he was also a resident of Stanwyck."

"I'm not sure you'll get much out of him. Didn't you say he now has the mental capacity of a five year old?"

"We thought we'd interview the infirmary doctor and perhaps the warden. It might turn up nothing, but you never know."

"Okay, sounds like a plan. Listen, I've gotta run. I'm due in Cunningham's office in a few minutes. What you've told me is very timely. Let's reconvene first thing tomorrow in my office."

After Delray disconnected, Frost said, "There's one thing about today that bothers me…"

"And what's that?"

"If he's lived off the grid successfully for this long, why now? What's changed."

"The only thing I can think of is the newspaper cutting."

Frost frowned. "You mean that good Samaritan thing he did for the school?"

Bridgette recalled the image in the newspaper article of Paul Johnson standing alongside his workmates accepting a plaque of gratitude. "It was only a tiny slip-up and only a local newspaper, but it showed his picture, assumed name and place of work."

"So how is that a slip up?"

"Almost every newspaper is published online these days. Most of the small ones for free."

"So what are you saying? Someone's been trawling the

Internet for ten years trying to find this guy. That sounds like an awful lot of effort to me."

"I guess it depends on how badly you want someone dead."

Thursday 8:03 AM

Bridgette's smartphone buzzed. Deep in thought, she didn't want to be disturbed, but when she saw whose number it was, she pressed answer. "This is a little early for you, isn't it?"

Renée Filipucci laughed. "Hi Bridgette. I'm just calling to let you know we're running a front-page story you're mentioned in."

"What story?"

"One of our reporters has made a link between the disappearance of Paul Johnson and the murder of Paul Ringwood. The headline is, 'The man who was murdered twice?' I think you're going to get a lot of press hassling you today."

Bridgette's heart sank. Vancouver Metro had been very careful about how much information they'd given to the media. She knew there was nothing she could do about it now. "Who's the reporter?"

"Joe Lyndall."

Bridgette knew Lyndall by reputation. He'd been a crime reporter for over twenty years and had good sources.

Filipucci added, "Look, I gotta run. Keep your head down today, okay?"

"Thanks for letting me know, Renée."

"I'll see you at the gym tonight." Then she hung up.

Bridgette swore as she put her phone back on the desk. A voice behind her startled her. "Doesn't sound like your day is getting off to a good start?"

Bridgette turned to see Levi Frost entering his cubicle. She shrugged then gave Frost a quick rundown of the breaking media story.

"Has there been a leak somewhere in our office?"

"Possibly, but Lyndall is a talented reporter and always has his nose to the ground. He's speculating of course, but he has a good instinct for these things. Someone in the media was bound to make the connection sooner or later. Lyndall's just ahead of the curve."

"This isn't going to make the chief happy."

"I'm more worried about Assistant Commissioner Cunningham. He has a tendency to panic when cases get a lot of media coverage. He'll make life hell for us."

Bridgette checked her watch. "We should get going, but I need to talk to the chief first. If he doesn't know about the headline yet, Cunningham will make him aware of it very soon."

"So what's the plan? Are we heading to Stanwyck for interviews?"

"Yes. I've set some up starting late this morning, but first I'd like to go to Vancouver prison and interview the doctor who cares for Alex Hellyer. And maybe even Hellyer too, if we can."

Frost frowned. "You think we're going to learn something useful?"

"The prison is on the way. I think it's important to have as much background as we can before we get to Stanwyck."

Frost stroked his chin. "He's been in jail for ten years and has brain damage. How much help can he be?"

Bridgette cocked her head on one side and shrugged. "We won't know until we try."

Frost raised his eyebrows. "Personally, I think it's a waste of time."

Bridgette was about to reply but paused when she saw Delray striding towards them waving a copy of the morning paper. He pointed to the front-page headline. "Have you seen this?"

After being delayed for almost an hour by a 'please explain' meeting in Assistant Commissioner Cunningham's office, Bridgette and Frost arrived at the Vancouver maximum security penitentiary at ten AM.

The journey had been quiet. Frost appeared to be sulking over Bridgette's insistence they visit the prison first. She ignored his oddly childish behavior and used the time to plan the day ahead.

The razor wire that topped both the inner and outer steel perimeter fences reminded Bridgette of how seriously the prison took its security. Upon arrival at the guard house out front of the administration wing, Bridgette wound down her window and flashed her badge.

A young male guard leaned towards an intercom. "Help you?"

"Detectives Cash and Frost from Vancouver Metro police. We have an appointment to see Doctor Shriver."

The guard studied their badges then nodded and pressed a button on a console.

As the heavy double gates slid apart, she heard the guard's voice through a speaker. "Park over on the left in general parking and make your way into the Admin Block. I'm sure you know the drill from there."

Bridgette thanked the guard then waited until the security gates had opened enough to allow the vehicle to enter.

She said, "Have you been here before, Levi?" as they drove across the parking lot towards a building signposted Administration.

Frost looked up at the two-storey brick and concrete facility that housed four thousand of the state's most dangerous criminals. "More times than I care to remember."

After parking the car, they entered through glass doors into a sterile reception area that reminded Bridgette more of a hospital than a prison.

They approached an overweight receptionist dressed in civilian clothes who was sitting in front of a computer behind reinforced glass. The receptionist kept her waiting for two minutes before she turned towards her and said, "How may I help?"

"Detectives Cash and Frost to see Doctor Shriver. We made an appointment earlier."

The woman turned to her screen again and after a couple of mouse clicks, pointed towards a security screening area. "I'll get you both to go through the security door. There's a waiting room on the other side. I'll let Doctor Shriver know you're here."

Bridgette thanked the receptionist. After getting through

the screening process, they sat on hard plastic chairs in a small reception area along with six other people. Bridgette tried to make conversation with Frost, but it was hard going. He was easy enough to talk to about anything related to the case, but when the topic drifted beyond that, Frost closed up. It was twenty minutes later before a man in his early forties appeared at the far end of the waiting room. Wearing a white lab coat over gray slacks, the slim man scanned the people in the waiting room. Bridgette noticed the stethoscope around his neck and said, "Doctor Shriver?"

"Yes. You must be Detective Frost."

"Detective Cash actually." Turning towards Levi Frost, who was now out of his chair, Bridgette added, "This is Detective Frost."

Shriver nodded at Frost and said, "If you'll follow me, I'll take you to our meeting room."

Bridgette raised her eyebrows at Frost as they followed Shriver. The doctor's body language was reserved, almost cold, and she wondered if he would cooperate. Frost gave her a subtle nod as if to say, 'I picked up on that too.'

The doctor led them up some stairs at the end of the hallway. They crossed a landing which led onto a long, enclosed walkway. Without breaking stride, Shriver said, "We'll take the overhead walkway, it's quicker."

The walkway was about ten feet wide and easily as tall. It had floor-to-ceiling glass paneling that gave Bridgette and Frost an aerial view of the facility. The walkway was around eighty yards long and she looked down as they passed over an outdoor prison exercise yard. Bridgette figured they were a good forty feet above ground as she studied the scene below. The inmates were huddled in small groups and seemed oblivious to the visitors' presence. Bridgette wondered which men were the predators and which were the prey as they jostled for position in the single spot that was bathed in sunlight. The swagger and body language of two men caught her attention. Frost moved closer to Bridgette and asked, "Why are we walking to the other end of the complex?"

Without looking back, Shriver answered, "I'm the only doctor in the infirmary at present. And I don't like to be too far from my patients in case of emergencies."

In an effort to break the ice, Bridgette said, "Do you get many, Doctor?"

"Drug overdoses mainly. Despite our rigorous screening, prisoners still manage to get illicit drugs."

They walked on in silence until they got to the end of the walkway before heading down a set of metal stairs into a hallway on the first floor. Shriver opened a door on the right and led them into a meeting room that Bridgette didn't find much different to any of the small meeting rooms they used in Vancouver Metro. There was a flat TV screen on one wall and a small push button console and speaker on the conference table.

Shriver sat on one side of the table and motioned his visitors to sit on the other. He waited until Bridgette and Frost were settled before he said, "I understand you have found the body of the man Alex Hellyer was supposed to have murdered?"

Frost responded, "We've recovered the body of a man we believe may be Paul Ringwood, but nothing is confirmed yet. We're still waiting on the DNA report."

Shriver said, "And how long has he been dead?"

Frost answered again, "About two weeks."

Shriver snapped, "How very unfortunate."

Bridgette interjected, "Our visit today is to gather as much background as we can. Your patient…"

Shriver interrupted. "Why would you be wanting to know about Alex? If it is Ringwood, and he's only been dead for two weeks, my patient is clearly innocent of his murder."

"Alex and Ringwood both lived in Stanwyck at the time of Ringwood's disappearance and…"

"When will Alex be released? Surely you're not planning on keeping him here any longer than is absolutely necessary. He's clearly an innocent man."

"As soon as a formal ID is made, an appeal process can commence. I believe our police commissioner is already in discussions with the relevant judiciary. But that's not something Detective Frost or I can comment on."

Shriver pushed a Manila folder across the table and said, "I printed out Alex's medical file. As his doctor, I don't see how I can help you beyond that. You can look at it but not take it with you."

While Frost opened and scanned the file, Bridgette said, "How long have you been Hellyer's physician?"

"I've been here five years and have treated him all that time."

"What can you tell us about him?"

"Not much to tell, really. He's got the mental capacity of a five year old. He's a cooperative patient who sleeps most of the day. He can feed himself with a spoon and use the bathroom, but beyond that he's almost helpless. He'll need special care when he's released."

"So is he housed in the infirmary or in the general population?"

Shriver rolled his eyes. "He wouldn't last five minutes in the general population."

"How did it happen?"

"How did what happen?"

Frost entered the conversation abruptly. "His injuries. Apparently he was a fully functioning adult when he arrived."

Shriver shrugged, "I wasn't here then. As I'm sure you're aware, prison is a tough place. Apparently when he first arrived another inmate tried to rape him, but Alex put up a fight. He was bashed and found unconscious in the shower block. He was in and out of a coma for over a week and was never the same once he came out of it. He was diagnosed with a brain injury and some paralysis in his right arm. He had physiotherapy early on, but it didn't seem to make much difference."

Shriver shook his head in disgust and then added, "And now we find out he was innocent the whole time and should never have been here in the first place."

Frost said, "The system's not perfect."

Shriver retorted, "Tell that to his mother."

In an effort to defuse the hostility, Bridgette said, "Could we see him? Perhaps talk to him?"

Shriver crossed his arms. "I don't see the point. He can't help you. Clearly he was here when this recent murder happened and like I said, he has the mental capacity of a child. He can barely remember what he had for breakfast, let alone anything that happened ten years ago."

Bridgette said, "Doctor Shriver, I respect your position, but I would like to…"

Shriver cut her off. "I don't mean to be rude, Detective, but if you want to talk to Alex, you'll need a court order. Unlike the system that put him here, I try not to judge and I do my best to look after all my patients regardless of their background, circumstance or alleged crimes."

Without waiting for a reply, Shriver pressed a button on the center console. A moment later a man's voice said, "Yes?"

"This is Doctor Shriver in meeting room four. I have two detectives here who need an escort back to the front gate. Can you be here in two minutes?"

After the guard agreed, Shriver said to Bridgette, "I have one thing to show you and then I must get back to work. Follow me."

They followed Shriver further down the corridor before pausing in front of a long glass window on the left. Bridgette didn't need Shriver to explain where they were as she looked into a room that contained six hospital beds arranged in a row.

Prisoners occupied three of the beds. Two appeared to be sleeping, but the third was clearly awake and raised the middle finger of a handcuffed hand in their direction. Shriver pointed towards a table at the far end of the room where a woman and man were sitting. The woman wore a white uniform, while the man was dressed in an orange jump suit — traditional prison attire.

Bridgette watched as the man who had sandy brown hair, a slim build and a wispy three-day growth, struggled to raise a spoon from a bowl to feed himself. She guessed his age at around thirty and had no doubt who she was looking at as his right arm dangled limply by his side.

She watched as the man lifted the spoon towards his face. A tremor in his hand caused some of the food to spill before he finally got a morsel into his mouth. The nurse made no attempt to help him, but sat alongside him watching his every move, her gestures encouraging him to keep on trying.

Shriver interrupted Bridgette's thoughts as he said,

"That's Alex Hellyer. Ten years ago, he was a free and able-bodied man. Now look at him. They all watched for a moment as Hellyer attempted to put the spoon back in the bowl. Bridgette felt sorry for him as she could see the tremors in his hand making the most basic of tasks difficult. She also noticed the movements of his head, almost as if he was constantly nodding to himself.

Shriver said, "The guard's here. Time to go."

Bridgette and Frost turned to the guard who said, "I'll get you to follow me now."

Bridgette said to Shriver, "Thanks for your time this morning, Doctor. We appreciate it."

Shriver responded, "I hope you can understand now why I won't let you interview him." Then he turned and walked back to the infirmary.

As they followed the guard up the stairs to head back across the walkway. Frost murmured, "Well, that went well. Are we going for a court order?"

Bridgette thought about the day ahead. It was crucial to find out all they could about Paul Ringwood, particularly if he'd had a relationship with Alex Hellyer.

Bridgette answered, "Maybe," as they passed over the exercise yard.

"Maybe?"

She wondered again whether Hellyer had been set up for the alleged murder ten years earlier or if he'd simply been in the wrong place at the wrong time. "Let's see what comes from our trip to Stanwyck."

Thursday 3:41 PM

Delray looked up from the report he was reading when his desk phone rang. He read the number on the digital display and muttered, "What does he want now?"

"Delray."

Never one for small talk, Assistant Commissioner Cunningham cut in, "I need to see you at four PM sharp, Chief Inspector."

"Certainly, sir. And what will we be discussing?"

"The status of the Ringwood case. I've got the media crawling all over me and I want an update."

"I can give you an update over the phone now if you like?"

"Let's discuss it in person."

Delray rolled his eyes and said, "Yes, sir. I'll be there at four."

"Who's your lead on this case? It would be good to have them join us as well."

"That would be Detective Cash, sir."

There was silence on the end of the phone before

Cunningham said, "Putting her in charge of this investigation was a mistake, Chief Inspector."

"With all due respect, sir, she's closed out three murder cases in her first year and provided great help with several other cases as well. She may only be twenty-eight, but with an IQ of 151 and…"

"We don't need to go over her resume again. I've heard it all before and that's not what I'm worried about. You know her reputation as well as I do. Two dead officers in three cases. It's a wonder that anyone in your team will work with her."

"Again, with all due respect, sir, my team understand we do a dangerous job and they're backing her a hundred percent."

"That's not what I'm hearing."

Delray shut his eyes. "Sir, if there's nothing else, I'll see you at four."

Five minutes later, Bridgette paused in the doorway to Delray's office and said, "You wanted to see me, Chief?"

"I sure do. Come on in, Bridgette."

Once she'd settled into a chair Delray said, "I'm meeting with Cunningham in a few minutes. He wants an update on the Ringwood case. Apparently, the media is crawling all over him wanting to know what's going on."

Bridgette had caught an early news bulletin before she'd headed into work and knew that it was a lead story. "Yes, I know. They're calling it the man who was murdered twice."

Delray rolled his eyes. "You can see why that's attracting media attention."

Bridgette nodded.

Delray asked, "Where's Frost?"

"He's reviewing CCTV footage that's coming in from Bolton. We've got two of their detectives working the neighborhood where Johnson lived. They're trying to piece together what happened. One of his neighbors has a security camera on his driveway and we got a partial image of the traffic that comes and goes on that road."

Her boss nodded his approval. "Well, that could be useful." Glancing at his watch, Delray added, "I don't have much time. Give me a quick rundown of what happened today."

Bridgette gave as concise an overview as she could. She started by telling Delray about their visit to the prison and being stonewalled by Shriver. Then a brief summary of the visit to Stanwyck, and how it had yielded little new information.

She closed by saying, "I visited a few of Paul Ringwood's relatives and friends from ten years ago. I didn't learn much other than he seemed to be a decent guy who went off the rails at a young age after his father died. Apparently, when he disappeared he was trying to put his life back together."

"So he didn't try to contact anyone afterward?"

"No one I spoke to seemed to be covering for him. In fact, they all looked quite shocked when they heard the news."

Delray nodded. "What about his mother?"

"His mother died six years ago. There's a sister who apparently lives on the West Coast who we're still trying to track down. I also visited his old house, but it was sold some time ago and I'd need a warrant to take a closer look."

"What about the police? Surely the detectives who worked the case should be able to tell you something?"

"One of them died a few years back, and the other has retired. Stanwyck police don't have a current address for him."

"As he was a former public servant you should be able to get that information from the State Records Department. Frost's wife works there as a matter of fact." Delray paused for a moment and raised an eyebrow. "Speaking of Frost, how's it working out?"

Bridgette didn't want to paint a grim picture of their working relationship, even though she could already see problems developing. Tactfully, she answered, "It's early days yet, Chief. He's happy enough to talk about anything related to the case, but beyond that he's not saying much. I guess that's understandable given what he's been through."

"I'm sure it will take time. So, I take it you're happy to continue working with him?"

Bridgette nodded.

"Do you need any extra help?"

"I think we're okay for now unless you think it would look better with the assistant commissioner to have a team on it."

Delray rolled his eyes again. "Don't worry about Cunningham. This is about what's best for the case. Teams can be good, but they can also become unwieldy."

Delray chewed on the tip of his glasses for a moment. "See if you can track down the detective who worked the original murder case. If he's like most old school detectives, only a fraction of what he knows will be actually written down. We'll reassess after we find out more."

Bridgette promised she'd make it her number one priority while Delray glanced at his watch again. "I have to go. I can't keep Cunningham waiting."

As he got up to put his coat on, Delray added, "By the

way, I got a call from Ray Warner about an hour ago. He confirmed a DNA match for the body and the hair on the hairbrush from Paul Johnson's place."

Bridgette's heart skipped a beat as she thought of the heavily pregnant Carrie Singleton now having to raise a child on her own. "Has anyone informed Carrie yet?"

"I phoned Bolton Police straight after I got the call from Warner. They're sending out a female police officer and a counselor to break the news to her."

"Well, at least that will give her some closure."

"Let me know if you get any grief from Records about getting that detective's name and I'll pull a few strings for you."

Bridgette promised she would and headed back to her desk.

It was fifteen minutes before the official five PM closing time when Bridgette entered the government office block across the road from the Vancouver Metro's South Precinct building. The State Records department was located on the first floor. Bridgette opted for the stairs. Hopeful of getting an address for the retired Detective Ron Burns before the day was out, she decided to make her request in person, rather than by phone call or email which were much easier to ignore.

With closing time just minutes away, Bridgette was relieved to see the department was almost empty. She approached a long administration counter and addressed the younger and more eager looking of two government employees with the name badge Danny.

Bridgette introduced herself, showed her badge and

asked if she could see Paula Reid. The young man's face dropped as he answered, "I'm sorry, Detective, do you have an appointment?"

"No. My boss, Chief Inspector Felix Delray, sent me. Apparently he knows Paula quite well."

Danny frowned. "Hang on," he said picking up a desk phone.

After dialing a number and waiting a moment, Danny said, in a hushed tone that Bridgette could barely make out, "I have a Detective Cash here to see you. She says this is…"

Danny stop talking and listened intently for a moment, before putting the phone down. He smiled and said, "I can help you. It's the address of a retired detective you're after, right?"

"Yes, Danny, that's right. Thank you."

The young administrator produced a paper form from under the counter. "Sorry, most of this work is done by computer now, but that will take longer. If I can get you to complete this form and sign it, I'll get you what we have on file."

Bridgette filled out the one-page form. As she handed it back, he smiled and said, "Hopefully this won't take long."

Bridgette decided to push her luck and said, "Do you have someone working here by the name of Jasmine Frost?"

Danny nodded. "Do you know her?"

"Not really. I work with her husband. He's a detective like me."

"I have to go out back and pull up the information you need from our computer system. If I see her out there, I'll let her know you're here."

Bridgette hadn't been after an introduction and called out, "Please don't bother her," but Danny had already disappeared through the door.

Two minutes passed before the door swung open again. Bridgette expected to see Danny returning, but was surprised when a woman about thirty years of age appeared instead. She was tall and slim, with long ebony hair, charcoal eyes and olive skin. She could have easily passed for a model. She made Bridgette feel awkward as she looked her up and down before saying, "Are you the detective?"

"Yes. My name is Bridgette Cash."

The woman took another step toward the counter and said, "You work with Levi, right?"

"Yes, and you must be Jasmine?"

The woman grimaced. "What's he done now?"

Taken aback, Bridgette responded, "Nothing, he's just started with our team and I thought it might be nice if..."

Jasmine cut her off. "Levi and I are separating." Then added with an amused look, "He hasn't told you that yet, has he?"

Embarrassed, Bridgette said, "No."

Jasmine moved a step closer. "He's not a great communicator is he?"

Bridgette flushed. "We're still getting to know each other."

Jasmine glanced at her watch and said, "If there's nothing else, I have real work to do."

Bridgette was going to say, 'Nice to meet you' and make an apology for taking her away from her work, but decided Jasmine's rudeness didn't deserve any extra effort and settled for, "Of course," before watching the woman turn and head back through the doors to the back office.

Bridgette let out a long breath as she thought about her partner. She wondered if the break-up had been recent. It would account for some of Frost's moodiness over the last two days. As she pondered his home situation, the door opened again and Danny returned.

Handing her a printed sheet of paper, Danny declared, "This is the new address for Ronald Burns. Apparently, he recently moved into a retirement complex."

Bridgette smiled and thanked Danny for his time, pleased at least one person had been pleasant. As she headed back down the stairs her phone buzzed. She recognized Frost's number even though it wasn't programmed in.

Frost said, "Where are you?"

"Across the road in the government office block getting information on Ron Burns' address. What's up?"

"I've been reviewing the CCTV footage we got from the guys in Bolton. I think we might have something."

Thursday 5:09 PM

After returning to the homicide room on level four, it took Bridgette several minutes to find Frost. He'd opted to take over one of the small meeting rooms at the far end of the floor in preference to working in his cubicle. Frost had written a mass of notes on the whiteboard and was immersed in his laptop at the conference table when she entered. She thought about the unpleasant conversation she'd just had with his wife but decided not to bring it up. His personal life was none of her business.

She said, "Hi, Levi. I came back as soon as I could," as she scanned the notes he'd written on the whiteboard.

Without taking his eyes off the screen, Frost murmured, "Pull up a chair, I've got something to show you."

Bridgette found it hard to take her gaze off the whiteboard as she sat down. While she had a thousand questions, she was confident Frost would tell her what she needed to know.

"I've spent two hours going through the security footage we've got from the Bolton Police." Pointing to the whiteboard, he added, "I've summarized the key points. We'll get to those shortly."

"Okay."

"So this is the CCTV footage from the house a few doors down from where Johnson, who we believe is really Ringwood, lived."

Pointing at his computer screen, Frost added, "This camera has a partial view of the road. I've been through nine days of footage so far. A week before his disappearance and two days afterwards."

"You've done all that in two hours?"

"It doesn't take long. There's not much traffic on the road. You can go a whole hour and not see anything."

Frost pointed at the monitor. "This is the footage of Ringwood's truck leaving for work on the morning he disappeared."

Frost clicked his mouse and the video sprang to life. Bridgette saw the grainy image of a truck appear on the right of the screen and then disappear again a second later.

Frost clicked his mouse again to pause the image and pointed to the bottom of the screen where the video's date and time had been recorded.

"You can see that he left for work at 6:35 AM which seems consistent with what his partner told us when we interviewed her. We don't see his truck again until late that afternoon — just after six PM, in fact."

With another click the screen sprang to life again. This time the grainy video image was much darker. A vehicle with its lights on appeared. Frost paused the video again. He pointed to the whiteboard and said, "I've noted down all the patterns I've seen with cars that use this road over the course of the week."

"And you think they're all neighbors?"

"Very likely. Most of them seem to come and go at roughly the same time each day. There were three exceptions — two delivery vans which came and went in the space of about ten minutes each, which I'm not overly worried about. But this…" Frost pointed to a white van with a black side stripe on the screen, "this van came up the road at 3:48 PM on the day Ringwood disappeared — two hours before he came home."

Bridgette moved in a little closer to study the grainy image. "The image quality isn't good enough to pick up any facial features of the driver."

"I'll ask the tech guys to see if they can digitally enhance this. It's a long shot, but you never know."

Another click and the image of the van disappeared off the screen. He said, "Now this is where it gets interesting. We don't see that van again until 7:02. Watch."

The same van, now set against the dark backdrop of night flashed by.

"I'm almost certain this is the same van from earlier. You only have to look at the stripe on the side."

Bridgette studied the screen for a moment and then nodded. "I agree."

"I find it curious. This van arrives two hours before Ringwood gets home and leaves less than an hour afterwards. And it never makes another appearance in any of the other footage."

Bridgette knew where Frost was going; Ringwood lived on a cul-de-sac. "So what are you suggesting?"

"I think whoever was in that van is involved. We'll check for deliveries with the neighbors, but I can't see the timing being a coincidence."

"What do you think happened?"

Frost pushed back from the table. "We can't prove any

of this, of course, but I think whoever was in that van drove up the road somewhere and parked out of sight, waiting for Ringwood to come home."

"We can check with the neighbors if they saw that van. That shouldn't be hard to do."

Frost nodded. "I think they then went back to the house, got the drop on Ringwood, maybe clubbed him or knocked him unconscious then threw him in the van and drove away."

Bridgette frowned.

Frost said, "You don't agree?"

There were no blunt trauma injuries on the victim. The only injury they found was the gunshot wound, and some scars on his arms." Bridgette cocked her head. "What if he was shot with a gun with a silencer on his patio rather than somewhere else."

"That would explain why the patio was wet."

"Washing it down is a quick and effective way to get rid of the blood."

Frost let out a long breath. The frozen image on the screen juddered a little as if it didn't like being on pause. "I would have liked to get a visual on the number plate, but the camera is pointed at the wrong angle."

"Perhaps we can get some security video from businesses in the surrounding areas? Maybe he stops to get gas or something?"

"I'm working on it. I've got the Bolton police scouring the area for other CCTV footage as we speak."

Frost rewound the video and paused it with the blurry white van in the center of the screen. "I wouldn't mind betting Paul Ringwood is in the back of that van and is already dead."

Bridgette mused, "It's plausible, but it begs the question…"

"What?"

"If he's in the van and already dead, why would you drive for three hours before you dumped the body?"

Friday 8:14 AM

Bridgette looked up from her computer screen as she caught sight of Levi Frost. An early riser, she was regularly at work before seven each morning. Frost seemed to have a different routine and never arrived before eight; today was no different.

They had worked until well after seven the previous evening reviewing the Bolton CCTV footage. Bridgette suggested they should get one of Vancouver's digital analysts to improve the grainy image. They needed a better picture of the van and its driver, and Frost had made a note to handle it first thing the next day.

Keen to get the day off to a good start, she said, "Good morning, Levi," as he entered his cubicle and took a seat.

Frost began pulling things out of his backpack as if he hadn't heard her.

Bridgette tried again. "Morning."

Again, Bridgette was greeted with silence. After giving him a few moments to settle in, she leaned over top of the divider and said, "When you're ready, it would be good to compare notes and plan out the day ahead."

Frost scowled. "I'm going to work on my own today."

"Oh … Why?"

"You didn't tell me everything about your trip to government records yesterday, did you?"

"I met your wife if that's what you're referring to?"

Frost got up from his chair. Even though Bridgette was five feet ten, Frost towered over her. Seething, he jabbed a finger at her. "You have no right to interfere in my private life."

Taken aback, Bridgette kept her voice calm and even. "I thought it would be nice to say hello, seeing as how I was already there and…"

Frost interrupted. "Well, you thought wrong!"

Bridgette was conscious the other detectives were watching them. In an effort to diffuse the situation, she said, "I think we should use one of the work rooms to talk about this?"

Frost took a step towards her and said in a low voice, "Let's get one thing straight. I don't want or need your help."

Bridgette's jaw dropped. Before she could get an apology out, Frost turned his back on her. Although embarrassed and angry at the injustice her overriding emotion was one of concern for Frost as he stormed off toward the elevator.

She sighed and shook her head as she wondered how yesterday's friendly outreach to his wife had backfired so badly.

The Cold Light of Day

Bridgette left the Vancouver Metro south complex almost immediately after her run in with Frost. No point hanging around to wait for his mood to improve, she thought. Giving him space was probably the best thing she could do.

She had phoned the retired detective, Ron Burns, to setup an interview. Burns had sounded wary over the phone and only agreed to the interview if they met in the town and not at the retirement village where he was living.

The forty-minute drive to Stanwyck gave her a chance to think about the incident in the office. If Frost's marriage had been in good shape, she couldn't imagine him having that kind of reaction. But if, as his wife had suggested, they were now separated perhaps there was more to the story.

She felt guilty — she hadn't meant to pry — that was not her style. She was disappointed that her efforts to get to know him were in tatters but what else could she do? It was in her nature to be concerned. There had been four suicides over the past two years in Vancouver Metro and she had almost been one of them while she'd grappled with her father's murder. She decided to talk it through with Carol Sanders, Vancouver Metro's resident psychologist. And Delray too, if he asked.

Now seated in a window booth at the Style Coffee Shop on Main Street in Stanwyck, she glanced at her watch. It was 10.21 AM and Burns hadn't shown up. She'd chosen a window seat to soak up some morning winter rays but as black clouds gathered, she shivered. An omen for the day ahead?

She pulled her jacket around her while a man in a heavy, woolen overcoat limped determinedly towards the coffee shop. He had a ruddy complexion with thinning salt-and-pepper hair, and she guessed he was in his mid-sixties. Although Bridgette had only been on the force a short time, she had developed a sixth sense for picking out cops amongst a crowd of strangers.

She was fairly sure the man in the overcoat was Ron Burns as he pushed through the glass doors. The man scanned the patrons until his eyes rested on Bridgette. She had given him a vague description of herself but needn't have bothered; she was the only person under thirty-five in the coffee shop apart from a waitress. Bridgette extended her hand as Burns walked towards her. "Detective Burns, I presume?"

Burns replied, "Retired detective actually," and shook her hand.

"Thanks for seeing me on such short notice."

Burns sat down. "No problem."

"Would you like coffee?" said Bridgette raising her hand to attract the waitress' attention.

Burns said, "Are you paying, or is Vancouver Metro?"

Bridgette smiled. "My department is paying for this one."

"Well, that's a first." Burns got up and took his overcoat off and hung it on the back of the chair. "Make it black, and hot … please," he grinned at the waitress.

"Sure thing, Mr. Burns, just like always."

Surprised by the familiarity, Bridgette also smiled at the waitress, "I'll have a peppermint tea, please."

"I figure whatever it is you wanted to talk to me about must be important if it had to be straight away."

"Yes it is. And again, thanks for seeing me on such short notice."

Burns nodded. "So how can I help?"

"Does the name Paul Johnson mean anything to you?"

Burns eyes narrowed. "I went to school with a Paul

The Cold Light of Day

Johnson, but he's been dead almost twenty years. I'm sure that's not who you have in mind."

"What about Paul Ringwood?"

Burns ran a tongue over his lips. "What about him?"

"There's a news story about to break. A man called Paul Johnson was discovered murdered twenty miles from here at Barnett Lake."

"I read about that. The guy they found floating in the water."

Bridgette nodded. "But Paul Johnson was not his real name. We're pretty sure the body belonged to Paul Ringwood."

Burns eyes widened and he leaned back in his chair. "That's impossible. Paul Ringwood was murdered ten years ago."

"Well... that's the problem. The man who was dragged out of the lake had a dragon tattoo on his right bicep just above a large mole. When we searched through our database we came up with an almost perfect match for Paul Ringwood. He..."

Burns interjected, "But lots of men have tattoos these days and it's not uncommon for people to have moles on their arms. It must be a mistake."

Bridgette shook her head. "Because Paul Ringwood had a criminal record, albeit a small one, we had photographs, including one of the tattoo on file. Since then, the coroner has confirmed his identity through a DNA test."

Burns looked away. "It can't be."

"You never recovered the body?"

"We thought it had been dumped somewhere and would eventually turn up. There was blood all over his garage and we found the murder weapon at the suspect's house." Burns shook his head, blood draining from his face.

Bridgette spoke softly, "I know this must come as a shock to you, but it looks like Ringwood staged his own murder and then disappeared. Through our investigations we've discovered he'd been living off the grid in Bolton under the name Paul Johnson."

She paused as the waitress returned with their drinks. Burns absentmindedly stirred three spoonfuls of sugar into his coffee.

When they were alone again, she continued, "I know this will get messy. My visit today is twofold. Firstly, as one detective to another, I wanted to warn you. The media love stories like this and you may even need to leave town for a few days."

Burns nodded and kept stirring his coffee.

"The second is I figured you might take off when the story broke so I wanted to learn all I could from you before that happens. It's fairly obvious the original disappearance was staged. I'm hoping you could help me so that I can figure out why someone just killed Paul Ringwood … again!"

Burns took a large swallow of his coffee. He was breathing fast and Bridgette could see beads of sweat forming on the man's forehead. The color draining from his face prompted Bridgette to ask, "Are you okay?"

He was silent for a few moments then nodded and gulped.

Narrowing his eyes, he took a breath, "Paul Ringwood was a small-time drug dealer. I knew his father quite well. We'd gone to school together and he was a good man. Paul was only about fourteen or fifteen when his father died and he never really got over it. I tried to keep an eye on him, but trouble seemed find him and he got drawn into petty drug crime. One day I went to visit my sister who lived two streets away from where he was living. This was about a week before he was murdered, I guess. As I approached, the whole place was lit up like the 4th of July. There were three cop cars and an ambulance. Naturally I stopped and discovered Paul had been stabbed, but he wouldn't say who did it, or why, and didn't want to press charges."

"Was the stab wound serious?"

Burns shook his head. "It was more of a slash, minor, but it bled a lot. After he was released from hospital I visited him. We talked a bit about how life was working out for him. He told me he wanted to go straight, and I believed him. We talked for over an hour about what he needed to do to turn his life around, and I think in the end he trusted me. As I went to leave, I asked him again who had stabbed him and he gave me the name Alex Hellyer, but still didn't want to press charges."

"Did you know about Hellyer?"

"Not really. He was apparently selling drugs here in Stanwyck, and rapidly moving up the dealer hierarchy. He'd approached Paul on the street and warned him, saying that this was his territory so Paul couldn't sell there anymore. That escalated into an argument which was when Paul got stabbed. A week later he turned up dead, except he didn't actually turn up."

Bridgette said, "Yes, not really dead, just missing."

Burns nodded. "I got a call from several of his work mates from the local stone masonry where he worked. When he hadn't shown up for work, they went around to his house to check on him. They found the garage door half open and blood everywhere inside, but no trace of Paul. We feared the worst. We mounted a massive search including dragging lakes and rivers, but never found him. I always expected his body to show up one day."

"What made you turn it into a murder investigation?"

"His bank accounts hadn't been touched. Even though we didn't have a body, we presumed he'd been murdered. After four weeks the case was officially turned into a murder investigation. The violent incident with Hellyer made him the prime suspect. We soon found out Hellyer had been seen by a witness in the street early in the morning on the day Paul disappeared.

"We got a search warrant for Hellyer's house and found a partially burnt knife in an incinerator in his back yard. There was enough blood on it to get a DNA sample and we got a match for the blood we found in Paul's garage. We believed we had the murder weapon, a motive, and a witness that placed him at the scene of the crime."

Burns paused for a moment. He appeared to have aged ten years before Bridgette's eyes. "If what you're saying is true, then this is very embarrassing. But we thought we were doing our job, and a jury agreed."

Bridgette nodded. "We all make mistakes. Unfortunately, this one means that an innocent man has been in jail for ten years."

Bridgette returned to her car, unsure of what to make of the interview with Ron Burns. He seemed on the level, but something about his answers made her think he was holding back. While she sat and contemplated, she realized she should check in with Delray.

She took a deep breath as she dialed his number. If Delray had heard about her altercation with Frost that morning, there was no doubt he would throw her questions which would be embarrassing to answer.

Delray rarely wasted time with phone greetings, and this call was no different. "How did the interview go with Burns?"

"Hi, Chief. About as well as could be expected."

"And what does that mean?"

Bridgette said, "He was defensive," and then gave Delray a summary of the interview.

There was silence on the phone for a moment. Bridgette pictured Delray sitting in his office chair scratching his chin or chewing on one arm of his glasses while he thought.

"You think he's on the level?"

"I'm not sure."

"You're not sure?"

"He sweated a lot, but I think that has more to do with his health than anything else."

"He's not well?"

Bridgette mused, "He didn't say as much, but he didn't look well. But that said, his answers were evasive. I don't think he was giving me the full story."

"Well ... I guess if we were in his position we'd probably react the same."

"I'd like to interview him again in a day or two. I think I can learn more if I can gain his trust."

"Put something in the diary for early next week. You never know, he may be the key to solving this murder."

"Will do."

"Before you go, what happened with Frost this morning?"

Bridgette's heart sank. She was hoping to avoid this conversation — at least until she'd had another chance to talk to her partner. "You've heard already?"

"News travels fast around the office, Bridgette. You should know that by now."

She gave Delray a quick rundown of the encounter with Frost that morning and concluded by saying, "So I'm working solo today."

There was another pause before Delray responded, "I knew he had some marriage problems — he admitted as much, but I didn't realize it was this bad."

"I figured giving him some breathing space today was the best thing I could do."

"I think that's wise. Let's hope he's feeling better tomorrow."

"Yes."

"So what's the plan for the rest of the day?"

"I've got two more interviews here in Stanwyck and then I'll head back to the office."

"Come see me when you get back. I've got Cunningham crawling all over me, so I need to keep him up to date."

Bridgette promised she would and then disconnected. She sat for a moment and thought about the interview again. She frowned as she thought about Burns' answers and then nodded once to herself. Satisfied that she knew what was bothering her, she started the car. As she pulled a U-turn, she was already planning the questions she would ask the retired detective at their next interview.

Saturday 8:53 AM

Bridgette entered the coffee shop on Main Street a few minutes before nine. It was busier than the day before. She figured fewer people worked on a Saturday so had more time to linger and chat over coffee. She caught sight of Ron Burns in a booth in the back. She was surprised he was here early when he had been late for their last meeting.

After weaving her way through the tables, Burns acknowledged her presence with a nod.

Bridgette said, "Good morning," as she eased into a chair. "I didn't expect our second interview to be so soon?"

Burns frowned. "I'm not sure where to begin."

Bridgette wanted to say, 'At the beginning is always good,' but didn't want to appear condescending. "Wherever you feel comfortable."

After a deep breath, Burns said, "I was a detective here for close on thirty-five years and took an early retirement when our budget was cut."

Bridgette nodded.

Burns continued, "During my time we investigated

everything from stolen bicycles to bank robberies, and even the odd murder."

"Must have kept you busy."

"Being a town of just forty thousand, you'd expect it to be quiet at least some of the time, but it never was."

Burns paused while the waitress came and took their orders. When they were alone again, he continued. "We work differently to city cops."

"In what way?"

"Most people you investigate, you know nothing about. Here, we know almost everyone."

Bridgette nodded again. "True enough."

Burns frowned. "The point is, as local cops, we know a lot about the people we're investigating before we even start."

Bridgette said, "I see," to keep the conversation moving.

Burns let out a breath. "I need to tell you things about Alex Hellyer. Things you won't read in his case file. Things that happened a long time ago that will help you understand why Paul Ringwood disappeared."

"I'm listening."

"Fifteen years ago, I got called to the local hospital to take a statement from a woman. She'd been badly beaten — two black eyes and a cut lip. A clear case of domestic violence, but she didn't want to press charges. She claimed she'd fallen down some stairs, but I've never seen anyone get injuries like that from stairs. My partner and I visited her home to confront her husband. He laughed and shrugged it off, telling us to only come back if she pressed charges. He had a reputation as a heavy drinker and had been violent on more than one occasion in the past. But we couldn't arrest him unless his wife pressed charges, which she wasn't prepared to do. We warned him, but we knew there was little else we could do. Over the course of the next three years, this happened another four times."

"Did she ever press charges?"

Burns shook his head. "The same pattern would repeat itself. She would be admitted to hospital, her young son would go and stay with friends and eventually she and the son would go home again, and everything would be all right for a while."

"How old was the son?"

"Eleven when it started."

Bridgette let out a frustrated sigh. "Some women find it very hard to leave relationships even when they've been badly abused."

"I noticed a change in the boy over that three-year period. He was friendly and sociable at first, but over time he became withdrawn and moody."

In the course of her criminology studies, Bridgette had studied domestic violence and knew some of the wider impacts it could have on families. "It can be devastating," she said.

"The last time it happened, I wasn't on duty. The woman self-admitted to the hospital but was in a bad way. This time it was a fractured cheekbone. She stayed for about three days as I recall … that was the last time he ever beat her."

Bridgette's eyes widened. "He changed his ways?"

Burns shook his head. "Their house burned down. Early the morning after she'd been admitted, the fire brigade got a call. By the time the fire crew got to the house it was fully alight. They did a search after they put the fire out and found a body upstairs in the master bedroom."

"The husband?"

"Yes. He was a smoker and there was an empty Whiskey

bottle found in the charred remains of his bed. It looked like he'd been drinking and smoking and had passed out."

Bridgette raised her eyebrows. "The timing is very suspicious?"

"The fire crew investigated but found no signs of arson or forced entry."

"But you think it was deliberate?"

"It's irrelevant what I think. No charges were ever laid, and the coroner listed the cause of death as accidental."

Burns paused to collect his thoughts and then continued, "In time she made a full recovery, but not so the boy. He started getting in trouble at school."

"So was this Alex Hellyer?"

Burns nodded.

"How was he getting into trouble?"

"It was just little things at first. He was sassing teachers and being disruptive. He was expelled twice as I recall but was still an A-grade student. Then it got worse. When he was sixteen, he was caught peeping into a girls' change room. One of the girls caught him in the act and came out and challenged him. He denied it, of course, but the girl made a big scene. A week later the girl's cat was found strangled and hung up in a tree in their front yard."

"Hellyer?"

Burns nodded. "We were fairly sure it was him, but we had no hard evidence. No one saw him in the neighborhood, or at the scene of the incident. We brought him downtown and questioned him hard, but he denied it."

The waitress arrived with their drinks. Burns waited until they were alone again then said, "Over the next three years another seven cats or dogs were strangled and hung up in trees in either the front or back yards of family properties. They all had one thing in common."

"Hellyer?"

Burns nodded and took a sip of his coffee. "He not only developed a reputation as a peeping Tom, but he also started following some of the local girls."

"As in stalking them?"

"Not overtly, but yes. He would take a liking to a girl and suddenly start appearing in places he normally wouldn't frequent to be near her."

"Was he strange?"

"Very. A loner, but very intelligent. We took him to court a couple of times, but there was insufficient evidence. All the locals knew about him by then, but he was very smart, and we could never prove anything. It was very frustrating, and he seemed to enjoy the reputation he was developing. Then it escalated."

Burns took another sip of his coffee. "One of the girls who was being followed had a boyfriend. He took matters into his own hands and gave Hellyer a beating one night. He was a football jock and big. Hellyer was messed up pretty bad and spent a night in the hospital. After he was released, he went home and wasn't seen for weeks. Eventually he came back into circulation but kept a low profile. Nobody expected it to last."

Bridgette wasn't sure what Burns was getting at but responded, "Uh huh."

"Then one day out of the blue, the football jock disappears. He got up early one morning to go for a run, as he normally did, but never came back. We mounted an extensive manhunt, but there was no sign of him. His bank accounts were untouched, and it was totally out of character. After a couple of months of fruitless searching, we knew he'd probably been murdered, and we were fairly sure who was behind it."

"But you couldn't prove anything?"

Burns nodded. "He was our number one and only real suspect. But with no witnesses, no murder weapon and no body, we couldn't make a case. It was very frustrating."

"So then what happened?"

"We investigated hard for six months but never found the body or any evidence we could use against Hellyer. He was nineteen by then and keeping a low profile now that he was a murder suspect. We didn't expect him to surface again for a while, but we were wrong."

"There's more?"

Burns' bottom lip trembled. He looked up at Bridgette and said, "The bastard came after my daughter. I'm convinced it was payback for the investigation."

Bridgette's frowned. "Your daughter?"

"She was seventeen at the time. She'd just started working part-time at the ice-skating rink. She was walking home one evening after finishing her shift and took a shortcut through the park. That's normally a safe thing to do in a country town, but not…"

Burns closed his eyes. The anguish on his face as he recounted the memory was clearly visible.

Eventually, he added, "She was attacked from behind and forced to the ground. He wore a mask and tried to pull her panties down. He slapped her hard across the face when she started to scream and told her to shut up, but she didn't. She kept screaming and a passing car heard her and stopped to investigate."

Burns paused. Bridgette felt sorry for him as he continued, "The car stopping saved her life. When the attacker realized he might be caught, he let her go and ran off into the night."

The waitress arrived with a top up for their drinks. Bridgette said thank you without taking her eyes off Burns. There was a thousand-yard stare in his eyes and his chest began to heave.

"Are you okay, Ron?"

Burns closed his eyes again and said, "I'm going to need a minute."

Nearly two minutes later he began again. "My daughter was a mess. She needed counseling for the next three years. I was furious, I knew it was Hellyer, but I couldn't prove it."

They were quiet for a moment before Burns added, "My lawyer advised me not to tell you anymore but ... you need to know how Paul Ringwood fits into all of this."

Burns blew out a long breath and then took another sip of his coffee. A thousand questions raced through Bridgette's mind, but she didn't want to break his train of thought. There would be time enough for questions when he was finished.

Burns looked down at the table. "The altercation in the street that I told you about between Alex Hellyer and Paul Ringwood wasn't exactly true."

"Oh? So what really happened?"

"Hellyer had sexually assaulted Paul's sister, but she never reported it. Paul approached Hellyer and threatened to kill him if he ever came near his sister again. It was a stupid thing to do, but understandable under the circumstances."

"So what happened?"

"Paul expected Hellyer to back down, but he didn't."

"What did he do?"

"Hellyer laughed in Paul's face and said, 'You remember Carl Stockton?' And then walked off."

Bridgette frowned. "Who's Carl Stockton?"

"He was the sports jock who disappeared. It was a veiled

threat, but Paul understood exactly what he meant. Paul came to me to talk about it. I told him we were unlikely to get anywhere with the threat given Paul had been the aggressor. I tried to get him to convince his sister to testify, but she wouldn't. We still had no real hard evidence and without that there wasn't much we could do."

Bridgette took a sip of her peppermint tea as she thought back over the events that had happened ten years ago.

Burns massaged his temples. Finally, he looked up and said, "Two days later, Paul came to see me again. I'd been friends with his father before he died and by then he was beginning to trust me."

"He came to you for advice?"

"Kind of. Paul told me the morning after he'd threatened Hellyer, he'd got up like any other morning and gone into his kitchen to prepare breakfast. That's when he first noticed some things had been moved around."

"What kind of things?"

"Just little things — his toaster and kettle and some cutlery in a drawer. He asked his sister — who lived with him at the time — if she'd moved anything, but she said she hadn't touched a thing."

"Someone had been in the house?"

Burns nodded. "The following night he locked everything up extra tight and lay awake until well after two before he drifted off to sleep. In the morning he woke up as normal only to discover that their underwear had been switched."

Bridgette frowned. "Underwear? What do you mean?"

"His underwear was in a drawer in his sister's bedroom and hers had been moved to his room. He also discovered two of his large kitchen knives were missing. There was no denying it. Someone had been in the house and he was certain it had been Alex Hellyer."

"So then what happened?"

"Paul told me he was leaving Stanwyck. He figured if he stayed any longer, he'd go crazy or wind up like Carl Stockton."

Ron Burns paused and stared into Bridgette's eyes. "That's when I knew something had to be done."

Saturday 9:27 AM

Bridgette's world became small as she stared across the table at the retired detective. The hustle and bustle of the café faded into the background as she realized where Burns' story was heading. "So what did you do?"

"Hellyer was a murderer. There was no doubt in my mind he'd killed Carl Stockton. I was convinced Paul Ringwood would be next. I had to do something. We were getting nowhere with the murder investigation and I had my daughter to think of."

"So, how was Paul involved?"

"Paul told me he was thinking of starting afresh; a new life with a new identity. Somewhere where Alex Hellyer couldn't find him. It got me thinking, Paul moving away might solve his problem, but it wouldn't solve mine or the town's."

Burns held Bridgette's stare. "It didn't take me too long to convince Paul if he was going away to start a new life with a new identity he could leave his old life behind permanently."

"So you staged his murder?"

"I offered him twenty-five thousand from my savings and told him to think about it. If we faked his death, he knew it would mean cutting himself off forever from everyone he knew and cared about, but like me, he was convinced Hellyer would kill again. He was certain he was at the top of the list."

"Faking a murder is a drastic step?"

"Both Paul's parents were dead, and his sister had fled to the other side of the country vowing never to return. Paul was so terrified he'd be murdered in his sleep, he'd taken to sleeping in his car in different locations every night. There was little downside for him. He would be free to start a new life and put a monster in prison who wanted to kill him."

Burns glanced around the café and then added, "I'm not proud of what I did, but I have no regrets either. Alex Hellyer would have killed again. I'm certain of that."

"So you staged the crime scene in his garage?"

Burns nodded. "I had a contact in Bolton and arranged for Paul to get a new identity. I gave Paul the twenty-five thousand and then we carefully cut his arm to drain enough blood to make the crime scene realistic. I only got one phone call from him after that to let me know he was safe. That's when I went around to his house and set up the crime scene in the garage. I used some of his blood to smear on a knife and then planted it in an incinerator in the back of the property where Hellyer lived with his mother. The rest ... well, I'm sure you've read the case file."

They were silent while Bridgette digested everything Burns had told her. She wasn't sure what she'd expected from the interview but hadn't counted on such a frank admission.

"Why are you telling me this now? Surely you must realize you'll go to prison?"

Burns' shoulders slumped. He suddenly looked like a very old man; defeated, yet strangely relieved as he answered, "I gave up smoking in my early forties, but apparently it wasn't soon enough. I've got lung cancer and it has spread. The doctors think I've only got months. There are a few things I need to put right before my time is up and this is at the top of the list. The only thing I draw comfort from is that Hellyer has brain damage and can never return to his old life."

Bridgette felt for Burns as she watched him almost wither before her eyes. Burns said, "So what happens now?"

Bridgette sat back. "To be honest, I have no idea. I need to report this to my boss and I'm sure Internal Affairs will want me to file a statement. I imagine they'll be in touch with you."

Burns nodded, resolved to his fate. Bridgette didn't think there was any point continuing the interview any further. The former detective looked exhausted and there would be many more for him in the coming days.

They sat lost in their own thoughts. Finally, Bridgette said, "Someone from Vancouver Metro will be in touch with you soon, Ron, but there's just one more question I'd like to ask you before I go?"

"Sure."

"Could you prove that Alex Hellyer started the fire that killed his father?"

Bridgette knew Delray didn't normally work on Saturdays, but he'd want to hear about the bombshell she'd just learned from Ron Burns. She'd driven her own car, a '66 Mustang, out to Stanwyck that morning for the interview, but Delray always struggled to hear her over the engine noise, so she decided to call him before she set off on the hour-long trip back to the city. The first attempt to contact him at home had failed with Delray's wife informing her he was on his way to work. She dialed his cell number and got an answer on the third ring.

"I've just pulled into the basement. Can you hear me okay?"

"I can hear you fine, Chief."

"How did your interview with Burns go?"

"I've just finished. I got more than I bargained for which is why I'm ringing you now."

"Okay, let me have it."

"This may take a while. Do you want me to call you back in a few minutes when you're in your office?"

"No. I won't be distracted down here, so shoot."

Bridgette spent the next few minutes recounting the details of her meeting with Ron Burns. At the end of her summary, Delray said, "Well, I didn't see that coming."

"Neither did I."

"So what made him want to give it up now? Surely he's smart enough to realize he'll get prison time for this if it's proven."

"He's got lung cancer and only has months to live. I think this has been playing on his conscience for a long time, and he's got nothing to hide now that Ringwood's dead and Hellyer can't hurt anyone anymore."

There was silence on the phone for a few seconds before Delray murmured, "God, what a mess. I'm going to have to call Cunningham right away. Internal Affairs will be all over this. Do you think he'll run?"

"I don't think so, but I can't say for sure. From what I gather his health is deteriorating rapidly."

"I've got some phone calls to make. How soon will you be back here?"

"Give me an hour. When do you think you'll be seeing Cunningham?"

"I'm not sure. Why do you ask?"

"It's not only Burns we have to worry about, but Alex Hellyer as well."

"You're right. If Burns is on the level, Hellyer has gotten away with murder and we shouldn't…"

Bridgette interrupted, "Two murders."

"Two?"

"Burns thinks he killed his father as well. He was burned to death in a house fire just a few hours after the last domestic violence incident with his wife. And I don't think it was a coincidence."

"But wasn't he only a boy?"

"He was fifteen. The fire happened at around two in the morning. Burns thinks he snuck out of the friend's house where he was staying and went home to let himself in to start the fire. The father was a heavy drinker and probably already unconscious. There's a good chance he never knew what happened."

"You really think that's possible?"

Bridgette studied the black clouds in the sky as they rolled in towards Stanwyck. She realized she was going to be driving home through heavy rain as she answered, "Given the timing and his history of violence, I'd say it was Hellyer's first murder."

"This just gets better and better. I'll see you back here in an hour. If you can't find me, I'll be in Cunningham's office."

Delray disconnected, leaving Bridgette alone with her thoughts. Suddenly she felt cold and started the engine to get the heater running. She sighed as she thought about the fresh developments in the case. Burns admission, if proven correct, answered a lot of questions about what happened ten years ago when Ringwood disappeared. While she had no reason to doubt his story, she would have to check it. He'd lied to her once and there was nothing to stop him from lying again.

After checking for traffic, she pulled out onto Main Street to head back to Vancouver. The drive would provide valuable thinking time to process everything she'd learned that morning. As she changed gears, she thought about her visit to the Vancouver penitentiary the previous day. The scene with Alex Hellyer trembling as he struggled to eat his breakfast played over and over in her mind. She tried to focus on the case again and realized despite everything she learned that morning, she was no closer to finding Ringwood's killer.

Saturday 1:27 PM

Bridgette sat alone in Delray's office waiting for his return. She had a fair idea he was still with Cunningham on level four and figured he would be back as soon as he could. She could have gone back to the Homicide room to wait, but there were still a few detectives working that afternoon. The quiet of Delray's office gave her the thinking time she needed. She had barely moved in twenty minutes while reflecting on what she had learned that day.

Deep in concentration, she had a picture in her mind of all the facts she had assembled. Like a visual whiteboard, she moved the pieces around as she processed the information she had gotten from Ron Burns against the backdrop of what she already knew.

Her concentration was broken by Delray's voice. "Sorry Bridgette, that took a lot longer than I expected."

"No problem."

Delray settled into his chair. "Have you been here long?"

"Not too long. How did it go with Cunningham?"

Delray rolled his eyes. "Let's just say he's not happy."

Bridgette thought about responding 'he rarely is,' but decided it wasn't her place to criticize a senior officer and settled for, "I guess you told him about my meeting with Burns?"

Delray grimaced. "He flipped out. The man murdered twice is a bad enough headline but throw in a corrupt cop staging a murder — the media will have a field day when they find out. I almost feel sorry for him."

"Does Cunningham know about Hellyer being a real killer after all?"

"I told him, but he wasn't interested. All we have right now is an accusation and no proof. We can't breathe a word of it to the media. It will only make us look worse."

"There'll soon be a bunch of lawyers beating a path to Hellyer's door."

Delray nodded. "And the last thing we need to do is give them ammunition for a libel suit as well."

"So I guess you'll want me to see IA and make a statement?"

"In time. Cunningham is aware of the information you learned today, so let them come to us. In the meantime, we have a case to solve and we need to focus all our energy on that."

Delray held Bridgette's gaze for a moment and said, "We'll try to keep this out of the media for as long as we can, but they will eventually find out about Burns. Once that happens, all hell will break loose. Cunningham wants a team on this from Monday and, for once, I agree with him."

Bridgette did her best to hide her disappointment. She realized it was the right call, but she had always preferred to work alone or with one partner rather than as part of a bigger team. As if reading her mind, Delray added, "I know you're not a fan of teams, Bridgette, but trust me this will help with your development."

"You're right. Just let me know what you want me to focus on and I'll give it a hundred percent."

Delray pushed back from his desk. "Right now, I'm not sure. What do you make of what you learned today?"

"I had been sure if we discovered why Ringwood disappeared ten years ago, we'd be very close to finding the killer. But I was wrong. I don't think we're any closer now than when we started, despite Burns' admission."

Delray scratched his chin. "This is getting very complicated."

"I've been trying to link the past to the present ever since I got in the car to drive back from Stanwyck. Maybe Ringwood's murder had nothing to do with what happened ten years ago? Maybe it was something recent while he was living as Paul Johnson that's behind it?"

"I'm tempted to shift the entire focus of the investigation back to Bolton."

"We're still working our way through other CCTV footage of the van that was seen on the road where Ringwood lived on the night of his murder. If we can get a license plate or a description of the driver, we're hoping that might open up a fresh line of inquiry."

"No luck so far?"

"I'm not sure. I haven't spoken to Levi since early yesterday morning. He was running the Bolton side of the investigation and I don't really know what he's found."

Delray grimaced at the mention of Frost's name. "I've been meaning to talk to you about Levi. He came and spoke to me late yesterday afternoon."

Bridgette could tell by Delray's body language that bad

news was coming. Her stomach tightened as she stared across the desk and asked, "What did he say?"

"There's no sugarcoating it, Bridgette. He told me he wants out. I asked him why and he wouldn't say. He said he'd made a mistake coming to Homicide and is requesting a transfer back to his old unit. I told him to give it another week and if he still felt the same way, I wouldn't hold him back."

Bridgette thought back to the last time she'd seen Frost when he'd stormed off after their argument. For once she didn't have a response and sat in silence contemplating where it had all gone wrong.

It was just after seven PM when Bridgette pushed through the heavy glass doors that led into the Chrome Bar and Grill. The bar and restaurant were a favorite hangout for Bridgette, Renée Filipucci and some of her other girlfriends from the gym. The decor was modern and even though the food and drinks were overpriced, Bridgette didn't mind. The higher prices generally meant a better class of clientele, which meant they could usually meet without being bothered by men every five minutes.

Bridgette scanned the bar area and spotted Filipucci sitting on a stool at the far end. As she made her way towards her friend, Filipucci frowned and said over the noise of the crowd, "You're not dressed?"

"Sorry, I've just come straight from work. I'm only staying for one drink and then I'm heading home."

Bridgette normally caught up with Filipucci and her other girlfriends from the gym every second or third Saturday night.

They would meet for dinner and sometimes go to a club afterwards. Bridgette and Filipucci would always meet half an hour before the rest of the girls showed up to catch up on the week.

Filipucci made a face. "The girls are going to miss you."

Bridgette grimaced. "I'm not going to be good company tonight. I've got a lot on my mind."

"With all the press you're getting on your case, I can understand."

Bridgette said, "It's more than that…" she paused while a barman took their order.

Filipucci ordered a vodka lime soda, while Bridgette settled for a mineral water.

After the barman left, Filipucci said, "So you were saying?"

"Levi wants to leave homicide."

Filipucci's eyes widened. "What! After only a week?"

Bridgette nodded. "We had an argument."

"What about?"

Bridgette summarized her meeting with Frost's wife and then the encounter she had yesterday morning with her new partner. "He accused me of interfering and told me to mind my own business. You don't think I interfered, do you?"

Filipucci shook her head. "Not by a long shot. You're not a social worker Bridgette, and if he's that sensitive, you're better off without him."

They paused for a moment while the barman served their drinks.

When they were alone again, Bridgette said, "I'm concerned for him. I don't think he's in a good place."

Filipucci didn't look convinced which prompted Bridgette to explain some of Frost's background, including the drug bust which had caused Frost to take stress leave. "I'm not sharing any secrets — this was all reported in the news except for his name."

"I remember the incident, but I wasn't aware he was the officer."

"Now you understand. Feeling responsible for the death of a young boy who took his last breath in your arms is something I don't think you'd ever really get over."

Filipucci twirled the straw in her drink. "What a mess. So what are you going to do?"

"My boss said he deserves a second chance, and I agree. He was only doing his job after all."

"It doesn't look as though he wants a second chance."

"I'm not prepared to give up on him yet. We have another week. Hopefully I can turn it around."

Filipucci looked doubtful. "Good luck Bridgette — you're going to need it."

Sunday 11:47 AM

After returning home from her drink with Renée Filipucci, Bridgette had taken a long shower and then heated a frozen meal. She rarely ate TV dinners but couldn't face cooking on a Saturday night. She tried watching HBO, but her mind kept returning to the case. At just after ten PM, she gave up and went to bed. She hoped she would sleep, but her dark bedroom only made things worse. Still awake at one AM and trying to figure out her next move in the case, she realized she still knew very little about the man who Paul Ringwood had become after he and Burns had staged his murder.

At just after eight o'clock on Sunday morning she called Carrie Singleton and asked if she could interview her again. To her surprise, Singleton agreed, and Bridgette spent most of her Sunday morning making the three-hour drive from Vancouver to Bolton. The drive gave her more time to think, and she reflected on Ron Burns' revelations about Alex Hellyer. The irony that a man who had quite possibly killed two people would soon be set free and compensated millions for wrongful imprisonment, weighed heavily on her mind.

It made her angry so she tried to push Hellyer out of her mind. She went back to basics and thought about the primary motives for murder: sex, power, money, justice, self-defense and revenge. The trip seemed to take no time at all as she mulled over each motive and how it might apply to her case. After turning into Singleton's driveway, she refused to give in to disillusion even though the motive for murder still eluded her. Bridgette switched off the engine and stared up at the house. She thought about her last visit and how Levi Frost had accompanied her. She wondered if they would ever work together again as she walked up the path to the front door.

She was taken aback when a short woman with grey streaks in her hair opened the door. She had been expecting to see Carrie Singleton, but said a pleasant good morning and flashed her badge as she introduced herself.

The woman responded curtly, "I know who you are. I'm Carrie's mother. Come in."

The woman led Bridgette into the same sitting room they had used for the interview on her first visit. The heavily pregnant Singleton sat in a sofa chair and made no move to get up as she greeted Bridgette. Singleton's mother paused in the doorway and said, "Carrie is too far along to be left alone now, so I'm staying here until after the baby is born." Turning to her daughter, the mother added, "I'm sure you don't need me here for this, so I'm going to head to the grocery store. Is there anything I can get you?"

After her daughter responded, "No," the woman turned to Bridgette and said, "Go easy on her," before she left the room.

Bridgette sat in a chair opposite Singleton. "It must be a big help having your mother here?"

Singleton nodded. "I'm not sure I would be managing without her."

Bridgette's heart went out to Singleton. The dark circles under her eyes were a tell-tale sign she wasn't sleeping, and her sad and pained expression suggested Paul Ringwood's death would take her a long time to get over.

She thought for a moment and then said, "I'm not going to ask you how you are Carrie, because I can see you're going through hell."

Tears trickled down Singleton's cheeks.

"I appreciate you seeing me again on such short notice. I can promise you we're doing all we can to find Paul's killer."

In a defeated voice, Singleton asked, "Are you any closer to finding out who did this?"

"I wish I could say yes, but the truth is, we don't have any strong leads yet, which is why I'm back here talking to you."

"I still can't believe he's gone," she said, looking at the door, "I expect him to walk in at any minute." Then she dissolved into tears again.

Bridgette didn't have any words of comfort and sat silently while she waited for Singleton to compose herself. When she thought she had recovered enough to continue, Bridgette said, "Since we last came to see you, we've been running two main streams of investigation. Bolton police have been running down leads here — mainly to do with the van we spotted on your neighbor's security video."

Singleton nodded. "They came and asked me questions about it, but I don't know anyone who has a van like that, and I don't think Paul did either."

"My partner and I have been trying to figure out what Paul's life was like before he changed his identity."

Singleton looked up. "What did you find out?"

Bridgette had debated how much to tell Singleton but decided it wouldn't be helpful to leave anything out to spare her feelings. "I found a man in Stanwyck who knew Paul and his family quite well. He's a former police detective and I've interviewed him twice now." She then explained everything Ron Burns had told her. Singleton listened in silence — spellbound — as Bridgette recounted the life story of Paul Johnson before he became her partner.

When Bridgette had finished, she added, "I know this is a lot to take in," and then stayed silent to give Singleton time to process everything she'd said.

Singleton blew her nose and wiped her eyes. "Before Paul died, I never really thought much about his past. But since then, I've thought about little else."

"From all reports, Carrie, Paul was a good man. He had two minor drug possession charges when he was a teenager, but he seemed to have gotten his life together when he left Stanwyck."

Singleton nodded. "This man he was running from, Alex Hellyer, could he be responsible? After all, I know people can organize murders from prison?"

"I've thought about that too, but it doesn't seem possible."

"Why?"

"Alex Hellyer was bashed shortly after he arrived at prison. One arm is paralyzed, and he has the mental capacity of a five year old. He can barely eat breakfast let alone orchestrate something as complex as a murder."

"What about a family member? Perhaps revenge on his behalf?"

"It's a line an inquiry we're pursuing. But so far, the only close relative or friend we've identified is his mother and she's in her mid-sixties."

Singleton frowned. "I can't see a woman in her sixties shooting Paul."

Bridgette wasn't as convinced but let the comment go. "As I drove here this morning, I almost convinced myself Paul's murder had nothing to do with his past. But there's one thing that continues to bother me."

"What's that?"

"If this has nothing to do with his past, why was his body discovered three hours away and so close to where he grew up? Bolton and Vancouver police are convinced he was murdered here, so transporting his body all that way for disposal has to be significant."

Bridgette studied Singleton's face for a moment and then added gently, "I'm not expecting you to have any answers Carrie, but anything you can recall may give us a vital clue."

Singleton struggled out of her chair and waddled over to the sideboard. After opening a drawer, she withdrew a folded piece of paper and said, "This has played on my mind ever since you told me about Paul. I showed it to you this last time."

Bridgette got up and walked over to Singleton. She knew before Singleton handed her the piece of paper that it was the newspaper clipping of Paul Johnson and his work colleagues.

Singleton said, "I've been wondering … could this have something to do with his murder? If someone from his past was looking for him, could this be how they found him?"

Bridgette unfolded the clipping and studied the image

of four young men posing next to a plaque out front of a school.

"I've thought about that too. I'm not sure if you remember, but I took a photo of this clipping on my phone last time. When I got back to Vancouver I checked the paper's website but found no trace of this or any other article about the school fire. I even did a wider Google search but got no hits for the fire or the restoration work Paul and his friends did. I called the newspaper and they told me because they're just a community newspaper with a limited budget, they swap out their online articles every two weeks or so to keep their server storage costs down. Once the article is removed, they fall off Google and other search engines fairly quickly.

Singleton held Bridgette's gaze. "But perhaps not quickly enough?"

Bridgette nodded as she stared at the clipping. "It's a possibility we can't discount."

Monday 7:58 AM

Bridgette checked her watch before she knocked on Delray's office door. She was two minutes early, but she didn't think he would mind. "You wanted to see me, Chief?"

"Come on in, Bridgette and close the door behind you."

Bridgette wondered why Delray had asked for the door to be closed. It was only ever closed when someone was about to be chewed out, but Delray's body language suggested that wasn't going to happen.

She watched Delray open his notepad to a fresh page as she settled into a visitor's chair.

"Like I said last time we spoke, Bridgette, we're turning the Ringwood case into a team investigation. We've got a meeting in the muster room at nine to go through all the changes. Cunningham has insisted he come and speak."

"I guess it's nice he's taking such an interest in the case."

Delray rolled his eyes. "He's worried about how this is playing out in the media. He's under a lot of pressure, which he will no doubt pass onto us. The reason I called you in now is because I wanted to explain the team structure to you in more detail. You're doing a good job, but there's a lot of moving parts with this case and we can't expect one team of two detectives to cover it all."

Delray put on his glasses. "Let me tell you about the new structure." He drew three circles on his notepad.

"We're going to have three teams; the Bolton team, the Barnett Lake team and the Stanwyck team."

Delray drew the initials TL and LG in the first circle and said, "Tony Lee and Lewis Grundy will lead the Bolton team. They'll work closely with the Bolton police, learning all they can about Ringwood's new life as Paul Johnson to see if we can find a motive for the murder. This team will be supported by others as required to go through all the CCTV footage coming in. We hope they'll be able to get an ID on the van seen leaving Ringwood's street on the night he disappeared."

Delray paused and drew the initials SM and JW in the second circle. "Sam McCartin and Jason Watts will lead the investigation at Barnett Lake and the surrounding area. We need to expand that investigation. I want everyone who lives within the immediate radius of the lake interviewed or re-interviewed. Somebody must have seen or heard something."

Delray paused again and drew the initials BC and a question mark in the third circle and then said, "I want you to lead the third team and continue your investigation in Stanwyck looking into Ringwood's past. Like you said, it makes sense if his body was dumped so close to where he lived before his fake murder, there has to be a reason. I think you're the best person to continue that investigation."

Delray put his pen down. "So that's the structure. We've got teams to investigate his past, the present and the place where he was murdered. Questions?"

Bridgette studied the diagram upside down for a moment and then pointed to the third circle. "Who's the question mark?"

"That depends…"

Bridgette frowned. "On what?"

Delray held her gaze and responded, "Are you happy to continue working with Levi or not?"

"After our run in, I wouldn't have thought you'd want me working with him?"

Delray took off his glasses. "Look, Levi has his problems and there's a good chance he won't be working here after this week, but his beef is not with you."

Bridgette shrugged. "It's your call, Chief."

"I don't think you'll have any more problems with him. But if you do, let me know and I'll move him to a different team."

Bridgette wondered if Delray had been talking to Frost again. She nodded. "Okay."

"Any more questions?"

Bridgette rose from her chair and pushed it back square to the desk. "Not for now. I think anything else I'm unsure of you'll cover at the nine AM briefing."

As she went to leave, Delray said, "Hang on a minute. Have you seen the paper today?" He slid a newspaper across his desk towards her.

She sat heavily into the chair again as she read the headline, 'Prisoner to be released. "Oh! No! It's too soon."

Delray nodded. "I couldn't believe it either. It looks like Alex Hellyer will be out of prison by the end of the week."

Bridgette walked back to her work pod, relieved that the muster was over. Delray had been concise in his explanation of the team structure, but Cunningham had waffled for over half an hour wasting everyone's time. She'd sat in the back of the meeting room, a habit she found hard to break, and noted Levi Frost didn't arrive until two minutes after the briefing had started.

Avoiding Delray's glare, Frost had opted not to sit and take notes like everyone else and had instead leaned up against a side wall, seeming to be only half engaged. Bridgette had figured by his body language he'd already decided on leaving and pondered if Delray's decision of placing Frost with her for the forthcoming week had been the right one.

She picked up a sealed envelope that had been left on her desk and heard Frost's voice behind her. "So it looks like I'll be working with you in the Stanwyck team."

Bridgette opened her mouth to apologize again for what happened on Friday but nodded instead; one apology was enough. "That's the plan."

Frost dropped his keys on the desk. "I've been out of the loop for a couple of days. What's been happening?"

Bridgette wondered how much she should tell him, but realized withholding information was not only petty, but unprofessional. "You heard about my second interview with Ron Burns in the muster room…"

Frost interrupted, "That was a bizarre confession."

"I think if I was dying from cancer, I'd want to put everything right too."

"So we now know why Ringwood disappeared. That's a start, I guess."

Bridgette nodded and peeled back the flap on the envelope.

"How do you feel about this becoming a team investigation?"

The question took her by surprise. For someone who seemed to be keen on leaving Homicide, Frost's question seemed odd.

"It's like the chief explained," said Bridgette, "lots of moving parts. We need a team to cover them all. Would you rather work alone?"

Frost shook his head. "So what's the plan for today?"

Bridgette answered, "I'm heading back out to Stanwyck to meet up with Ron Burns again." She pulled a piece of paper from the envelope. "He's got a lot of local knowledge that will be…" Bridgette paused as she scanned the contents of the letter. Then her face broke into a smile.

"What is it? Good news?"

"You could say that. It's my court order."

"Court order?"

Bridgette nodded. "The judge has granted us approval to interview Alex Hellyer."

Monday 11:29 AM

Bridgette and Levi followed the guard down same prison walkway they had used four days earlier. As they approached the infirmary, she wondered if Doctor Shriver had calmed down. She'd called him earlier to advise him that the court had granted her permission to interview Alex Hellyer.

Shriver had argued that it was a gross violation of his patient's human rights now that he had been pardoned.

Bridgette had tired of Shriver's grandstanding and threatened him with obstruction of justice if he didn't comply. The threat settled him enough for her to arrange an interview at eleven-thirty. Bridgette peered through the viewing window as the guard knocked on the infirmary door. There were four inmates in the hospital beds, none of whom were Hellyer. Bridgette noticed one unmade bed as she scanned the ward through the window. She then watched Shriver emerge from a room at the end of the facility. The scowl on his face was obvious as he walked through the infirmary. This is going to be difficult, thought Bridgette, but she was buoyed by the court order, which gave her all the legal back-up she needed and there was nothing he could do about it.

"I thought I'd seen the last of you, Detective."

"Good morning, Doctor Shriver," she said pleasantly.

Shriver stood in the doorway with an outstretched hand. "I want to see that court order."

Bridgette handed over the document. Frost raised his eyebrows at her while they waited.

After examining the warrant, Shriver said, "This is pointless, but I obviously can't stop you."

Shriver thrust the document back at Bridgette, then turned on his heel and walked back into the ward. Bridgette and Frost followed the doctor who headed towards the rooms at the end. Both rooms had floor to ceiling glass windows and full-length curtains, which Bridgette presumed remained open unless an examination was in progress. The curtains in the room on the left were drawn, but open in the room on the right, which was empty and sparsely furnished like most hospital rooms.

Shriver paused in front of the table and chairs where Bridgette had seen Hellyer eating breakfast on their first visit.

"Wait here. I'm going to check if he's sleeping or not. If he's awake, I'll bring him out." Almost as an afterthought, he pointed at the table, "This is where you'll be conducting the interview, and I'll be observing every second of it."

Once Shriver entered the room, Frost whispered to Bridgette, "Do we have to have him present for the interview? Can't we insist on privacy?"

Bridgette grimaced. "The court order gives us permission to interview Hellyer, but it doesn't say anything about privacy."

The door opened and Shriver appeared before turning back and mumbling something Bridgette only half heard. It sounded like, 'This way, Alex,' but she couldn't be sure.

Alex Hellyer appeared to be trembling as he reached out with his good arm and clutched Shriver's coat almost as if he was looking for instruction. Shriver led the prisoner towards the table then pulled out a chair. "Sit here, Alex."

Hellyer placed his good arm on the table for balance before he sat down.

Shriver said in a soft voice, "These two people are from the police, Alex. You don't need to be afraid, they can't hurt you. They just want to ask you some questions."

When Hellyer spoke for the first time, Bridgette wondered if he had sustained any throat injuries in the attack; his voice was high and squeaky like a young girl's.

Hellyer looked up at Shriver. "You stay here?"

Shriver put his hand on Hellyer's shoulder and said, "Yes, Alex, I'll be here."

"We'd prefer to interview Alex alone, if you don't mind."

Shriver shook his head. "Not a chance in hell. He's in a hospital and under my care, so I get the final say."

Bridgette knew it was an argument she wouldn't win and responded, "Very well."

Shriver said, "He gets tired when he has to concentrate. So let's keep this to fifteen minutes. And go easy on him."

Bridgette pulled her chair closer to Hellyer. She had agreed with Frost before they got to the facility that she would ask the questions and Frost would observe. Not knowing how well he could communicate, Bridgette decided to start with a few basic questions to judge his ability to interact.

She gave a brief smile and said, "Nice to meet you, Alex. Do you know my name?"

Hellyer shook his head and rocked backwards and forwards on his chair.

"My name is Bridgette, and this is Levi. We're police officers. Do you know what police officers do?"

Hellyer continued to rock. In his childlike voice he answered, "Put people in jail."

Bridgette nodded. "Sometimes we do, but only bad people."

Hellyer continued rocking without making eye contact. "Not bad."

Bridgette agreed, "No, you're not. Has Doctor Shriver told you that you'll be leaving here soon?"

Hellyer nodded. "Going home with my mom."

"That's right Alex. We want to ask you some questions before you go. Is that okay?"

"Okay."

"Alex, do you remember why you were put in jail?"

"No."

Bridgette continued to evaluate Hellyer's responses and body language as she asked, "Do you remember much about your life before you came to prison?"

"I lived in a house."

"With your mother?"

Hellyer nodded.

"What were the names of your friends?"

Hellyer stared off in the distance for a moment before he responded, "No friends."

Bridgette glanced at Frost who rolled his eyes and mouthed, "We're getting nowhere."

Bridgette tried a different tack. "Do you remember a man called Paul Ringwood?"

Hellyer stopped rocking for a moment and shook his head vigorously from side to side.

When Bridgette realized he wasn't going to say anything more, she pointed to the room he'd come out of and said, "Is that your room?"

Hellyer nodded. "Alex's room."

"Do you mind if my friend Levi has a look?"

Shriver growled. "You don't have a search warrant so that's not happening!"

Frost weighed in. "What does he have to hide, Doctor?"

Shriver declared. "This interview is over."

Bridgette didn't protest. She had seen enough. Shriver pulled Hellyer out of his chair. "I'm going to take you back to your room now, Alex."

Turning to Bridgette and Frost, Shriver snapped, "I'll get a guard to escort you out."

Ten minutes later they were making their way across the park towards their vehicle. Neither of them said a word until they'd settled in the car.

It was Frost who spoke first. "Well, that went well."

Bridgette was now getting used to Frost's sarcasm. She hadn't wanted to say anything until they reached the car. Partly because she was still going over the brief interview in her mind, and partly because she didn't want any guards or prison staff to overhear their conversation. "I'm not sure what to make of Alex Hellyer."

Frost frowned. "What do you mean?"

Bridgette tugged gently on her left earlobe while she was thinking. "The way he wouldn't answer the question about if he knew Paul Ringwood."

Frost shifted in his seat so that he could look directly at Bridgette. "I have a niece who's four, and she often shakes her head instead of saying the word, No."

"You could be right. But I think he was lying. He might not remember his friends, but I think he remembers Ringwood."

Frost nodded thoughtfully. "Well, we know for a fact five year olds are capable of lying."

After starting the engine, Bridgette responded, "I want to interview him again. But first we need to understand what brain injuries can do to an adult. Right now, we have no idea what's normal for him and what isn't."

"So how do we figure that out?"

"We need to talk to a specialist."

"You think that will help?"

Bridgette looked up at the penitentiary. "We're on a steep learning curve with everything on this case, and that includes Alex Hellyer."

Monday 12:46 PM

The drive out to Stanwyck was a quiet affair. Bridgette had tried to engage Frost in conversation as she drove, but after getting just yes or no answers for close to ten minutes, she gave up. Normally, she would have persisted, particularly as she was keen to see Frost stay with the Homicide team until he'd had a proper chance to see if he was a good fit or not.

But the peace gave her time to reflect on the interview with Alex Hellyer.

She played the interview back in her mind. All Hellyer's physical mannerisms were consistent with someone who had suffered brain damage. But the over-dramatized shaking of his head when he denied knowing Paul Ringwood was too much. The more she thought about it, the more perplexed she became.

While Frost gazed out at the rolling hills of the countryside as they sped along the freeway, she was thinking about Hellyer's physical condition. Were there any other physical injuries he might have sustained in the attack?

She thought about Shriver as well. What else did he

know? Despite his hostility, she wondered if he would let her interview him. Worth a try.

She turned off the freeway for the last few minutes of the trip into Stanwyck.

Frost said, "Are we meeting Burns at the coffee shop again?"

"No, at his house in the retirement village."

"I thought he didn't want us meeting him there?"

"I guess as his name is all over the newspapers with the story of Ringwood's double murder, he just doesn't want to be seen in public."

"I wouldn't either. When will Internal Affairs interview him?"

"That happened yesterday. Apparently perjury charges are being drawn up against him as we speak."

Frost went quiet again until they turned onto a road called Glenn Abbey Drive. "I'm surprised he's still willing to meet us."

"I think he's keen to appease his conscience."

Bridgette turned right onto a small sealed road towards Stanwyck Retirement Village and reduced her speed to match the limit of 15 mph.

They drove around a meandering circuit past a neat row of single-story brick and timber cottages.

Frost commented, "My aunt lives in one of these places. You've gotta be over fifty-five to get in, apparently."

Bridgette grinned. "It will be a while before you or I qualify."

"I stayed with her overnight once. I think everyone was in bed by eight o'clock."

Bridgette nodded. "I can see why you only stayed one night."

"What number are we after?"

"Forty-One," said Bridgette pointing at a house up ahead with a white picket fence. "On the left."

They pulled up out front of a small brick and timber cottage. The garden, like every other garden in the complex, was immaculate. Bridgette switched off the engine, and said, "I wonder how many more months he'll be able to live here before he has to go into a hospice?"

"He'll probably go to jail before he goes anywhere else."

"Maybe not. He's only got months to live."

Frost grimaced. "Not a lot to look forward to either way."

They walked up a stenciled concrete path and knocked on the front door. After almost thirty seconds with no answer, Bridgette knocked again.

Frost said, "You told him we were coming, right?"

"Yes. I called him about six o'clock last night and told him we wanted to see him today. I couldn't give him an exact time, but I told him it would be around midday."

Frost knocked on the door, this time much louder. "Maybe he's sleeping?"

While Bridgette called his cell phone number, Frost moved across to the front window and peered in.

"The curtains are drawn. I can't see a thing."

They listened for a moment hoping to hear his phone ringing inside.

Frost said, "Let's check around the back."

They walked around the side of the cottage and through a high gate to a small paved courtyard. Apart from three plants in pots and two timber chairs, the area was empty. Frost stepped onto a tiny patio and peeked in through the glass sliding door.

They were interrupted by a woman's voice calling out, "Can I help you?"

Bridgette turned to see an elderly woman with short gray hair and glasses glaring over the side fence at her. "This is private property!"

Bridgette held up her badge. As she walked towards the woman, she said, "Good morning, ma'am. We're police officers here to interview Mr. Burns."

The woman re-positioned her Coke-bottle glasses on her nose and peered at the badge. "Well, I'm afraid I haven't seen him ... not since last night. He was very distressed."

Bridgette asked, "Why was he distressed?"

"He showed me a headline in the newspaper. Something about a murder case he'd been involved with many years ago when he was still a police detective. He said he might have to go away for a while."

"Did he say where?"

The woman shook her head. "He didn't tell me anything else. Mr. Burns and I are not particularly close. I water his plants when he goes away and we say hello over the fence, but we keep out of each other's business."

"Did you see him packing for a trip?"

"No. I don't pry either, so I wouldn't know."

"So you didn't see him drive out of the complex last night or early this morning?"

"No, I didn't. But I know he's not here."

Frost said, "And why is that, ma'am?"

"His curtains are drawn. He normally has all his curtains open well before eight in the morning. Also, his lights went out at about seven thirty last night. He's a night owl and normally doesn't go to bed before ten."

Bridgette thanked the woman and headed back to the car with Frost.

Frost said, "What do you make of that?"

"For someone who supposedly stays out of her neighbor's business, she observes quite a lot."

It only took five minutes with the guard at the village's front security gate to confirm Burns had left the facility just after seven-thirty the previous evening and hadn't returned.

Bridgette called Delray to report Burns' disappearance, then she and Frost drove into Stanwyck.

As they approached the town center Frost said, "What I don't get is why run now? What is he afraid of? It's not as if the media is camped out on his doorstep?"

"I don't think it's the media he's worried about. Can you get the Internet on your phone?"

"Sure. What do you need?"

"Can you look up the online version of the Vancouver Tribune? I read last night that Hellyer's lawyer is getting him released on Friday."

"Surely they can't organize an acquittal hearing that quickly?"

"No. But the judge doesn't like the idea of an innocent man being in prison any longer than necessary. He's being released on a form of parole until his hearing. It would be good to know what time that story broke yesterday."

Frost logged into Google and searched for the Tribune. "It was published at six-fifteen last night."

"That can't be a coincidence."

Frost frowned. "Why would Burns be afraid of someone who is physically disabled and has the mental capacity of a five year old?"

"Perhaps Burns knows more than he's letting on? Maybe whoever killed Ringwood is gunning for Hellyer as well? Whatever the reason, he's gone, and we need to find him."

"So how do you plan on doing that?"

Happy that Frost was now engaging in actual conversation rather than just giving yes or no answers, she kept the thread going. "I'm hoping the APB on his car will turn something up. But if it doesn't, we can start with some of his old work buddies and see if they know of any places he liked to go to get away from it all."

"He doesn't have family?"

"Not here. His wife died a long time ago. He has a daughter, but she lives interstate."

"Well, that's sad."

Bridgette nodded. "Also, when I called the chief, I gave him Burns' cell phone number. They should be able to track his location from when it pings off cell phone towers."

"Provided it's switched on."

"Yeah."

"Well, that's a start I guess."

"Hopefully it's enough."

"Where are we going now? Who are we interviewing next?"

"Alex Hellyer's mother."

"I thought you said she didn't want to be interviewed?"

"She doesn't. I haven't made an appointment, but I'm hoping she'll be home."

"So what if she refuses to talk?"

"Now that her son is so close to getting out of prison, I don't think she'll do anything to jeopardize that."

"And if she refuses, we can always threaten to arrest her for obstruction."

Bridgette raised an eyebrow and glanced at Frost. "Let's hope it doesn't come to that."

"So what do you plan on asking her?"

Bridgette didn't have an answer. She'd conducted enough interviews to know the best ones were often the ones which you didn't prepare for. "That depends."

"On what?"

"How she answers our first question. If she's hiding something, we'll see it in her body language,"

"And if she is?"

"Then maybe we have a whole new line of investigation to work on."

Monday 2:06 PM

Bridgette and Levi pulled up in front of a two-storey timber house in Stanwyck. Bridgette guessed the house had originally been white, but with years of grime and neglect, it had turned a dull gray. The house was set back from the street in a middle-class neighborhood amidst an overgrown garden. The grass was almost knee high, which prompted Frost to say, "Are you sure this is the right place? The house looks abandoned."

"This is 129 Beaumont Avenue. It's the right address."

Frost frowned. "She's not big on home maintenance."

"She's lived here alone ever since her son went to prison, so I guess it's understandable."

"So, what's the plan?"

"We'll start with some general questions and see what comes of that."

"And what do you want me to do?"

Bridgette brushed her hair from her face. Even though the only question he had asked at the prison had gotten them thrown out, he was still her partner. "I'm happy to lead, but if you have a question, then go for it."

"I didn't exactly cover myself in glory with Shriver."

She smiled at Frost's recognition that tact wasn't his strong suit. "He was looking for any excuse to kick us out, so don't worry about it."

As they headed up the path through the weeds to the front door, she said, "We still don't have a motive for murder. The primary motives are power, greed, sex and revenge. The fact that Ringwood was shot and dumped the way he was probably rules out sex, but all the others are in play."

"I agree."

"While I still have an open mind, I'm leaning towards revenge if this is in any way connected to his past in Stanwyck. That's why we need to question Hellyer's mother."

"Do you think it's possible something bad went down in Bolton and his body was dumped back here to throw us off the scent?"

"That would imply they knew about his past."

Frost said, "Let's go see if she's home. I'm betting no one will answer."

Lauren Hellyer opened the door on the third ring, causing Frost to lose his bet. Alex Hellyer's mother was about five foot three with long gray hair that she'd pulled into tight bun. She was lean with a narrow mouth which made her facial features sharp. She peered over her glasses at them and said, "Can I help you?"

Bridgette flashed her badge and said, "Detectives Frost

and Cash from Vancouver Metropolitan Police, ma'am. We like to ask you a few questions, if you don't mind?"

Holding tightly onto the door, Lauren Hellyer made no move to let them in as she responded, "What about?"

"The murder of Paul Ringwood, ma'am."

The woman scowled. "You've got a nerve coming here after what you did to my son."

Frost said, "May we come in?"

"No, you may not!"

Bridgette responded evenly, "Fine, we're happy to stand here and ask you our questions. You'll be letting the cold air into your warm home, but it is your choice, ma'am."

"How long is this going to take?"

"I'm not sure. It depends on your answers."

"Do I need a lawyer?"

"That's entirely up to you, Mrs. Hellyer. If you request a lawyer, we'll drive you back to Vancouver and conduct the interview in our offices."

Hellyer scowled but opened the door. "I don't want you giving the neighbors anything to gossip about."

She led them into a sitting room. Bridgette guessed the furniture was older than she was. The flowery curtains were almost completely drawn, and Bridgette was relieved when Lauren Hellyer flicked on a light. She motioned Bridgette and Frost to sit on the lumpy sofa while she took a straight-backed timber chair opposite.

The woman sighed. "I know nothing about the murder of Paul Ringwood, so I expect this to be brief."

"Mrs. Hellyer, I'm sure you're aware that Paul Ringwood was only murdered a few days ago?"

Hellyer nodded. "I don't read newspapers or watch TV, but I found out when lawyers started calling me wanting to take Alex's case for wrongful imprisonment."

"Detective Frost and I are developing a list of suspects who would have a motive for wanting to see Paul Ringwood dead."

Bridgette let the statement hang in the air. Lauren Hellyer's mouth dropped as she looked from Bridgette to Frost. "Surely you can't think it was me? I thought he'd been murdered ten years ago. Like everybody else. A murder I might remind you that my son is still in prison for."

"We're conducting investigations in Bolton where he had been living but also locally here in Stanwyck."

Lauren Hellyer scowled, took a deep breath then leaned forward. "I have nothing to say to you."

"Don't you find it odd that his body was discovered not more than fifteen-minutes from where we're sitting?"

"I haven't given it any thought."

"He made a new life three hours away. Why would his murderer bring his body all the way back here?"

"I wouldn't know and frankly, if you ask me, that man got what he deserved. My son now has permanent brain damage because of what he did. He could have stopped all that by coming forward and telling the truth."

Hellyer paused to glare first at Bridgette and then at Frost before adding, "As far as I'm concerned, what goes around comes around."

"Do you know who else has visited Alex since he's been in jail?"

Hellyer let out a short cackle. "You can't be serious?"

"We're just trying to cover all angles."

"Nobody else visited Alex. Only me. And maybe an occasional lawyer. Alex's friends, if you could call them that, abandoned him before the trial. By the time he received his life sentence there was nobody but me … nobody."

Bridgette studied Lauren Hellyer's pained look. The woman had every right to be hostile. But while she had some sympathy for the woman, she was trying to solve a murder.

"Mrs. Hellyer, why do you think your son was framed for Ringwood's murder?"

"I have no idea. Why don't you ask that cop who arrested him?"

"Did your son know Paul Ringwood?"

"What's that got to do with anything?"

"We're not convinced the events of ten years ago aren't connected with his recent murder. We are trying to learn all we can."

Hellyer conceded, "This is a small town. I'm sure he knew him in passing."

"And what about you? Did you know Paul Ringwood or his family?"

"Not really. We kept to ourselves."

"So you wouldn't know if the Ringwood family had any enemies?"

"No."

"How long have you lived here, Mrs. Hellyer?"

"I've lived in Stanwyck all my life."

"I mean in this house?"

"Twenty-two years. Why is that important?"

"It's all part of gathering background information. I understand there was a fire here?"

Hellyer frowned. "Yes, but I fail to see what…"

Bridgette cut her off. "How often do you visit your son?"

"As often as they'll let me, which for maximum-security prisoners is once a fortnight."

"Have you always believed Alex was innocent?"

"Of course. After the fire and losing my husband, Alex was my rock."

"Were you surprised when you heard that Paul Ringwood had only been murdered two weeks ago?"

"I'm not sure how I felt. It was a lawyer who called me the morning the story broke in the paper. He informed me of what had happened and wanted to represent Alex. He was confident he could secure his release and that's all I was interested in."

"I see. So you had no knowledge of Ringwood's murder before that call?"

"No."

"Who was the lawyer who rang you?"

"Michael Grayson from Vancouver. Why is that important?"

"How did he find out?"

"About what?"

"The murder, Mrs. Hellyer."

Lauren Hellyer stood up abruptly. "Mr. Grayson is my lawyer and I'm not answering another question without him being present."

Two minutes later Bridgette and Levi were outside and headed back to their car. Frost spoke first. "Well, that was interesting."

"Yes, it was." She waited until they were both settled in the car with the doors closed before she added, "Especially because she's lying."

Frost raised his eyebrows. "Are you sure?"

Bridgette nodded and turned to stare up at the house. "She lied about how she found out about Ringwood's murder. It wasn't through her lawyer. A journalist from the Tribune rang her before the story broke, asking her for a comment. At that stage nobody outside the police and the newspaper knew."

"And how do you know that?"

"I have a good friend who is a sub-editor at the paper."

Frost frowned. "So why would she lie about that?"

Without taking her gaze off the house, Bridgette replied, "I'm not sure, but I'm more concerned about what else she's lying about."

Tuesday 5:09 AM

John Avery peered through bleary eyes at the green digital readout on his bedside clock. At just after 5 AM it was still two hours short of the time he usually arose in the morning. Normally a sound sleeper, the pressure in his bladder had woken him and he knew he wouldn't sleep again until he'd relieved himself.

He sat up in bed and glanced across at his partner, Francine Turello, who was still in a deep sleep and snoring softly.

Without turning on any lights, he padded across the hallway and into the tiny bathroom of the two-bedroom house he and Francine currently rented. The tiled floor was cold on his feet and while he could afford better, he liked the small cottage's location. Set back from the road at the foothills of a state forest, the remoteness made it much easier to watch who was coming and going. None of his business enterprises were legal and the less nosy neighbors and passers-by he had to worry about the better.

After relieving himself he paused in the hallway and

listened for the rhythmic breathing of Turello again. Satisfied that she was still asleep, he walked into the second bedroom. After closing the door and switching on the light, he paused for a moment to allow his eyes to adjust. The room had no bed and two of the walls were piled high with old storage boxes, most of which contained clothes Francine had worn once or maybe twice if she was lucky.

On the rear wall beneath the window sat a scarred, heavy timber desk that was home to his laptop, a tatty notebook and two pens. Because most of his business activities were illegal, he had little need for stationery, and record keeping was something he avoided.

Beneath the desk was a small floor safe about two feet high and eighteen inches wide. Even though it weighed a ton, Avery had bolted it to the floor as an extra security measure. After getting down on one knee, Avery worked the old-fashioned dial left and right with a practiced touch to enter the safe's combination.

After hearing a tiny click as the tumblers fell into place, he pulled down firmly on the lever to open the door. The safe had two shelves. The bottom shelf he used to store his three pistols and ammunition, but his focus went to the top shelf. He stared for a moment at the two plastic bags full of money before taking them out to count the contents.

He fumed as the count came up short on the first bag. Two days ago, the bag had contained over eleven thousand dollars. Today it would be lucky to be nine thousand. He counted the cash in the second bag, this time with more urgency. His anger subsided as the count came out at exactly thirty thousand — the proceeds from his most recent crime.

As he returned the cash to the bag, he marveled again at how easy the job had been. Less than three days' work from top to bottom after he'd been given the location. Waiting for Ringwood in the dark and shooting him as he got out of his truck had been child's play. If you didn't mind taking another human being's life, which he had no problem with; shooting apples in a barrel was harder.

He had no idea why he'd had to bring the body back to Stanwyck and still kicked himself for only asking for an additional five thousand. When his client had so readily agreed, he knew he should have asked for ten. He shook his head promising himself he would be better at negotiating on his next job, particularly as he was the one taking all the risk.

His thoughts returned to Francine Turello as he placed the bags back in the safe. Her cocaine habit was getting worse. Giving her the combination to his safe in a moment of weakness before sex had been a mistake.

He debated changing the combination, but he knew that would only cause another fight. He was over the fights and was growing tired of her dependence upon him. The sex was still great, but he now despised almost everything else about her. Better to have a more permanent plan he decided as he latched the door and spun the dial to lock the safe again.

He padded back to their bedroom and stood in the doorway for a moment listening to the cadence of her breathing. He was positive she was still asleep as he stared down at her sleeping form in the semi darkness.

He looked at the sawn-off shotgun which lay on the floor next to his bed. It had been his bedside companion for almost twice as long as Francine. Fortunately, he'd never had to use it, but he wondered if now was the time?

He studied Francine again as he contemplated what to do. In less than twenty seconds it could all be over. They were far enough away from their neighbors and he could muffle the sound with a pillow. A single blast would be all it would take, and he doubted anyone who heard it would think it was anything more than a truck backfiring. It would solve his problem about her stealing his money and he would finally be free of her hysterical rants.

He wondered how long it would take before she was discovered. He figured he would need forty-eight hours to make good his escape. With close to forty thousand in the safe and another twelve thousand in his truck, he had more than enough cash to fund a new life with a new name on the other side of the country.

As he pondered the question, he thought about the doctor at the penitentiary. He was positive there was more to Francine's cozy relationship with him than just siphoning money off Lauren Hellyer. Not that it really bothered him. He hadn't been exactly faithful, and it wasn't as if they'd had made any real commitment to each other when she'd moved in four years ago.

But the doctor bothered him. He called and texted Francine regularly. If she didn't answer, the last thing Avery needed was him poking around and discovering a body before he'd made good his escape.

Better to think it through properly, he thought. As he slid back into bed he decided to play it smart. A few phone calls today would be all it would take to organize a new identity. He would wait until Francine's next shift and then take his money and what else he needed to disappear.

Leaving without any drama was the smart play. He'd heard the cops were already making inquiries at the penitentiary. Connecting Ringwood to Hellyer was always going to happen and Francine would be wrapped up in that by association. This way, he could distance himself from the Ringwood job and be rid of Francine at the same time.

Avery lit a cigarette. Sleep was now impossible. He had plans to make and he would start with a few phone calls straight after breakfast.

He glanced across at Francine as she rolled over. Within seconds, her rhythmic breathing started again. They'd had a good run, but now it was time to move on.

Tuesday 8:17 AM

Francine Turello yawned and lit a cigarette — her first for the day. She been trying to cut back in recent times, but never seemed to be able to go beyond a day or two before being back to a full pack a day. She made herself a promise, 'no more than ten today' but knew the commitment would be hard to keep as she drew the nicotine into her lungs and felt the immediate buzz in her brain. She wondered about vaping as she stared around a bedroom that was barely large enough for a double bed and a wardrobe. Several of the other nurses had switched from cigarettes to vaping and seemed to be healthier and happier for it.

She coughed once and called out, "John," but got no answer.

Having only just woken up, she had no idea where her partner was which wasn't unusual. He was always out of bed before her but was never great at communicating his plans.

Turning slightly, she parted the Venetian blinds that covered the window just above their bed and looked outside.

She shifted her position until she could see between the shrubs in the overgrown garden. Shielding her eyes from the morning sun, she now had a clear view of their garage at the back of the house. John's truck was gone. She was alone.

Good, she thought, I have the place to myself.

After taking another drag of her cigarette, she picked up her smartphone and hit speed dial. She knew Shriver would be at work by now and hoped he wasn't busy.

The call was answered on the third ring. "Hi Francine, I can't talk for long. I have a meeting at eight-thirty."

"I've got to come in early today … for an interview with the cops. What's that all about?"

"They were here yesterday interviewing Alex."

"What did they want to know?"

"It looked to be fairly routine. I'm sure you've heard they found the body of the man they believe Alex murdered?"

"Yeah, the guy that's only been dead two weeks."

"It's only natural they would want to interview Alex."

"Are they on to us?"

"No. You're one of seven nurses being interviewed today. This is all routine and has nothing to do with our arrangement with Lauren Hellyer."

Turello blew a smoke ring. "I don't like it."

"Relax."

"What if they find out about the money?"

"They won't. There's no paper trail — it's all cash. We've got nothing to worry about. You back me up and I'll back you up. We'll be fine."

Turello took another draw. "What happens if Lauren Hellyer talks?"

"She won't."

"How can you be so sure? I could lose my job."

"That's not going to happen. I'm not letting them anywhere near Alex, and Lauren Hellyer has no time for the police after what they did to her son."

"Do I need a lawyer?"

"No. That will only make it look worse. They're just fishing for information. You stick to what I told you and you'll be fine. We have nothing to worry about."

"Is it true he's being released?"

"Yes. At the end of the week."

Turello swore. "I'm going to miss that money. Is there any way we can postpone his release?"

"I'm working on it, but it doesn't look good. His mother is insisting on his release as soon as possible."

Turello took another deep draw on her cigarette.

Shriver added, "When can I see you again?"

Turello rolled her eyes. "I'm not sure. John has been staying close to home of late."

"He must be going away soon. You could come and spend the night?"

Turello shook her head. "He rarely tells me what he's doing until he's ready to go away. I just don't know."

"Is he there now?"

"He's out the back working on his truck," she lied.

"Maybe we could go away for a weekend? You could say you're visiting your mother."

"Maybe. But right now, I just want to get through this. The cops are making me really nervous."

"You don't need to worry about that. It's all under control."

"Will you be there when I come in for the interview?"

"No. They're conducting the interviews in the main complex. Just relax, you'll be fine."

Turello rolled her eyes again. Shriver had no idea she'd

brokered the hit on Ringwood and that wasn't about to change. Avery would kill her if she ever breathed a word.

Deciding she'd learned all she could from Shriver for the moment, she said, "I'll call you after my interview."

She took a final pull on her cigarette then stubbed it out in an ashtray overflowing with butts on her bedside table. In no hurry to get up, she lay still and contemplated what she would do next. John would be furious if he found out she was being interviewed by the police. She would tell him later — after it had happened — and play it down as all being routine.

She thought about Shriver and their relationship again. Their affair had been exciting for the first few months, and the opportunity to earn some extra money babysitting Alex had been a bonus. But she was bored of him. Shriver was too strait laced for her and it would never work. With the money from Alex's mother coming to an end, now was the time to dump him, but maybe not just yet? Maybe not until this thing with the cops had blown over.

Life was becoming far too complicated, she thought, as she lit her second cigarette.

Wednesday 8:02 AM

Bridgette knocked on Delray's door. "Sorry, Chief, I know we were due to meet you at eight, but Levi has just texted me to say he's stuck in traffic."

Delray waved her in. "Good morning, Bridgette. We'll catch Levi up later."

She smiled and settled into a chair. "Any news on Ron Burns?"

Her boss grimaced. "I haven't heard anything, have you?"

"No, I keep calling and leaving messages, but so far nothing."

"Well, Missing Persons are on to it, so let's hope he turns up alive and soon."

Bridgette didn't share her boss' optimism but nodded anyway.

Delray continued, "Been out of the office for two days so I've got a lot to catch up on. Why don't you fill me in on your progress?"

Bridgette started by giving Delray a rundown of the

interview with Lauren Hellyer, and how the woman had lied about how she'd found out about Ringwood's murder. She mentioned the lack of any useful information from other interviews in Stanwyck, and then sat back.

Delray said, "So coming back to Hellyer's mother. Why do you think she lied?"

"I'm digging into her background but haven't found anything yet. She's got no criminal record and has kept her nose out of trouble in Stanwyck. Levi has been looking into her financial background."

"Levi spent a lot of time tracking dirty money when he worked in narcotics, so you've got the right guy on the job."

Bridgette nodded. "In two days he's almost got a complete picture of Hellyer's financial history both public and hidden."

Delray raised his eyebrows. "Hidden?"

"Levi traced records back to the time of the house fire and her husband's death. She collected close to nine-hundred thousand between her husband's life insurance and the insurance they had on their home. About three-hundred grand went into rebuilding the house and she still has about half of the original balance in her accounts."

"So the rest has been spent on living expenses?"

Bridgette shook her head. "No. It disappeared out of her account shortly after the house was rebuilt — almost three-hundred thousand."

"So where did it go?"

"After a lot of digging, Levi found the money in a trust account in her maiden name with the Roma Bank here in Vancouver."

Delray let out a soft whistle. "So how much is in there now?"

"There's still over a hundred thousand in the account, and this is where it gets interesting."

Delray leaned forward. "Okay."

"For the last four years, regular payments of five hundred dollars have been coming out of this account on a fortnightly basis."

"What's she doing with the money? Paying bills?"

"No. Every five-hundred-dollar amount has been withdrawn in cash."

"That's interesting."

"I did some cross checking to see if I could establish any patterns and it quickly became clear that the withdrawals were being made the day before she visited her son."

"So, what's she doing — paying someone at the prison for special favors?"

"We're still trying to work that out. I looked at the rosters and discovered a matching pattern. There's one nurse, Francine Turello who's been rostered on almost every time Lauren Hellyer has visited."

Delray frowned. "Almost every time? It doesn't seem…"

"There have been six occasions in four years where Francine Turello hasn't been roster-ed on when Hellyer's mother visited. On each occasion, the withdrawal wasn't made. Instead, a one-thousand-dollar withdrawal was made two weeks later prior to the following visit."

Delray leaned back and said, "That can't be a coincidence."

"Cash exchanges can be hard to prove. We're getting phone records for both Lauren Hellyer and Francine Turello to see if they've been in regular contact."

"This is great work, Bridgette."

"Francine Turello works almost exclusively on the afternoon and evening shifts. We interviewed her yesterday along with six other nurses, but she was nervous. We've also done a background check on her and she had some minor offenses for drug possession and petty theft, although that was some years back."

Delray scratched his chin. "So what's she providing to Hellyer that's costing his mother five-hundred a fortnight? Drugs?"

"His only medication at present is for his tremors and he has no medical record of dependency. We'll keep looking, but I don't think it's drugs."

"Hellyer gets his own room. Maybe that's a payoff?"

"He's had his own room for almost as long as he's been in prison. And that was long before Turello starting nursing there."

"So what's your theory?"

Bridgette slid a single piece of paper across to Delray. "What's this?"

"This is a copy of the newspaper article I got from Carrie Singleton when I first interviewed her. Paul Ringwood stayed off the grid for ten years. He worked for cash, never had a driver's license and all his possessions were in his partner's name. There was no trace of him anywhere except for this article which appeared in a local paper about a year ago. This was his only slip-up. He was rarely photographed and had no idea this one would wind up as a good Samaritan story in the local paper. Even though it was only on the internet for two weeks, it may have been enough time for someone…"

"But he's using his alias."

"Yes, but there's a photo of him, and he's a stonemason — not a common profession."

Delray looked up from the newspaper article. "So you're suggesting that someone tracked him down through this?"

Bridgette nodded. "It's a possibility we're exploring. If you're desperate enough to find someone and you're driven by rage and revenge, why not?"

Bridgette was quiet while Delray drummed his fingers on the table. "So where does the five-hundred a fortnight fit in?"

"I want to investigate Francine Turello's partner?"

"The nurse has a partner?"

"Yes. John Avery. I've only had time to do a brief background check on him, but he's got a rap sheet as long as my arm."

"What's he been convicted of?"

"Assault, robbery and an attempted murder charge which he was acquitted of."

Delray nodded. "Time to pay John Avery a visit."

Thursday 5:57 AM

What had started out for Bridgette as a suggestion for a short interview with Francine Turello's partner, John Avery, had quickly escalated when Delray became aware of Avery's criminal record.

Still reeling from the loss of one of his senior officers in an arrest that had gone horribly wrong the previous year, Delray had insisted on coming with them to Avery and Turello's residence.

It was still dark when the team assembled at the meeting point on Higgins Road.

Bridgette had organized a search warrant and Delray was in no mood to take risks. The cottage backed onto a forest in an isolated location with no close neighbors. He had called in a favor with a colleague in Operations and had two uniformed constables join the team to assist. When she had asked about the additional officers, Delray had conceded it was probably overkill but with Avery's record he wasn't taking any chances.

They assembled about two hundred yards from the

laneway that led to Avery's property and under Delray's direction would make the rest of the journey on foot. The conditions were close to freezing and Bridgette would have normally worn gloves. But in the unlikely event she would need to use her gun, she knew gloves would make the task impossible.

Using a single flashlight, Delray brought everyone in close. Brigitte cupped her hands together and blew warm breath on her fingers as Delray addressed the group.

"All right team, it'll be daylight in nine minutes so that will give us plenty of time to walk up the lane. I'll approach the front with Constable Dunstan, and I'll get Detectives Frost and Cash to take up a position around the back."

Turning to face the younger of the two constables, Delray added, "Constable Jordan, I'll get you to wait on the lane. We're not expecting trouble, but the man we want to interview has a record and you can never be too careful. Any questions?"

When no one responded, Delray switched off his flashlight and moved away from the assembly point with everyone following close behind.

The plan was for the group to move as one down Higgins Road and then disburse when they got near the house. Conscious that Frost was walking beside her, Bridgette gave him a quick thumbs up. Under normal circumstances, Delray would have asked them to serve the warrant. But he had confided to Bridgette that because of Frost's recent trauma, he wasn't prepared to take a chance on him if there was a confrontation at the front door.

Bridgette understood and admitted she would have done the same thing if she had been in Delray's position. She wondered if Frost realized Delray had broken with tradition. If he had, he wasn't saying anything, at least not to her.

As the group walked up the gravel road, Bridgette focused on the job ahead. They had all studied images of the property on Google maps and were familiar with the layout. The house wasn't much bigger than a cottage with a separate detached garage and workshop. The property sat on about two acres of land and was covered in trees that would make visibility around the house difficult if things got complicated. Bridgette, like Delray, hoped the raid would turn into a non-event and that Avery would cooperate.

Bridgette glanced up at the sky as they walked. The dark backdrop was slowly turning blue-gray signaling dawn was just minutes away. Bridgette felt her heart race when the silhouette of the house became visible as they walked up over a rise in the road.

Delray nodded to Jordan that this was as far as he wanted him to go and then signaled to Bridgette and Frost to disperse. Bridgette nodded once then moved off quickly with Frost towards the side of the house. They had plotted a path through the trees on Google Maps and Frost fell in behind her as they crept stealthily around the side to the rear of the house.

Bridgette was relieved that she could see no lights on inside. Hopefully that meant Avery and Turello were still sleeping. They continued until they got to the rear corner of the house. Bridgette paused and peered around. She could just make out the back porch, an old exercise bike and a rusted wheelbarrow lying on its side in the long grass. They moved quickly around to the rear to set up in position.

As she debated where they should stand, Bridgette noticed the floorboards on the porch were weather beaten and had lifted in several places. She whispered to Frost, "I think we'll stay here. If we go up on that porch and it squeaks, we're likely to alert anyone inside."

Frost gave her a thumbs up. They positioned themselves below the porch, directly in line with the back door. Bridgette checked her watch — one minute to go until Delray would give the signal. They pulled out their hi-vis yellow vests which had the word Police printed in bold letters on both the front and back and quickly fitted them over the top of their bullet-proof vests. Frost nodded to Bridgette to show he was ready and they pulled their Glocks from their holsters.

Bridgette kept an eye on the two-way radio she was carrying in her left hand for Delray's signal. She felt a rush of adrenaline and was somewhat surprised by her response to the situation.

A moment later the light on the two-way flashed red. Bridgette whispered, "Here we go," as she heard pounding on the front door followed by Delray's booming voice, "Police, open up."

Thursday 6:04 AM

Bridgette tensed when Delray's voice broke the early morning silence. She and Frost waited, their eyes focused on the back door, straining to hear any movement inside the house. Above the heavy pounding at the front, Delray's voice thundered a second time, "Police, open up — now!"

Bridgette kept her eyes fixed on the door. She could hear sounds coming from inside.

Delray's voice boomed a third time, but it became background noise as the back door burst open.

Bridgette raised her weapon and shouted, "Police, stop…" as a man brandishing a shot gun appeared in the doorway.

Her command was cut short as she saw a flash and felt the concussive blast of a weapon fired at close range. Frost reeled backwards and the man shoved Bridgette in the chest and charged between them. Losing her balance, she fell back and hit her head heavily on the ground.

She was not sure how long she was out for — probably only seconds — but when she came to, it was difficult to focus and her head was throbbing. As her vision cleared, Bridgette saw Frost writhing on the ground next to her. She crawled over to him. It looked as if he had taken the full blast to his chest, but the bulletproof vest had saved him. But her relief was short-lived when she noticed his left arm was bleeding. She peered up through the new light of dawn but could see no sign of Avery or Delray.

Returning her gaze to Frost, she said, "How bad is it?"

Holding his chest, Frost groaned through gritted teeth. "The son of the bitch shot me."

Frost's voice sounded like he was under water, but Bridgette knew her hearing would return soon. She nodded at him and pointed to her ears. "Can't hear too well. You've been hit in the arm."

Frost studied his arm for a moment and then ran his good hand across his face and neck. "Just my arm — I'll live."

Bridgette put a hand on his shoulder to stop him from getting up. "Stay put. I'll get help."

Before Frost could respond, Delray appeared from around the side of the house and barked, "What the hell happened?"

"Avery had a shotgun. Levi's been hit," said Bridgette.

Delray knelt down beside Frost and said, "How're you doing?" as he studied the wound.

Frost mumbled, "Shotgun pellets. I'll be OK."

Dunstan appeared in the doorway holding a stunned Francine Turello by her arm. She was dressed in a skimpy nighty and seemed oblivious to the freezing temperatures as she howled in protest.

Dunstan said, "The house is clear. There were only the two of them inside."

Delray radioed Jordan to call an ambulance then turned

back to Dunstan. "Cuff her, put something warm on her, then bring her out here. You can keep an eye on Frost until the Ambulance arrives while we go find Avery."

He turned to Turello. "Where would Avery go?"

Turello extended her middle finger at Delray and retorted, "How should I know? I'm not his keeper."

Delray turned to Dunstan and said, "I'm gonna need you to call Jordan and get him up here. Explain what's happened and that we're a man down. Avery has probably headed into the forest."

Turning to Bridgette, Delray said, "Bridgette you go watch the garage just in case he doubles back to get a vehicle. Keep your two-way on and don't take any unnecessary risks. I'm going to head into the forest to see if I can find him."

Bridgette nodded at Delray but didn't leave Frost until Dunstan had dragged two chairs off the porch and positioned one next to her partner.

Locking eyes momentarily with Levi, Bridgette noted his pale color and hoped the ambulance wouldn't be long. She touched him briefly on the shoulder and murmured, "I'd better go. You hang in there." He gave her a nod, winced a little then wished her good luck.

Bridgette headed to the garage that backed on to the west corner of the house. It was an aging timber structure that had faded to gray from countless years of weathering. Big enough to hold four cars, the side door was locked, but the two front doors were wide open.

She stopped short and peered inside. The garage was dark and she had difficulty seeing anything beyond a red pickup truck and an old blue Toyota Corolla.

Bridgette removed a slim flashlight from a side pocket then placed her left hand over her right which was holding her Glock. She positioned her feet in a modified Weaver stance and shone the light into the garage. The Glock followed the beam as she scanned the back of the garage.

There was a workshop of sorts in the rear, complete with an array of wood-working tools, but little else. She noticed two tarps on the floor, but the rest of the area was empty. Bridgette focused the flashlight briefly on the truck and the car. She couldn't see anyone inside either vehicle and got down on her knees to check under each one. She found no sign of the man and stood up again. Taking a deep breath, Bridgette crept forward to check inside each vehicle. Scanning left to right for any sudden movement or an ambush, she stopped just short of the driver's door of the truck and shone the beam of the flashlight inside the cabin and rear cargo area. Empty. Swinging the beam to her right, she checked inside the Corolla. It too was empty.

She blew out a breath then headed outside again. After switching off the flashlight, she ran about thirty feet from the garage's entrance, peering down the driveway in the hope that the medics would arrive soon. She looked out towards the forest but couldn't see any sign of Delray. A sudden movement caught her eye. She saw a figure disappearing into the forest. The figure was shorter than Delray and slimmer. Avery. Bridgette sprinted after him, over the side fence and into the woods.

The pine forest was dense, tree trunks and low branches hampered her sight and movement. Bridgette was thankful for the dawn — at least now she could see. After about fifty yards she stopped. At first all she could hear was her pounding heart but in the distance she could hear the sound of someone crashing through the trees up to her left. It could have been Delray or Avery. Bridgette pushed on, branches swinging back into her face. Her right hand hung on to her Glock, while her left cleared the foliage away. She moved forward another fifty yards and then stopped to listen again. The sounds seemed to be coming from her right this time. She was confident it was Avery zigzagging through the forest to throw her off.

Changing direction again, she was conscious that the further she went into the forest the less likely it was the others would know where either she or Avery were. Then she realized she didn't have her two-way with her.

Bridgette was furious with herself. She had dropped it when her head had hit the ground when Avery had pushed her over and forgotten to retrieve it — even though Delray had told her to.

Above the sound of her labored breathing, she heard Avery's footfall, this time much closer. Too close. Bridgette couldn't see more than ten or fifteen feet in front of her in the dense woods. She took another two steps then stopped to listen again before creeping forward cautiously. She strained to hear any sound that would disclose her quarry's location but heard nothing. Bridgette scanned the ground in front of her. It was covered in dry leaves and twigs which would crackle under her feet giving her position away. She crept forward, carefully navigating her way between branches and tree trunks.

There was light ahead. Even though she had lost her sense of direction she continued and found herself at the edge of a small clearing no more than twenty feet wide and fifteen feet deep. An almost vertical rock wall closed off the clearing on the far side. It looked to be about sixty feet high, an effective barrier for her, and for Avery. As her brain registered that he knew the area much better than she did, she realized he could be hiding close by and watching. While she pondered which direction to continue the search, the silence was broken by the sound of a shot gun being slammed shut and primed.

She turned to her right and found herself staring into the barrel of Avery's shot gun. In an almost pleasant voice he said, "Drop it."

Thursday 6:27 AM

Bridgette dropped her gun, her heart pounding as she stared into the barrel. Avery moved forward until there was only about eight feet separating them. He was around forty, average height and lean with unkempt hair. Bridgette barely noticed any of this as she held her breath, her body paralyzed with fear.

She forced her mind to think through her options. The distance was too far for her to lunge forward to grab the weapon. It wasn't the first time she'd stared down the barrel of a gun. She had to stay calm. Breath, Bridgette, breath. She tried not to think about what a shotgun blast this close to her face would do to her. She willed herself to look beyond the gun barrel and directly at Avery.

"Are you alone?" he said in a shaky voice.

His eyes kept darting from left to right. She didn't think he would shoot, it would give away his position.

"No. There are other officers searching these woods right now. But how close they are, I'm not sure. Better to give it up now."

Bridgette kept her breathing even; her heartbeat was steadying. She realized Avery was just as scared as she was. Her eyes were drawn back to the barrel of the gun which was still pointed at her. It seemed like an eternity before Avery said, "Do you have handcuffs?"

"In my side pocket."

"Show me and no sudden movements."

Bridgette had only got her hand as far as her hip pocket before she heard a familiar voice. "Put the weapon down and your hands above your head, Avery."

Delray was standing about ten feet behind Avery, his gun pointed at the man's back. Bridgette wasn't directly in his line of fire but if Delray's shot went wide, she knew she could be hit.

Avery kept his gaze fixed on Bridgette. The shotgun remained pointed at her face as he called out, "I don't think so. From this distance I won't miss."

Delray shot back, "And neither will I."

Bridgette noticed Jordan appear at the edge of the tree line on the right-hand side of the clearing. He stayed in the shadows and she was fairly sure Avery hadn't seen him.

Avery kept his gun steady and aimed at Bridgette's face and made no move to surrender. The forest was silent again.

It was Delray who spoke first. "The smart thing to do is to drop your weapon, Avery. Otherwise you won't get out of this alive."

Avery sneered. "Looks like we've got ourselves an old-fashioned stand-off."

The forest fell silent again. Bridgette prayed Avery wouldn't do something stupid that would get them both killed. Her pulse started to race again.

As if realizing he needed to de-escalate the situation, Delray said, "I'm not willing to see you gun down one of

The Cold Light of Day

my officers so here's my offer. We will move to the left-hand side of the clearing and I'll put down my weapon down in front of me. You've only got a single cartridge in that shotgun and you won't have time to reload before whoever is left standing shoots you."

Delray paused to let his words sink in. "This is your only chance to escape ... the smart thing would be to take me up on my offer."

Avery squinted at Bridgette. She felt some comfort knowing that she wasn't alone even though Avery's gun was still pointed at her face. Part of her felt detached, as if this was happening to someone else. Having two colleagues backing her up was one thing, but if Avery chose to fire, she wouldn't be able to avoid the blast. She kept an eye on his trigger finger wondering how a man like him got himself into this sort of trouble. He looked no different to thousands of other men his age, and she wouldn't have given him a second glance if she'd passed him on the street. It was only the words that came out of his mouth and his violent actions that set him apart.

When Avery broke the silence, he seemed to have made a decision. He kept his eyes on Bridgette, but the gun barrel dipped a little when he spoke. "OK. I'll take you up on that offer. Now move!" He jerked the gun at Bridgette as he added, "But do it nice and slow."

Bridgette edged towards Delray without taking her eyes off Avery.

Avery's gun followed Bridgette's every move. He now had Delray and her in his sights. "Throw your gun on the ground like we agreed."

Delray placed his gun on the ground.

Turning to Bridgette, Avery said, "Handcuff yourself to him and throw me the key."

Delray growled, "That wasn't part of the deal."

Avery laughed. "I need a good head start and this will buy me some time." Avery stepped forward and aimed at Bridgette's face again. "You got three seconds."

Delray said, "Don't be stupid, Avery. Right now, you have a chance to get away. You pull that trigger you're as good as dead."

Bridgette felt her heart beating in her throat as she stared down the barrel of the shotgun again; one black hole less than four feet from her face.

Avery just laughed. "One, two…"

"Avery!" A voice from inside the forest shouted.

Avery turned towards the voice. Bridgette ducked just as a shot echoed around the clearing and Avery's head exploded in a pink mist.

As the sound dissipated, everyone was motionless, staring at Avery's body and his shotgun that now lay at an odd angle across his upper torso.

Delray spoke first, "Is everyone okay?"

Bridgette breathed a long breath; thankful she was still alive. She knew the ringing in her ears and the rapid beat of her heart would soon subside, but not so the image of the dead man who lay only a few feet in front of her.

She mumbled, "Yes," and watched as Jordan pivoted, dashed back to the tree line and threw up.

Everyone swallowed hard.

Delray put a hand on Jordan's shoulder once he'd rejoined them. "Good job, Danny, you just saved two lives and prevented the escape of a violent felon."

Bridgette had been in his position and knew he was going into shock. He was talking rapidly and not making much sense, a natural response. Taking someone's life, regardless of the circumstances, was something he would need help to come to terms with.

Delray nodded at them. "This was great work. There will of course be an investigation, but I'm proud of you both. But for now we need to get this scene secured. Bridgette can you radio in and get the coroner and forensics here? We need to search the house."

"Can I borrow your two-way Chief, I dropped mine back at the house?"

Delray glared at Bridgette, then passed her his.

After finishing the call, she stared down at the blood that was pooling around what was left of Avery's head; she knew she too would need some help.

Delray came and stood alongside her. "It's been a rough day and it's only just beginning."

Without taking her eyes off Avery she said, "Rougher for some than others."

"I'd like you to go back to the house now and stay with Frost. Dunstan's going to be needed to direct the forensics team and I don't want Frost being left alone. You okay with that?"

Bridgette nodded. "There's nothing more I can do here, anyway."

Bridgette picked up her pace once clear of the trees and jogged through to the back of Avery's property where she could see Levi still lying on the ground. He looked gray. As she climbed over the back fence, he lifted his head to look in her direction.

The sleeve of his left arm was now entirely red. It was hard for her to tell whether the bleeding had stopped, but she felt relieved to hear the ambulance pull into the driveway.

Bridgette crossed the backyard and knelt down beside Levi. "You had me worried there for a moment."

He nodded once. "Did you find him? Where are the others?"

Bridgette nodded. "They're coming, but they're slower than me!"

"What about Avery?"

"He's dead."

Francine Turello burst into tears.

Dunstan asked, "So what happened?"

Bridgette would have liked to give them a run down but now was not the right time in front of Turello.

"I'm sure the chief will give you a full explanation when he comes back, but right now let's get Detective Frost taken care of."

Dunstan said, "So no more casualties for our team?"

Bridgette shook her head as she watched the two medics hurry across the rear lawn, one carrying a large medical kit and the other, a portable stretcher.

The taller of the two men nodded in Bridgette's direction and said, "Ma'am, we got a report of a shooting. Is this the only casualty?"

Bridgette decided the medics only need to be told about the living and not the dead at this point and said, "Yes, this is Detective Levi Frost. He took the full brunt of a shotgun blast when our suspect came out of the house."

Bridgette moved back as both officers dropped to their knees and began assessing Frost's condition.

Dunstan sidled up beside Bridgette. "Sounds like it got ugly up there?"

She said, "It could have been worse," as she glanced at

Francine Turello who was now slumped in a chair, covered in a blanket and crying softly.

Dunstan went to ask another question but thought better of it when Bridgette shook her head.

Taking the hint, he said, "I'm taking the suspect back inside to get her dressed. Will you be okay out here?"

"I'll be fine."

Bridgette watched as Turello was led back inside the house and then turned back to look at the medics as they treated her partner. They had removed his bullet-proof vest and had cut away the left sleeve of his shirt. His arm was covered in blood, but both men remained calm, which she took as a good sign. As they wrapped his upper arm in a pressure bandage, Bridgette asked, "How bad is it?"

The taller officer looked up and said, "The vest saved him. He's got about a dozen pellets in his arm that need to be removed, but apart from that and some severe bruising, he'll be on the mend in a day or two."

After completing the bandaging and putting in an IV drip, Bridgette watched them lift Levi onto the stretcher.

She asked, "You mind if I ride in the ambulance with him?"

"No problem."

Thursday 7:42 AM

The first few minutes of the trip back to Vancouver in the ambulance were quiet. Bridgette could do little but watch while the bumpy road caused Frost to close his eyes and grimace in pain. It was only when they were on the freeway and the ride had settled down that he opened his eyes again.

She was thankful the second medic had chosen to ride up front, leaving her free to talk to Frost in private. Once he had finally relaxed, she asked, "How's your arm?"

"I'll live, although when he fired … I feared the worst."

"So did I."

Frost managed a brief smile. "Thank God for bullet proof vests."

Bridgette nodded.

Frost shifted on the stretcher to get more comfortable and then said, "It all happened so fast."

"It usually does. One minute you're in control and the next you're wondering if you'll live long enough to take another breath."

"Do you think they'll make me take time off?"

"I would have thought so. Aren't you going to need surgery?"

Frost looked down at his arm. "The medic who bandaged me said they might get all the pellets out with tweezers."

"Even so, you will need recovery time."

"Maybe. I don't feel too bad."

Bridgette raised her eyebrows. "The chief might have a different opinion. Particularly if you're transferring back to Undercover."

Frost frowned. "You heard about that?"

"The chief thought, as your partner, I had a right to know."

Frost frowned. "I was hoping he'd keep that confidential."

"I don't think he's told anyone else."

Frost nodded but said nothing. They were quiet for a moment before he asked, "Why are you doing this?"

"Why am I doing what?"

"Riding with me in the ambulance."

"I'm not sure if you know much about my history, but I almost didn't survive my first case. My partner and I were tracking a serial killer, and it all got out of hand. I'm sure you're aware my partner was shot and killed?"

Frost grimaced. "I heard he was a good guy."

"He was the best."

"That must have messed you up?"

"I barely escaped with my life. I'm only alive today because of what he did … and I still feel guilty I survived and he didn't. I was also dealing with my father's death at the same time … it all got on top of me."

"I can imagine."

"The chief made me take leave. He used to call me every day just to see how I was doing."

Bridgette closed her eyes and paused for a moment, surprised at how difficult it was to recount the events of that time. She felt her throat tighten and the palms of her hands begin to sweat. "I was standing in my bathroom, just staring at the mirror. I'm not sure how long I'd been there, maybe an hour or more, but I was a mess. At that point in my life I wasn't even sure if I wanted to continue living, let alone be a police officer."

Frost nodded. "I know that feeling, pretty serious."

Bridgette nodded. "I was holding my service pistol when the phone rang. It was the chief. I debated whether to even answer, but I knew if I didn't, he would have had someone swing by to check on me and that was the last thing I wanted. So, I put the gun down and took his call. We talked for a while and that seemed to help. I remember him telling me we were a team, and that we were all hurting, all in this together … I'm not sure how long I sat on the floor after the call, but eventually I took the bullets out of my gun and put it in my bedside drawer. I never picked it up again until I went back to work."

Bridgette opened her eyes and looked at Frost. "Delray made me feel like I was part of a team and that I mattered. It helped me back then, and it still helps today. That's why I'm riding with you to the hospital."

Frost was silent for a minute. "I'm starting to understand how things work in Homicide."

"It doesn't work the same in Undercover?"

Frost shook his head. "Not so much. You work alone a lot of the time and you can quickly blow your cover if you're seen in the company of other cops."

"I've had regular counseling since that incident, and it

helps ... a lot. I'm not sure of your situation but talking to someone can help."

They were quiet for a while, lost in their own thoughts until Frost said, "It will be tough now that Avery's dead. You can't exactly interview a corpse."

"Let's hope we have some luck searching his house. Who knows, we may get most of the answers we need."

"Do you think he killed Ringwood?"

"Probably, but unless Francine Turello confesses or we turn up something from the search of his house, we may never know for sure."

"We will have to push her hard. She had to be in on it. There's no doubt in my mind that she's the connection to Hellyer and his mother."

"Why do you think he did it?"

"What? Kill Ringwood?"

"Yes."

"I think he was hired and did it for money pure and simple."

Bridgette nodded. "That's what I was thinking. The connection through Francine Turello links him to Hellyer, but not directly to Paul Ringwood or his alias, Paul Johnson."

"So, if he was just a hired gun, who put him up to it? The mother? Hellyer himself? Or someone else?"

Bridgette thought for a moment. "That's the sixty-four-thousand-dollar question. From what we know of Hellyer, he's not capable..."

"But we know his mother has been paying Francine Turello five hundred bucks a fortnight."

"Yes, but that doesn't necessarily link her to the murder. It could just be a payment to keep her son comfortable and safe inside prison. We'll need a lot more than that for a murder conviction."

"Hellyer's mother needs to be interviewed again."

"She will be, just as soon as we get through what happened today."

"Do you think it could be someone else?"

Bridgette thought for a moment. "Possibly. We are only beginning to scratch the surface. If we keep digging, who knows what we'll turn up?"

"I've been thinking about Ron Burns. Do you think he's really as sick as he's making out? Maybe he hired Avery?"

"I've checked with some of his former work colleagues. They all say he's got cancer and his condition is deteriorating. So I don't see what he's got to gain from killing Ringwood now."

Frost nodded. "I've also been thinking about Ringwood and his drug dealing past. Maybe he started dealing again and got on the wrong side of someone?"

Bridgette half smiled. "It's good to see that you're thinking about the case, Levi."

"I'm still part of the team."

"It's a line of investigation Tony Lee in Bolton is still looking at along with trying to run down the identity of the white van."

Frost closed his eyes. Bridgette asked, "Is the pain getting worse?"

Frost opened his eyes. "No, I was just thinking about Avery. I mean, why did he run? Surely he knew it wouldn't end well?"

Bridgette sighed. "I'm not sure. Who knows what goes through a criminal's mind when they're faced with the prospect of spending the rest of their life behind bars?

Maybe he knew his chances of escaping alive were slim, but that was better than the alternative."

They were both quiet again as they tried to make sense of what had happened.

Bridgette allowed her mind to wander. She thought about Levi Frost's past twelve months as she watched him close his eyes. After having a young boy die in his arms and needing to take leave to recover, she wondered what impact today's shooting would have on him now he was trying to re-launch his police career.

She hoped sharing her story would help.

Without opening his eyes, Frost said, "So tell me, what happened in the forest?"

Thursday 6:51 PM

It had been a long day for Bridgette, and she was keen to get to the gym. She paused on her way to the elevator at the door to Delray's office and knocked lightly.

Delray looked up from a report he was reading and said, "Hey, Bridgette, you heading home?"

"About to, but I thought you'd appreciate some good news."

"After the day I've had, any good news would be very welcome."

"Ron Burns called me about ten minutes ago."

Delray raised his eyebrows. "Well, that is good news. Is he okay?"

"He seems to be. He was in his car heading back to Stanwyck. Apparently he's been out of cell range and only just got my messages. He apologized and is happy to meet me again."

"Did he say where he's been?"

"No. I didn't push it, but I'll ask when I see him next. I

gather he's got some remote place he heads to when he wants to get away."

Delray murmured, "We could all do with one of those places once in a while."

"How's the team holding up?"

"Okay, but Avery's property was taken over by Internal Affairs, so we didn't get a lot done."

"That's going to slow us down."

Delray motioned her to come in and sit for a moment. "I guess it could be worse. While they gave nothing away, the body language of the lead IA officer suggested it looks like a fairly open and shut case. I'm hoping they'll be done tomorrow and we can get back to focusing on our investigation."

"Have you heard any more about Levi?

"He'll be released soon. All the shotgun pellets have been removed and he should be as good as new in a few days."

"That's a relief."

"I've told him not to come back to work until he gets medical clearance. I think he's trying to organize an appointment for tomorrow morning."

"He seems keen to get back to work?"

Delray nodded again. "He told me he's feeling part of the team now and doesn't want to let us down."

"That's positive."

"I didn't push it, but I'm hoping he might reconsider going back to Undercover."

"Well, a couple of days convalescing will give him time to think."

"Exactly. Time to think right now is a good thing for him."

"How's Danny Jordan?"

Delray sighed. "He says he is all right, but I'm not so sure."

Although eager to get to the gym, Bridgette was also keen for an update and asked, "So, did the team find anything interesting at Avery's property today?"

Delray scowled. "Once IA arrived, everything went on hold. The team spent the rest of the day in interviews and getting statements."

"I can imagine. I spent about three hours with them when I got back."

"We did find a bag full of cash in a locked safe and some weapons, but nothing that links Avery directly to Ringwood's murder, yet. We've got Ballistics testing all the weapons we seized to see if we get a match for the bullet that killed Ringwood. I haven't heard anything yet, but I hope to get the results in the morning."

"So the team will be back out there tomorrow?"

"Yeah, after our morning muster. I want to review everything we know about the case and make sure we're all on the same page."

"Sounds like a plan."

"I know you're keen to get to the gym, but how are you holding up?"

Bridgette had had better days. "I spent some time with Levi at the hospital and when I came back here, I spent about an hour with IA. Then I tried to interview Francine Turello after she was released."

"And how did that go?"

"A waste of time."

"Her lawyer give you trouble?"

Bridgette shook her head. "She was high on something. I'm not sure what, but I couldn't get any sense out of her. Her lawyer said she'd been medicated after what happened to her partner. So, I've rescheduled the interview for tomorrow afternoon."

"Well, let's hope she's better tomorrow."

"We need you to re-interview Hellyer's mother as well."

"After what happened today, that has to be a priority. I can't see Avery working for anyone else."

"I'm not so sure it's just Hellyer's mother working with Avery and Turello."

Delray raised his eyebrows. "Why do you think that?"

"How did she find Ringwood's location? When we visited her house, the furniture and everything in it looked older than me. I could be wrong, but I think she'd struggle to turn a computer on, let alone do complex web searches to find someone living off the grid."

"Maybe that's something Avery did for her, or perhaps Turello? Or maybe she hired a PI?"

"Maybe…"

"You don't think so?"

"I'm not sure. We need to keep digging."

"Well, let's hope we turn up some solid evidence tomorrow."

Bridgette tugged at her left earlobe. "There's one question I continue to lose sleep over. Why the three-hour drive before dumping the body?"

Friday 8:03 AM

Tony Lee was three minutes late and the last of the small group of detectives to enter the muster room. Delray, normally a stickler for everyone being on time, scowled when Lee mumbled, "Sorry, Boss."

In no mood for time wasting, Delray ignored the apology, approached the whiteboard and studied the timeline and notations that Bridgette had put together for him.

"This timeline is a summary of all the key facts that we know about the case so far. I've asked Bridgette to put it in chronological order as I think that's the best way to review the facts."

He turned to face his detectives. "You've all been running different parts of the investigation and we need to consolidate our knowledge now to make sure we haven't missed anything. Any questions before we start?"

All detectives shook their heads.

Delray nodded. "Please interrupt if you have questions. It's important we're all on the same page by the end of this meeting."

Jason Watts said, "I've got a question, Chief."

Delray nodded. "Shoot."

"How's Levi?"

Delray was about to respond, but instead stood with his mouth agape, staring at the back of the room as Levi Frost walked in and leaned against the back wall. Apart from his arm being in a sling and his shirt not being buttoned up properly, Bridgette didn't think he looked too bad.

Delray broke the silence. "Levi, you're supposed to be on sick leave. What are you doing here?"

Frost shrugged. "I have an appointment with the Chief Medical Officer at ten. I thought I'd just sit in on this meeting first … if that's okay?"

Delray frowned. "Technically, you're not supposed to be here until you get a medical clearance."

"I'm a little sore, but other than that I feel okay, boss. Besides, I was bored at home."

"Hmm. Well, it's good to see you up and about. We'll leave it to the doc to decide whether you stay or go home, but for now, have a seat."

Delray waited while Frost settled into a chair next to Watts before turning back to the whiteboard. Pointing to the left-hand side of the board, he said, "Let's start with some background."

He pointed to Paul Ringwood's name and said, "The victim was a stonemason who has lived in Bolton for ten years under the alias of Paul Johnson. By all accounts he led a quiet life and was a devoted partner to Carrie Singleton who is now nearly eight months pregnant with his child. From what we've been able to piece together, he was shot dead as he tried to enter the back door of his house just over two weeks ago. We have no clear motive yet and he had no enemies in Bolton that we are aware of."

Delray then pointed to the beginning of the timeline. "Let's go back ten years. Ringwood lived in Stanwyck. He had two minor convictions for drug possession, but they were years earlier and apparently, he was trying to go straight. Everybody in the town seemed to like him — everybody, that is, except Alex Hellyer. With me so far?"

Everybody nodded. "Okay, let's talk about Alex Hellyer for a moment. Ten years ago, he was also living in Stanwyck. By all reports, he had a troubled childhood. His father used to beat his mother regularly; badly enough that she was hospitalized on more than one occasion. Hellyer's father died in a house fire early one morning. He was home alone that night as a result of yet another beating he'd given his wife which had put her in hospital. Young Alex was staying with a family friend like he always did when his mother was hospitalized. Hellyer liked to drink heavily and smoke in bed. The coroner ruled it an accident, but some of the local police think Alex snuck back to his house that night and deliberately started the fire. Nobody knows for sure, but it seems too much of a coincidence. Fast forward several years and Alex Hellyer is now a troubled teen, a loner, and fast developing a nasty reputation as a peeping Tom. Perhaps even more troubling, he has taken to revenge attacks against the family of any girl who reported him."

Delray surveyed the upturned faces of his detectives. "Anybody care to inform the group of what he liked to do for revenge?"

McCartin said, "He started killing their pets if memory serves."

Delray grimaced. "Yes. He liked to hang them up in trees. Theatrical and disturbing. What's more disturbing is he was never caught. From all reports Hellyer is highly intelligent and very cunning."

The Cold Light of Day

Delray nodded in Bridgette's direction. "While we can't prove this, we think he allowed himself to get caught in the peeping Tom act, all as part of a bizarre power trip he may have been on."

Delray looked around the room. "Questions?"

Jason Watts mumbled, "That's one sick puppy."

Delray said, "I agree, but it gets worse. One of the girls he'd been following had a boyfriend, Carl Stockton. Stockton gave Hellyer a beating to warn him off. One morning the boyfriend went for a run and never came home. His body has never been found, but Hellyer remains the number one suspect."

Delray paused to look at the timeline again. "What I've told you so far doesn't prove Hellyer, or anyone in his family killed Ringwood. It's just a theory right now, but it's the best we've got. I'm going to let Bridgette take it from here. She's led the investigation in Stanwyck. It's better that you hear the rest from her."

Delray nodded at Bridgette who rose from her chair.

Bridgette said, "After graduating high school, Hellyer started a college degree. Not long after that, he started selling drugs to support his lifestyle. We're not sure how they crossed paths but Hellyer was developing a reputation as a mid-level drug dealer in his hometown. Ringwood hadn't been using or selling for at least a year, but Hellyer threatened him anyway. They had a confrontation, and it all went downhill from there."

Bridgette went on to explain everything she'd learned about Hellyer from her interviews with Ron Burns before adding, "In the end, Ringwood feared for his life. He'd been threatened on multiple occasions by Hellyer, so much so, that he began sleeping in his car in random locations for fear he'd be murdered in his sleep at home. Ringwood was desperate to get out of Stanwyck for good and formed a close bond with Detective Ron Burns. Together they hatched a plan to fake his murder so that Ringwood could escape and start a new life — and Burns could finally put Hellyer in jail."

Delray interrupted. "I'm sure you're all aware that Burns — who has since retired — has been arrested. He's currently out on bail but because he's got terminal lung cancer he may never go to trial."

Delray motioned Bridgette to continue.

Bridgette nodded. "Fast forward ten years. Paul Johnson, as he is now known, is living in Bolton and looking forward to the birth of his first child. He has a steady job as a stonemason and is leading a quiet life. No trouble with any authorities that we know of. His partner, Carrie Singleton, knew he had a past, but he never told her any specifics — probably for her safety as much as anything else. Ringwood kept a low profile, lived off the grid and his real identity seemed to remain a secret."

Watts piped up again, "We skipped over Hellyer. What's the deal with him?"

"Alex Hellyer was framed and then convicted for Ringwood's murder and has been serving a life sentence."

Delray responded, "A murder we now know never happened."

Bridgette nodded. "Correct."

Watts said, "But Burns and others are convinced he's a psychopath."

Bridgette answered, "There's no proof he killed either his father or Carl Stockton, but…"

Lee interrupted, "There are a lot of coincidences here."

McCartin said, "I hear Hellyer has permanent brain damage?"

Bridgette nodded. "He was bashed unconscious shortly after starting his prison sentence. According to the doctors, he suffered brain damage and now has the mental capacity of a five year old."

McCartin said, "So even though he has the most to gain from the present murder, he's probably not capable of setting it up from inside?"

Bridgette shook her head. "He has permanent tremors and paralysis from the beating. I don't think he's even capable of tying his own shoelaces."

Delray stood up and looked around the room. "Everyone with us?"

After a chorus of nods, Delray continued. "Detective McCartin raises a good point. Hellyer does have the most to gain and we've discovered a link between Alex Hellyer's mother and one of the nurses at the Vancouver penitentiary. Her name is Francine Turello, who you'll remember from yesterday's raid. She works in the infirmary mostly at night and it appears she's been receiving fortnightly cash payments of five hundred dollars from Hellyer's mother. For what exactly, we're not sure. It could be for protection or special treatment. We're going to interview her again today, but so far, she's not talking."

Delray pointed to the name John Avery on the whiteboard and continued. "Her partner is, or was, John Avery. Avery had a long criminal record, which included armed robbery, assault and attempted murder. We decided he was worth interviewing but we all know what happened yesterday. While we haven't found a direct link to the Ringwood murder yet, we did find close to forty thousand in cash in his house and more money in his truck. One bag in his house contained thirty thousand dollars."

Watts commented, "That's ballpark for the going rate for a professional hit."

Delray nodded and looked around the group again. "Questions?"

When nobody responded, he turned back to face the board. "We don't have anything concrete to link Avery directly to the murder. No witnesses, no confession. We've taken weapons from Avery's house but none of them match the bullet that killed Ringwood, so no murder weapon yet either. The only association is through his partner and her relationship to Hellyer and his mother. But that's not enough to build a solid case, so we need to keep digging."

Bridgette said, "Of course, we could be wrong with this line of investigation. Avery may have run because he thought he was being arrested for some other crime he'd committed."

Delray added, "Bridgette raises a good point. For all we know, Ringwood could have started dealing again and run afoul of someone in Bolton. So we need to keep all lines of inquiry open."

Lee asked, "Any news on the van seen on the Ringwood's street on the night of the murder?"

Delray shook his head. "We're still trying to track it down."

McCartin frowned. "Let's say it was Avery in the van. Why would he risk a three-hour drive back to Stanwyck with Ringwood's body in the back? Surely it would have been less risky to dump it locally?"

Delray grimaced. "You're not the only one who's losing sleep trying to figure that one out."

Watts said, "It's almost as if the killer was making a statement with the location of the body."

Bridgette replied, "What do you mean?"

"The location is close to where he originally lived. It's like they wanted him remembered as Paul Ringwood, not Paul Johnson."

Bridgette tugged on her left earlobe as she considered Watts' answer. Delray held up a finger to his lips indicating that Watts should stay quiet. He'd seen Bridgette in this deep thought process before and didn't want her being interrupted.

After a few seconds, Bridgette walked to the whiteboard. She murmured, "You could be right, Jason, but what if it's something more basic than that?"

Watts frowned. "Like what?"

Without taking her eyes off the whiteboard, Bridgette responded, "Let's say, the killer left the body at the house in Bolton, or disposed of the body somewhere else, but close by…"

Delray chimed in, "Okay."

"What would have happened when the body was found?"

Delray looked perplexed. "The Bolton police would have handled the case, not us."

"Exactly," replied Bridgette, then added, "And if that happened and the body had no ID, what would the local police have done?"

Delray mused, "They would have first looked for a match against local missing persons."

Bridgette nodded. "Exactly. Carrie Singleton had already reported her partner missing. They would have quickly made a match. A match to Paul Johnson, not Paul Ringwood."

"I'll be damned," said Delray.

McCartin looked puzzled. "What are you talking about?"

Bridgette answered, "If Ringwood's body had been found in the Bolton area it's likely he would have been identified as Paul Johnson by his partner and his true identity would have never been discovered."

McCartin nodded. "I think I see where you're heading with this."

Bridgette turned back to the whiteboard. "Taking the body out of the Bolton area takes away the possibility of a simple match to a local missing person."

Frost chimed in for the first time. "And makes it almost certain that a DNA check would be run to help identify the victim."

Bridgette added, "And because of his record, his DNA is in the system as Paul Ringwood, not Paul Johnson, meaning…"

Frost completed the sentence. "Alex Hellyer gets cleared of a murder he couldn't have committed … because it never happened."

Bridgette picked up a marker and circled the name Alex Hellyer. "And that would explain why the killer had to drive south for three hours to dump the body."

Friday 9:12 AM

It was another fifteen minutes before Delray released the team.

Although keen to see part of his team back in Bolton continuing the investigation, Delray had to continue the search of Avery's house and property.

After shuffling assignments for his detectives, Delay asked Bridgette to come to his office as soon as he'd finished a phone call to Assistant Commissioner Cunningham. Knowing she had a few minutes to herself, she made her way back to her cubicle and was surprised to see Frost sitting at his desk staring at a blank computer screen.

Bridgette could tell by his vacant look that something was wrong. "How are you feeling, Levi?"

"Maybe a bit sore, but I'm all right."

"So I guess you're pushing for a clearance to come back to work today?"

Frost's gaze was not focused on her as he answered, "That's the plan."

Bridgette frowned as she studied her partner for a

moment. She'd seen that same pained expression in her own eyes a few months earlier and knew it had nothing to do with his physical condition. Knowing she could be called in to see Delray at any moment, she pushed for an answer. "Are you sure you're okay?"

Frost waved her off with his good arm. "I'm fine. Like I said, a little bruised that's all."

Frost couldn't maintain eye contact which prompted her to say, "I'm not buying it. Something's wrong and I'm not talking about your arm."

Frost shook his head. "Don't push it, Bridgette."

"Keeping it bottled up won't help, Levi."

There was a moment's silence before Frost said, "When I got home last night, my wife wasn't there. I hadn't told her about what happened out at the Avery place and she'd had no idea I'd been to hospital. I thought at first she'd just been working late, but when she wasn't home by eight, I began to worry. I tried calling her, but it just went to voicemail. I sent her a text message and got no response to that either."

Frost brushed his fingers through his hair. "I waited another half hour and then tried calling again, but still got no answer. I wasn't sure what to do, so I called her mother."

Frost let out a long, shaky breath. "Her mother has always been very kind to me. She apologized and said Jasmine needed some space and had moved out. She tried to tell me why, but I wasn't listening. I just hung up."

Frost closed his eyes for a moment. "I checked our wardrobe and sure enough, pretty much all her stuff was gone. I think she must have been planning it for weeks."

Bridgette wasn't sure what to say and settled for, "I'm sorry, Levi," which she knew was hopelessly inadequate. She was about to add, 'If there's anything I can do,' but decided that was a platitude that wouldn't help.

Frost let out a short laugh. "You know the funniest thing about this?"

Bridgette shook her head.

"I phoned one of her closest girlfriends a bit later. Just to try and understand where it had all gone wrong. You'll never guess what she said?"

"What?"

"She's been seeing a guy two floors below in our apartment block for almost six months — she's been having an affair right under my nose."

"I'm really sorry, Levi."

Through gritted teeth, Frost said, "I have no idea where she's living. For all I know, she may have just moved two floors down. As you can appreciate, I want to spend as little time as possible in my apartment block."

They were quiet for a moment. Bridgette had no words that she could offer and put a hand on his shoulder and said, "For what it's worth, we're all here for you."

Frost nodded. "Thanks. It's totally blindsided me. I knew we had some issues, but I didn't see this coming."

Bridgette glanced to her right and saw Delray coming out of his office.

Frost said, "You need to go talk to the chief and I need to get to my medical examination."

"Are you sure you'll be okay?"

"I'll be fine. And please, don't mention this to anyone. I'll tell the chief when I'm ready, but it may be a day or two."

Bridgette nodded. "Okay."

She paused for a moment and then added, "Let me know how you get on with your medical. If you don't get a clearance, I think it would be good for us to meet anyway."

Frost sucked in a deep breath. "I don't have a lot more to say about it right now."

"We can talk about the case, I mean?"

Frost grimaced. "I'll see what the doc says."

Bridgette glanced at Delray who was signaling her to come to his office. "I'll call you later, Levi."

Bridgette only got as far as Delray's office door before her boss looked up at her from his desk. "I noticed you talking to Levi just now. Is he all right?"

Bridgette hesitated. She didn't want to betray Frost's confidence. "He said he was fine, but I'm sure it wouldn't hurt to talk to him yourself."

"I intend to as soon as I've received a briefing from the doctor. Have a seat, Bridgette, we've got a lot to talk about."

After Bridgette had settled, Delray said, "I want to re-interview both Lauren Hellyer and Francine Turello this afternoon. They're both holding out on us and I'm sure one of them has the information we need to crack this case wide open."

"Okay, what's the plan?"

"I want you to run both interviews. You think better on your feet than any other detective I know, and now that we're without Frost, I'll be your backup."

Somewhat surprised, Bridgette responded, "Shouldn't you be leading as the senior officer?"

Delray shook his head. "You're closer to this than I am, but I'll be there for backup. Both of them will have lawyers and I'll play referee if I need to."

"Okay. Who are we going to interview first?"

Delray pulled off his glasses and placed them on his desk.

"Good question. I wanted to talk to you about that. I'm thinking Lauren Hellyer. It will be very hard for her to deny that she's been paying someone at the Vancouver penitentiary. If we can get her to admit that she's been paying Turello, that will give us something to use on Turello in the second interview. And if that happens, maybe we can get her to open up about John Avery and find out what she really knows."

Bridgette nodded. "What time do you want to start?"

"I've told Hellyer's lawyer to be here at noon and Turello's lawyer at two PM. I want them to know they're both being interviewed today. We might be able to use that to our advantage and play them off against each other."

Bridgette looked at her watch and was relieved. "That gives me time to prepare."

"You're going to need it. They've both hired the best defense lawyers Vancouver has to offer."

Friday 12:07 PM

The interview rooms were located in a special section of the Vancouver Metro complex that included state-of-the-art recording equipment and holding cells. Lauren Hellyer, who was voluntarily coming in with her lawyer, would be interviewed in one of the rooms that looked like a small conference room. The theory was the less threatening the surroundings, the more a suspect would talk. Bridgette doubted the theory would work on Hellyer but hoped her strategy and list of questions would get results.

She glanced at her watch. They were running late. Delray waved her concern away. "Let them sweat. What do you know about Hellyer's lawyer?"

"Not a lot. I've heard he's smart and likes high-profile media cases."

Delray nodded. "Frankly, I didn't think Michael Grayson would take on a client like Lauren Hellyer. He normally deals exclusively with celebrities and A listers."

"Well, it's getting his name back in the media spotlight, just where he likes it."

As the elevator doors opened, Delray added, "Grayson is rude and arrogant. He likes to ride roughshod over everyone, particularly cops. But I'm sure you can handle that."

"Good to know," said Bridgette, following Delray down a government-green-painted corridor where closed doors displayed the numbers of each room.

Although Bridgette didn't think she was nervous, she felt butterflies in her stomach. She wanted to perform well in front of her boss and was excited by the prospect of what they might uncover.

They entered a small, white room and sat down at a timber conference table. The room looked no different to dozens of other meeting rooms in the complex, except for the high-tech video camera and microphones that were connected to recording equipment in an adjacent room. Bridgette noticed the small signal lights on the cameras and knew their technical team were in position and ready to start recording.

She locked eyes with Grayson who was already seated on the opposite side of the table with Lauren Hellyer. Grayson was in his early sixties, lean to the point of being gaunt, and looked a lot older in real life than he did on TV.

Bridgette figured Grayson wasn't one for small talk when he said sarcastically, "So good of you to keep us waiting, Chief Inspector Delray. I see nothing has changed."

Delray ignored the jibe and said, "This is Detective Bridgette Cash. She is one of the lead investigators on the Paul Ringwood murder case and will conduct the interview today."

Grayson gave her a curt nod. "I've heard about you. You're developing an interesting reputation."

Bridgette decided that comment wasn't worth a response and faced Lauren Hellyer whose gray hair was pulled back off her face in a ponytail that accentuated her harsh features.

Delray went through the preliminaries, advising Grayson and Hellyer that the interview would be recorded before saying, "I'm going to hand over to Detective Cash now. She will ask most of the questions."

Bridgette started by getting Hellyer to state her name and address for the record and then asked her a few basic questions about how long she had lived in Stanwyck and how often she visited her son in prison. For the most part, Grayson scribbled notes on a standard yellow legal pad. When Bridgette felt she had established a rhythm with Hellyer, she withdrew a sheet of paper from a folder and slid it across the table.

"I'm sure you're aware, Mrs. Hellyer, that the prison records all visits to inmates."

Hellyer responded haughtily. "Of course, I am."

"This report shows all of your visits over the last three years. A quick analysis would suggest that you visit your son regularly, in fact, at least fortnightly."

Grayson and Hellyer scanned the report for a moment before Hellyer looked up over her glasses. "I would need to check these dates, but I don't see why it's important. I visit Alex every two weeks and I would visit him more often if I was allowed. I'm not sure what you're getting at here?"

Grayson weighed in. "Where are you going with this, Detective?"

Bridgette withdrew another sheet of paper from her folder and slid it across the table. "We've tracked down an obscure bank account in your name Mrs. Hellyer ... or should I say, a bank account that's in a trust linked to you."

Bridgette spun the page around and gave Hellyer and Grayson a few moments to read the contents.

"As you can see, this statement shows a list of withdrawals that date back three years. You'll notice the dates of the withdrawals are all two weeks apart and always on the day before you visit your son in prison. I'm sure you remember the pattern. Care to explain what you do with the money?"

Hellyer looked flustered as she turned to Grayson, who said, "You don't have to answer that, Lauren."

Without taking her eyes off Hellyer, Bridgette said, "The withdrawals are all for the same amount — five hundred dollars."

Bridgette waited for a response, but Hellyer just glared at her. Bridgette continued, "I'm happy for you to study these two sheets of paper, but I'm sure you'll agree there is a pattern here. You've been withdrawing five hundred dollars the day before you visit your son in prison. Would you care to comment on that, Mrs. Hellyer?"

Grayson fired back, "Mrs. Hellyer won't be commenting on this until I've verified the accuracy of the statements you're making."

Bridgette glanced at Delray and then produced a third sheet of paper from her folder. Rather than sliding the paper across the table, Bridgette held it up and pretended to read it instead.

"This makes interesting reading. There are three data anomalies on both the withdrawals and the prison visits, and they all align with one member of the nursing staff at the prison."

Bridgette looked up from the page at Hellyer. "This member of staff wasn't working on any of the three days you visited without making a withdrawal the day before."

Bridgette placed the piece of paper on the table and turned it around so that it was facing Lauren Hellyer. Before sliding the paper across the table, she added, "I'm sure you're familiar with the name Francine Turello?"

Hellyer looked uneasy as she glanced across at Grayson and explained, "Francine is one of the nurses at the penitentiary who looks after Alex."

In an almost casual tone, Bridgette responded, "I find it interesting that you consistently withdraw five hundred dollars on the day before you visited the prison ... except when Francine Turello wasn't on duty. Care to explain that?"

Grayson retorted, "Mrs. Hellyer won't be answering that until we've had time to compare the records that you purport are from the prison and the bank account you allege she operates. Until we are in a clear position to understand if this data is accurate, she will not be responding."

Delray interjected for the first time. "All right, let's cut to the chase here shall we? You know as well as we do, Mrs. Hellyer, that you've being paying money to Francine Turello to look after your son in prison. As far as we're aware, you haven't committed an offense, although I'm sure Ms. Turello will have some explaining to do to her employer and the tax office."

Delray paused and looked from Hellyer to Grayson. "You can stall all you like, but we will get our answers."

Lauren Hellyer's features softened slightly. As she was about to speak, Grayson interrupted her and said, "I think we need to meet in private Lauren to discuss this matter before we go any further."

Hellyer shook her head. "I've got nothing to hide. Yes, I have been paying Nurse Turello to look after my son and I don't apologize for that. My son was a fully functioning adult when he went into that prison, and within months they'd reduced him to a mere shell of himself with the mental capacity of a five year old. If it was your child, you would do the same."

"What was the money for?" asked Bridgette.

Hellyer scowled. "You can't be very familiar with prisons, Detective Cash. There are predators everywhere … sexual predators who care about nobody but themselves. No one is safe from them, not even in the infirmary. I've been paying Francine Turello to protect my son. He's suffered enough and I wanted to do all I could to make sure he's not molested. The money helps get him his own room at night and makes sure he's watched." As an afterthought, Hellyer leaned forward and spat out, "I make no apologies for what I've done. But that doesn't make me guilty of anything other than wanting to protect my son."

Bridgette had done enough interviews not to be fazed by the verbal volley. "Did you hate Paul Ringwood?"

Grayson exploded. "That's an outrageous question, Detective, and I'm instructing my client not to answer it."

Bridgette kept her gaze locked on Hellyer as she asked the next question. "Do you know a man called John Avery?"

Hellyer's eyes widened just slightly. "Should I? I have no idea who you're talking about."

"John Avery is Francine Turello's partner. We have mounting evidence to suggest he's involved with the murder of Paul Ringwood."

Grayson said, "My client has told you that she doesn't know this man. Move on."

Bridgette leaned back in her chair. "Tell me about your son? He's an only child, isn't he?"

Hellyer's eyes narrowed. "You're the detective. I'm sure you know everything there is to know about him."

"When he was young and going to school … what was he like?"

Grayson interjected again. "Why is that relevant?"

"I'm sure you're aware of your son's record as a juvenile, Mrs. Hellyer. More than one incident where he was caught as a peeping tom? He was also questioned extensively over the disappearance of a young man from Stanwyck who is now listed as murdered … a man who had an altercation with your son."

Hellyer glared back at Bridgette but said nothing.

Bridgette continued, "Also, your son was questioned in relation to the killing of a number of pets, coincidentally that were…"

Grayson interrupted. "You're on a fishing expedition here, Detective, and I'm instructing my client not to answer any of these questions. Unless you can make a direct link between my client and Paul Ringwood, you're wasting your time."

Bridgette said, "You've led a hard life, Mrs. Hellyer. For that, I'm very sorry. Not only has your son been falsely imprisoned and almost beaten to death, but you too, have had your fair share of suffering."

When Hellyer didn't respond, Bridgette continued. "In working through the background of this case, I understand your husband used to beat you. So severely in fact that you were hospitalized on more than one occasion."

Grayson said, "None of this is relevant, Detective. Move on quickly or I'm going to terminate this interview."

Delray shot back, "That's not your call. We'll let you know when the interview is over."

"If you continue to harass my client like this, I'm making a formal complaint to the Commissioner."

"Be my guest," said Delray, adding "You can contact

him on this number," and slid a business card across the table.

Bridgette ignored the exchange and kept her focus on Hellyer. "Your husband died on the same night as your last beating which hospitalized you, didn't he?"

Hellyer snapped, "You've got no idea what you're talking about."

"Don't you find that a coincidence? Of all the nights for a fatal house fire, it's the night you're in a hospital?"

Grayson said flatly, "My client is not answering any of these questions."

Bridgette leaned forward and in a voice not much above a whisper said, "Did your son start that fire, Mrs. Hellyer?"

Friday 2:05 PM

Bridgette and Delray sat alone in the interview room. It had been several minutes since Lauren Hellyer and her lawyer had stormed out. In that time, they'd barely spoken a word. Lost in their thoughts, both were disappointed with the outcome.

Delray tried to hide it as he commented, "Good question about the fire."

"It certainly got a reaction."

Delray nodded. "When she leapt out of her chair and bellowed at you across the table, I thought we'd have to restrain her."

Bridge gave a brief smile. "I think Grayson thought so as well. Getting her to concede she was paying five hundred dollars a fortnight proves she loves her son but nothing more."

Delray scratched his chin. "We're a long way from having enough evidence to link her to Ringwood's murder, let alone charge her."

"Particularly now Avery is dead."

Delray took off his glasses and rubbed his eyes for a moment. Bridgette could see he was exhausted and knew the case was taking its toll on him. She asked, "Are you still getting heat from upstairs?"

"While this is playing out on the evening news, I'll be getting heat from upstairs."

Bridgette nodded. After a few seconds, Delray put his glasses back on and pointed at her sheet of questions. "So what's the plan of attack for Turello?"

Bridgette hooked her dark brown hair back behind her ears as she considered the questions she planned to ask their next interviewee. With an IQ of 151 and a photographic memory, she didn't need the sheet of paper and intended to ask the questions from memory and in an order determined by how the interview played out.

"I want to focus on the plastic bag we discovered in her house with the thirty-thousand in it. I'm hoping if I ask the questions in the right order we might trip her up."

"And now that we have the fingerprint results back with a match for hers on the bag, she can hardly deny she knew anything about it."

"My bet is she will deny she knows anything other than it existed."

Delray nodded. "She wouldn't be the first suspect to say she found it and put it straight back without asking questions."

"Avery has a history of domestic violence with former partners, so if her lawyer is smart that's the answer they'll come up with."

"So what's your follow-up question?"

"I've got three. It will depend on how the interview flows as to which one I use."

Francine Turello's lawyer was a short, stocky man. He was in his early forties with thinning hair that he'd plastered in place with so much product that Bridgette didn't think it would move even in a hurricane. She had heard a lot about Gideon Best and his reported links to organized crime. Commonly referred to as 'the Beast' by Vancouver police, Bridgette had no doubt he would be every bit as formidable an opponent as Grayson had been earlier. With a reputation for doing whatever it took, legal or illegal, to get a client off a charge, Best had barely acknowledged her presence when he entered the interview room with his client and sat in the same seats Grayson and Hellyer had occupied two hours earlier.

Turello looked very different out of her nurse's uniform. She was tall with olive skin and her brown shoulder length hair was stylishly cut. Bridgette figured the Valentino designer jeans and Ena Pelly leather jacket she wore would have cost close to a thousand dollars.

After going through the formalities and then sitting through a lecture from Best on his client's innocence, Bridgette finally asked her first question eleven minutes into the interview.

She started by going over some of Turello's background: where she was born, where she lived and what she did for a living. For the most part, Turello cooperated, but some of her answers were vague, prompting Bridgette to ask further clarifying questions.

In a few minutes, they'd established that Turello, now thirty-two, had been working as a nurse on and off for eleven years since graduating just before her twenty-second birthday.

Best sat on the edge of his seat, his eyes fixed on Bridgette, his body language suggesting he was poised to strike like a cobra with an objection the moment he thought a question was out of line.

Best got his first opportunity when Bridgette asked, "Now Ms. Turello, about your criminal record…"

Best interjected, "Were not here to talk about what my client has done in the past. Everything is on file and there's nothing relevant to this case."

Unfazed, Bridgette continued, "How long have you worked at the Vancouver Penitentiary?"

Turello looked at her lawyer. Best nodded and she replied, "Nearly four years."

"And where and when did you meet John Avery?"

"I met him about five years ago in a bar in Vancouver."

"Now, about the five hundred dollars a fortnight you've been receiving from Mrs. Hellyer. Who approached who?"

Turello looked puzzled. "Sorry, what do you mean?"

"It's a simple question. Who initiated it?"

Best jumped in. "My client said she doesn't know anything about any money."

Bridgette slid the same three sheets of paper across the table towards Turello that she had shown to Lauren Hellyer. Bridgette said, "Maybe this will refresh your memory," and then explained the pattern of withdrawals and deposits.

Turello looked defeated as Bridgette continued, "I'll ask you again, who initiated it?"

Turello looked at Best and then said, "Mrs. Hellyer approached me. She was worried about the care her son was getting and wanted to know if I could do anything extra to help."

Bridgette nodded and scribbled something on a scratchpad in front of her before asking, "And about the thirty thousand we found in the plastic bag at your house. I…"

Turello shot back, "I know nothing about it."

Bridgette held Turello's gaze easily as she responded, "We found your fingerprints all over the bag. Care to explain?"

Best interjected. "My client says she knows nothing about the bag. You should…"

"This is the fingerprint report from the lab for the plastic bag," declared Bridgette, presenting the report. "Read it for yourself. Your client's fingerprints, as well as those of John Avery, are all over the bag."

Turning her gaze back to Turello, Bridgette continued, "I'll ask the question again. What do you know about this money?"

It was Best who responded. "You don't have to answer that question, Francine."

Bridgette could see from the anxious look on Turello's face that she was rattled. Deciding to change tack for a moment, she commented, "Don't you think it strange?"

Turello frowned. "What's strange?"

"What John Avery allegedly did for a living?"

Turello said flatly, "He was a private investigator."

Bridgette pulled another sheet of paper from her folder and passed it across the table. "He was a lot more than just an unlicensed private investigator. This is his charge sheet from the last five years. Assault, resisting arrest, being in possession of stolen goods. It seems your partner was involved in a lot more than just PI work."

"I know nothing about any of that."

Bridgette raised her eyebrows. "And yet he was your partner. Do you really expect us to believe that?"

Turello looked at Best who simply shook his head.

Bridgette pulled a plastic bag from her folder and slid it across the table to Turello. The bag was about seven by four, had a small green logo on both sides and a friction seal across the top.

"This is the same type of bag that we found the money in at your house. Did you know that it's only used by three banks in Vancouver?"

Turello shook her head. Bridgette rattled off the name of the three banks and then said, "Did Avery bank with any of those?"

Turello said, "Not that I know of."

"And what about you, Ms. Turello? Do you bank with any of those banks?"

"I've never stepped foot inside any of them in my life."

Bridgette nodded and looked from Turello to Best. "That's interesting…"

"What's interesting?" asked Turello, in an exasperated voice.

"I'm sure you're aware that these three banks all have security cameras which record their customers coming in and leaving during opening hours…"

Bridgette paused for a moment. "We are currently going through all the security footage from the last month for each bank to determine whether you or John Avery paid them a visit."

Turello's mouth dropped.

"Would you like a glass of water, Ms. Turello? You've gone awfully pale."

Friday 3:55 PM

The interview with Francine Turello went for over two hours. Bridgette was mentally drained and thankful for the few minutes of silence and alone time at its conclusion while Delray took a bathroom break.

She replayed the key points of the interview in her mind while consulting the few notes she'd written on her scratchpad. She shook her head in frustration at how little progress they'd made.

Delray broke the silence when he returned to the room. "Well, how do you think that went?"

Bridgette looked up at her boss. "Not great."

Delray slumped in a chair opposite. "I didn't expect a confession, but Best made it almost impossible."

"He steered her away from saying anything incriminating."

Delray let out a sigh. "Whatever she's paying him, he earned his money today."

Bridgette circled the phrase '40K–bank' that she'd written.

"Did you notice her body language when I asked about the bank?"

"You mean the one about going through the security footage?"

Bridgette nodded.

"I wasn't aware we were going through any bank security footage?"

"We're not. I just threw that in to see what response I'd get."

"She didn't look comfortable."

"Yes, I think we actually should go through all the security footage from the banks."

"Do you think we'll find her on it?"

Bridgette frowned. "Maybe ... she got very nervous. If we can find footage of her or Avery, we have grounds for another interview."

"I like it. Perhaps it's something we can get Watts or McCartin to look into."

"If we can find footage of her going into any of those three banks in the last month, she has lied to the police and will have a lot of explaining to do."

Bridgette was interrupted by the buzz of her phone. She recognized the number and said, "I should take this call. It's the brain injury specialist I asked to examine Alex Hellyer's medical file."

She placed the phone on speaker so that Delray could listen.

"Detective Bridgette Cash."

A well-spoken woman replied, "Good afternoon, Detective, this is Doctor Monica Longmire from the Bolton Hospital Brain Injury Clinic. I've finished my examination of the file you sent me on Alex Hellyer."

Bridgette said, "Thank you for getting back to us so

quickly, Doctor. You're on speaker, and I have Chief Inspector Delray with me. What have you found?"

"I've been through the file you provided and the video tapes as well."

Bridgette glanced at Delray who was a picture of concentration as he stared at the phone. She repeated her question. "And what did you find?"

"Well, let me preface everything I'm about to say by telling you I can't be sure of my diagnosis until I've examined the patient myself. We will need to run some of our own independent tests."

"We understand this is just a preliminary finding, Doctor. If we think it's worthy of exploring further, we'll make the necessary arrangements."

"Well then, I'll email you the report, but given there are some anomalies, I thought I'd call you first."

Bridgette looked at Delray. "Anomalies? What are you referring to, Doctor?"

"Well, after reading the report and studying the videos, there are two really. The first is his body tremor. I think your concerns about its consistency are valid and warrant further investigation."

"So, what are you saying?"

"My research suggests the long-term symptoms someone would suffer from after this type of brain injury would be mild at worst. Most patients with similar injuries suffered in say a car accident or a fall, make almost full recoveries with physiotherapy. So much so, that you'd barely notice the symptoms if you were observing them in everyday life."

"Interesting."

"The second anomaly is the paralysis of the right arm. I would need to run additional tests."

Bridgette frowned. "The scans in the report didn't help you?"

"They're almost ten years old. And, unless there is an underlying physical injury that I'm not aware of, I don't see that kind of paralysis being caused by a brain injury, spinal yes, but a simple brain injury, no."

Delray raised his eyebrows at Bridgette and said, "This is Chief Inspector Felix Delray here, Doctor. Good afternoon to you. I have to say your findings are very interesting. Can I put it to you this way — do you think it's possible the patient has been faking his injuries?"

Doctor Longmire replied, "When Detective Cash first approached me, this was clearly at the forefront of her mind," she paused, "based on the evidence I have in front of me, I'd say it's a very strong possibility."

After disconnecting, Delray looked at Bridgette and said, "You suspected he was faking it all along, didn't you?"

"I had my suspicions. That's why I asked her to request his records from the prison because Shriver wouldn't let me take them out of the infirmary. She obviously got her court order."

"Then how come you picked up on it when nobody else did? What about all those doctors at that prison? Are they blind? Or worse, complicit?"

"We have to remember that nothing is confirmed yet."

"Even so, we know Longmire is only hedging her bets until she's made an examination. But you and I can read between the lines."

They were silent for a moment before Delray asked, "What made you suspect it was all a ruse?"

"It wasn't so much the head tremor as the way he responded to my question about if he knew Paul Ringwood or not."

"What did he say?"

"He didn't say anything, but his tremors stopped, and his only response was to shake his head dramatically like a child would."

"But isn't he supposed to only have the mental capacity of a five year old?"

"Yes, but all his other answers were consistent with an adult with an intellectual disability. His reaction made me wonder if he was lying."

"So, if Hellyer's handicap is a ruse, we have to completely rethink his involvement in Ringwood's murder."

Bridgette was still processing the information provided by Longmire and simply nodded in response. While it didn't surprise her, it threw up a whole new set of possibilities.

Delray continued. "So could he orchestrate all this from a prison hospital bed?"

"I'm not sure, Chief, but I'm thinking Turello is now far more involved than I first thought."

Delray frowned as he asked, "What do you mean?"

"It's on record that he sleeps most of the day … so what's he doing at night in that private room?"

Delray scratched his chin. "Probably not sleeping."

"Ringwood's only slip up as Paul Johnson that we're aware of was allowing that photo and article about him to be on the internet for two weeks. Although it didn't have his real name, it had enough information to identify him and his location. It may have cost him his life."

"So what you're saying is that Hellyer is the one who found him through the internet?"

"It's possible."

Delray said, "So how does he get to the internet? Are there computers in the infirmary?"

"Only one at the nurse's workstation. But that's too open. Other inmates would have seen what he was doing and called him out."

"So what then?"

"Maybe a smart phone? Turello could pass it to him each night and collect it in the morning before the end of her shift with almost no risk of discovery."

"That makes sense. He gets his own room and privacy to search all night, then sleeps all day."

"So, her five-hundred-dollar fee was for a lot more than just a private room."

"We need to interview Alex Hellyer again."

Delray shook his head. "I can't believe they're releasing him on Monday."

"We need to interview him this weekend before he leaves prison. Otherwise, we might never get another chance."

"Let's set it up for tomorrow. Alex Hellyer has a lot of explaining to do."

Saturday 6:12 AM

Levi Frost padded across the small hallway that separated his bedroom from the bathroom. His morning routine was normally the same: relieve himself, shower and dress, followed by breakfast.

Today was different. Not because he was now living alone, but because of what confronted him in the bathroom mirror. He barely noticed the stubble on his face and the bags under his eyes as he stared at his upper body. Naked from the waist up, Frost focused on the solid mass of angry purple that spread from the middle of his chest to past the bicep of his left arm.

He was told the bruising and pellet wounds would be painful for at least a week. He gritted his teeth and bent his left arm, cautiously rotating it at the shoulder. He closed his eyes as pain shot from his shoulder through his neck and into his brain. He found the experience of the physical pain was drawing him back to memories of the boy; memories that were still raw and more painful than anything else he'd ever experienced.

The Cold Light of Day

He let out a long breath. There were still nights where he'd wake up in a cold sweat as he relived the incident; holding the boy in his arms, trying helplessly to comfort him as he watched him take his last breath. It was a memory he could never erase, and he lived in hope that one day he would wake up and it wouldn't be the first thing he thought about.

He stared up at the ceiling. He had come to realize in his thirty-five years that he was much better at blocking out physical pain than emotional pain. He closed his mouth and pursed his lips — breathing in and out through his nose.

He continued the deep breathing until he felt more in control and then lowered his head to stare at his reflection again.

His gaze was drawn to a small glass shelf on the left-hand side of his mirror. The shelf was normally empty, but today it held a bottle of Oxycontin pills that had been prescribed by his doctor. He picked up the bottle and turned it slowly in his fingers. He'd used the pills before with a previous injury and knew they would take the pain away almost immediately. But he also knew how addictive they were. He'd battled addiction before and wondered how many he could take this time before he needed them for more than just pain management? Ten? Twenty? A whole bottle?

Frost put the bottle back on the shelf and studied the bruising on his battered body again.

He wanted to go back to work as soon as possible, but he wasn't entirely sure why. He definitely didn't want to be spending any more time than necessary in his apartment, but that didn't mean he had to be at work.

He wondered if it was the camaraderie he was starting to feel with the Homicide team. He hadn't felt that in a long time. Frost leaned in closer to the mirror to get a better look at the bags under his eyes. He'd barely managed two hours sleep, but was still eager for the day to begin. The Ringwood case intrigued him, no doubt about it. Maybe that was why he told the doctor he was fine and eager to return to work.

He pulled back from the mirror and let out a long sigh. There was a lot still to play out. The mother was the obvious suspect, but there were others in the mix as well. He still wondered about Ron Burns. Could the retired detective have been involved? Maybe Ringwood wanted to come out of hiding? Despite his failing health, was Burns capable of killing Ringwood to hide their crime ten years earlier.

He decided he would talk to Bridgette about it as soon as he got to work. His thoughts drifted to his partner while his reflection in the mirror stared back at him. Bridgette had what he liked to call the 'X factor.' It wasn't just her IQ that made her stand out. He'd come across plenty of cops with high IQs but being able to leverage that intellect so effectively as a police officer was rare. She was humble and downplayed her abilities, which he liked. But he could also see from his short time in Homicide why Delray placed so much faith in her.

Frost glared at the bottle of pills and felt tiny beads of sweat form on his forehead in response to the pain when he rotated his arm again. He picked up the bottle and this time unscrewed the cap. Peering inside, he knew just a couple of the tiny green tablets would give him the relief he craved. Frost tilted the bottle until two of the tablets spilled into his hand. 'Maybe just today?' he thought.

Frost looked into the mirror and grimaced. "Who are you kidding?"

The pills had once ruled his life and he knew if he

started, it wouldn't be long before they would control him again. He felt a wave of relief flood through his body as he upended the bottle and watched, transfixed, as the pills bounced around the basin before disappearing down the plug hole.

Holding out his left palm, he studied the two remaining pills and debated whether to take these just to get him through today. He looked into the mirror again, as if he was seeking advice from his alter ego. The face that stared back at him reminded him of who he had been six months ago; someone he desperately wanted to avoid meeting again.

He tilted his palm and watched the last two tablets tumble into the basin and disappear down the drain. He turned the faucet on and let the water run as if to underline the decision he'd just made.

He looked into the mirror once more and watched a bead of sweat trickle down his face. He knew the pain would eventually go, but the next few days would be hell. He was ready for that. He'd lost his wife but wasn't going to lose his career as well.

The hot water in the shower made him groan with pain as soaped his face and body. He made a mental note to call a cab to take him to work after he was dressed. Driving a car today would be madness.

Bridgette glanced at her watch. It was just after eight AM and she'd been at her desk for almost two hours. Unable to sleep after Dr. Longmire's revelations about Alex Hellyer, she got up at four-thirty and headed to the open-all-hours gym for an early morning workout. She'd spent the time while exercising going over the two main suspects in the

Ringwood case: Lorraine Hellyer and Francine Turello. The interviews the day before had been disappointing. Being 'all lawyered up' as Delray termed it, had meant neither suspect had provided any useful information to advance the investigation.

She stared down at her meager notes. Lorraine Hellyer's payments to Turello didn't prove she was involved in a murder any more than Turello's fingerprints on the bag of cash did.

Bridgette pushed back from the desk and massaged her neck. Closing her eyes, she begrudgingly accepted they were still a million miles away from solving the case. Without a ballistics match for any of Avery's weapons to the bullet they'd removed from Ringwood, or a witness, or any credible DNA evidence at the crime scene, she knew they had no case. She let out a long sigh, realizing this was the first time in her career she was on a case which was close to stalling.

Her thoughts were interrupted by the sound of approaching footsteps. She twisted her chair around expecting to see her boss but was surprised to see Levi Frost walking towards her. His movements looked stiff and he seemed to be putting on a brave face.

She cocked her head and asked, "Where's your sling?"

Frost gingerly put a bag he'd been carrying down on his desk and said, "I don't really need it."

Bridgette frowned. "Is that wise? You must be in a heap of pain?"

"I'll manage. I've been through worse."

Determined to steer the conversation in a different direction, Frost added, "So how did the interviews go yesterday?"

"Almost a complete waste of time. Both Turello and

Hellyer have engaged high-powered lawyers and it was impossible to get a straight answer on anything. But ... there has been one development."

Frost pulled his chair around to Bridgette's cubicle. "What?"

Bridgette told him about the phone call from the doctor at the brain injury clinic. Frost's eyes widened as he listened.

Frost shook his head. "That son of a bitch has been faking all this time?"

"We're not a hundred percent sure, but it's looking that way."

"He could have set this whole thing up from behind bars. It's all beginning to make sense. So what's next?"

Bridgette picked up an envelope from her desk and handed it to Frost.

"We have a court order to re-interview Alex Hellyer — this time without his doctor being present. I want to confront him with Dr. Longmire's medical opinion. I'm sure he'll play dumb, but hopefully we'll get him on the defensive and learn things the others aren't telling us."

Frost raised his eyebrows. "Do you think that will work?"

"It's worth a shot. Right now, every other lead we've had has been exhausted. Unless we come up with something new, we're dead in the water."

"So what are you going to ask him?"

"I just want to get him talking. I want to ask him about his routine, who visits him, what he thinks of the prison. Anything to get him talking. Once I establish a rapport, I'll hit him with what we learned from Longmire. Hopefully, he'll slip up and we can call him out as a fake."

"And if that fails?"

Bridgette looked at Frost. "We'll cross that bridge if we come to it."

Saturday 10:55 AM

Bridgette and Frost went through the same rigmarole as they had on their previous visit to the Vancouver Penitentiary. After going through the security checks, Frost lost his patience after twenty minutes in the waiting room.

"Why's Shriver taking so long?"

"I don't think he's here yet."

"What do you mean?"

"I don't think he works Saturdays. I only spoke to a nurse to set up the interview, and she kept me waiting for almost ten minutes. I could hear her speaking to Shriver in the background on a different phone. At first I thought he was just somewhere else in the facility. But the more I listened, the more I got the feeling he wasn't here at all."

Frost screwed up his nose a little, a habit Bridgette noticed he did often when asking a question. "So, what? He's still driving in?"

"Maybe. That would explain why we're still waiting."

"Does he know about the second court order?"

"I told the nurse that Dr. Shriver wouldn't be required, but I'm not sure she passed that on."

Frost grinned. "Man, he'll go apoplectic when he finds out."

Bridgette grinned. "You might be right." She studied her partner for a moment. After everything he'd been through in the last few days, she was glad to see him returning to normal. "How are you feeling?"

"I'm okay. The doctor says I'll be in pain for another week or more, but I'm happy to ride it out."

"What are you taking?"

"Just some pain killers."

Bridgette cocked her head. "Really? Are you actually taking them?"

"Well … not really."

"So you're operating today without any medication?"

"Pretty much."

She wasn't sure that was wise but decided to keep her opinions to herself. They waited two more minutes before Shriver appeared dressed in civilian clothes minus the doctor's coat he normally wore. The frown suggested he didn't look happy as he strode toward them.

Bridgette rose from her chair. Before she could get out a greeting, Shriver snapped, "I don't appreciate being called in on my weekend off, Detective. Couldn't this have waited until Monday?"

"Good morning, Dr. Shriver. Mr. Hellyer will be released on Monday and our court order only gives us permission to interview him here before his release."

Shriver stood with his hands on his hips. "So what are you hoping to learn from a second interview that you didn't learn from the first?"

"I'm sorry, I'm not at liberty to discuss that."

Shriver laughed. "I'm not sure what you're playing at here, Detective, but I'm going to hear all the questions anyway."

"I'm sorry if there's been a misunderstanding. When I spoke to the nurse, I made it clear the interview was just with Mr. Hellyer, Detective Frost and myself. You won't be required ... or permitted."

"I won't allow it!" said Shriver, pointing a finger at her. "Alex's diminished mental capacity makes him very fragile. There's no way in all good conscience as his physician that I can allow that."

Bridgette calmly showed Shriver the court order. "This court order is very clear. It grants us a private interview with Alex. As I said, just Detective Frost and myself."

Shriver's face turned red as he snatched the papers from her hand.

"Please. Go ahead. Read it for yourself," said Frost with a subtle nod. Bridgette could tell by his tone that he was enjoying the exchange.

After reading the document, Shriver fumed, "I can't accept this. This is absolutely crazy."

Conscious that everyone in the waiting room was now staring at them, Bridgette said, "Is there somewhere we could go to discuss this privately?"

Shriver didn't seem to be listening. "Surely he has a right to a lawyer, or at the very least his physician or a communication assistant?"

"Alex is not a suspect, we are seeking background information only. The court order specifically states that nothing he tells us can be directly used against him, and we won't be recording the interview."

"Wait here."

Frost raised an eyebrow and said, "Well, this is getting interesting," as they watched Shriver storm off.

Bridgette and Frost sat in the waiting room for another two hours. In that time, she made three phone calls; the first to Delray informing him of the setback, and the other two to the judge's office that had issued the order.

The first call to the judge's office took close to half an hour. Bridgette learned that Shriver was disputing the court order and there would be a delay while the judge considered whether the challenge was legitimate or not. Bridgette ended the call disappointed that the judge was looking for a compromise. After waiting another hour, she got the ruling she expected when she called back. The judge was amending the order saying the second interview with Alex Hellyer could still go could go ahead, but only under the supervision of a doctor or approved carer.

Frost's respect for Bridgette was growing. When Shriver returned to the waiting room with a faxed copy of the amended court order, he did his best to rub it in as he waved it in front of Bridgette's face. "My hands are tied, Detective. I have to do what's in the best interest of my patient. I'm sure you understand."

She took the setback in her stride and politely asked Shriver if they could now proceed with the interview.

As they followed Shriver to the infirmary, Frost almost forgot about his pain while he wondered how Bridgette would handle the interview now that Shriver would be present.

After being ushered into the same small conference room

they had used on their previous visit, Shriver disappeared to collect Alex Hellyer. Hardly a word was spoken between the two detectives while they waited. Frost knew enough about Bridgette to know that she was deep in thought, thinking about the questions she would ask Alex Hellyer.

Frost had seen a lot of cops conduct interviews, but he hadn't seen anyone operate quite like Bridgette. She had an uncanny ability to think on her feet, changing tack frequently to keep the interviewee off balance. He likened her to a boxer; one good punch to get them off balance followed up by more precise blows, not necessarily as heavy, but targeted and well timed. He wondered if Shriver would feel so smug after his patient got through round two with her.

While they waited, Bridgette picked up the faxed copy of the revised court order and re-read the contents before passing it to Frost who had his eyes closed. "Are you okay, Levi?"

"I'm fine. The pain occasionally catches me off guard is all."

Frost could see by the look on her face she that wasn't convinced. He glanced at his watch and changed the subject.

"How long is he going to make us wait?"

"I'm not sure. It's the same interview room as last time and the infirmary is just down the hallway."

"I think Shriver is preparing Alex. It doesn't take this long to get a patient from an infirmary that's almost next door."

"I agree."

Frost was about to ask Bridgette what her opening question would be when the door opened. Shriver led Alex

Hellyer into the room and settled him in a chair on the opposite side of the small conference table.

Shriver said to Hellyer, "These are the two detectives I was telling you about, Alex. They've come back to ask you a few more questions."

Turning to face Bridgette and Frost, Shriver added in a firm voice, "And they're not going to take up too much of your time either."

Frost opened a notebook he'd brought along for the interview. While the court order prevented them from recording anything, he was free to take notes. Today, like most of the other interviews he'd done with Bridgette, he was there to provide backup, take notes and ask the odd question when needed.

Bridgette wasted no time in asking her first question. "When do you get out of prison, Alex?"

Hellyer looked at Shriver, who nodded. "Go ahead, Alex."

Hellyer stared down at the conference table. "Monday."

"That must make you very happy?"

Hellyer mumbled, "Yeah," without looking up.

"Are you looking forward to going home to live with your mom again?"

"Yeah."

Bridgette persisted. "I bet your mom is looking forward to having you home again?"

"I guess."

Frost continued to study Hellyer as Bridgette asked a few more introductory questions. Something was definitely different, but he couldn't put his finger on it.

"Do you think you'll miss the nurses when you leave here, Alex?"

Without looking up, Hellyer nodded.

"Who's your favorite nurse?"

Hellyer shrugged his shoulders.

"Do you like Nurse Turello?" When she didn't get a response, Bridgette added, "Does your mom speak to Nurse Turello?"

"Sometimes."

"Did you know your mom has been paying Nurse Turello money to look after you?"

Shriver exploded, "That's not an appropriate question, Detective."

Bridgette held up the court order. "You have a right to be present, Doctor, but you have no say over the questions I ask."

Shriver shook his head. "This is an inappropriate line of questioning, Detective, and you know it."

Frost couldn't suppress a smile as he watched his partner respond, "My hands are tied, Doctor. I have to do what's in the best interest of the case. I'm sure you understand."

Shriver turn bright red. Bridgette continued with her questions.

After another few minutes of general questions, Shriver seemed to have calmed down but then interrupted. "How much longer, Detective?"

"I'm not sure, Doctor. But I'm finding this interview very helpful."

Shriver frowned. "Really? How so?"

"How long has Alex had his tremors?"

Shriver look slightly perplexed. "Ever since the attack that caused his brain injury."

Frost suddenly realized what was different about Hellyer and weighed in for the first time. "Do the tremors come and go, Doctor?"

The Cold Light of Day

Shriver looked at his patient. "No, they're constant. He even has them in his sleep from time to time."

Hellyer sat motionless with his head down staring at the table.

"Care to explain why the tremors have stopped, Alex?" Frost said. "Perhaps it's a miracle from God?"

Hellyer didn't move a muscle.

Frost leaned forward. In a voice just above a whisper, he said, "Or perhaps this has all been a little charade, Alex? Maybe you've been faking the entire time, but now you're getting out you don't need to pretend anymore?"

Hellyer remained still with his head down.

Frost demanded, "Look at me, Alex. I know you're not deaf."

Hellyer raised his head and made eye contact with Frost. After holding Frost's glare for a moment, he winked and then lowered his head.

Saturday 2:17 PM

Felix Delray normally felt comfortable in Commissioner Blaine Underwood's office, but not today. Located on the fourth floor, the Commissioner's executive suite was almost the size of Delray's entire homicide room that housed twelve detectives and support staff. Underwood was a small, stocky man with a neatly trimmed beard and a buzz cut. Both the beard and hair had once been red but were now pure white. Pressures of the job perhaps. Delray had worked well with Underwood and he hoped that wouldn't change after today's meeting. He appreciated Underwood's intellect and his fair no-nonsense approach to policing.

Underwood was a far cry from Delray's direct boss, Leon Cunningham, who was sitting beside him. Cunningham was tall and lean, a stickler for the rules, and a nightmare to work with.

As Underwood turned the laptop around on his massive oak desk so that all three could see the screen, he said, "While we weren't at liberty to film the interview, the penitentiary security cameras were still operating in the meeting room. There's no sound, but the video is still damning."

Underwood said "I've fast forwarded through to the part of the interview which I'm most interested in."

Delray felt his gut tighten as he stared at the image on the laptop. The still image from the security video showed three men and a woman sitting around a conference table.

Underwood looked across his desk and said, "Can you both see?"

Delray and Cunningham nodded.

Underwood pressed a key on his keyboard before adding, "There's no sound, but you'll get the general idea," as the video came to life.

All three men watched in silence as the video played. Delray could see Bridgette and Frost sitting on one side of the conference table with Hellyer and his doctor on the other. By the body language and lip movement in the video, he could see that Bridgette was asking the questions.

Underwood commented, "It's coming up in about five seconds."

Delray felt a sheen of sweat spread across his brow as the interview continued. He focused on Levi Frost. Within the space of two seconds, Frost's body language changed dramatically. It was clear that Frost was talking, but it was impossible to know what he was saying. Delray saw Frost lean forward, seemingly to ask a question, then could barely watch as Frost rose from his chair, leaned across the table, and grabbed Hellyer by the neck.

Delray heard Cunningham mutter, "Appalling," as both Bridgette and the doctor jumped out of their chairs. Delray watched the screen as Bridgette wrenched Frost's hands away from Hellyer's neck, while the doctor fussed around with his patient.

They saw Shriver fly into a rage as the video captured him waving his arms around, pointing first at Bridgette, then at Hellyer, and then at Frost who hurriedly backed away from the table.

Underwood pressed pause. "I'm not sure we need to see any more of this right now. In a moment one of the prison guards comes in while the doctor takes Hellyer back to the infirmary."

Underwood looked from Cunningham to Delray and said in an even voice, "Clearly Detective Frost's behavior is unacceptable and he'll need to give us an explanation." He grimaced and then added, "Needless to say, if the press finds out about this, this is going to get out of control very quickly."

As Delray and Cunningham nodded, Underwood said to Delray, "Where is he now?"

"He's in my office, sir. I thought it best to keep him out of the Homicide room until we figure out what we're going to do going forward."

"Is he alone?"

"No. Detective Cash is with him."

Underwood nodded. "I think that's wise."

Cunningham interjected, "Sir, respectfully, I'm not sure that we need too much of an investigation on this one. Clearly this officer has overstepped the mark and I'm recommending his immediate dismissal. We have all the evidence here in this footage that we need. Anything other than a dismissal…"

Underwood held up a hand. "Stop. We're not jumping to conclusions. We'll follow due process regardless of the initial information presented. Are we clear?"

Cunningham nodded, but then replied, "Respectfully, sir…"

Underwood ignored the deputy commissioner and turned to Delray. "Have you had an opportunity to hear Detective Frost's side of the story?"

Delray let out a long breath. "I have some information, sir, but frankly, Detective Frost is very upset with himself and I haven't pushed it too far just yet."

Underwood nodded. "What about Detective Cash? Have you spoken to her?"

"Yes."

"And what did she have to say?"

Delray took his time and chose his words carefully. While Underwood might be prepared to play fair, Cunningham would look for any opportunity to cut Bridgette out of his team.

"We've been working under the assumption that Alex Hellyer received a severe brain injury as a result of a prison assault early on in his sentence."

"That would be ten years ago?" said Underwood.

Delray nodded. "That's correct, sir. Hellyer was in a coma and hospitalized for several weeks after the attack."

He then described Hellyer's physical disabilities before Underwood clarified, "And he now has the mental capacity of a five year old?"

"That's what the medical report said."

"Okay, so what caused the behavior we've just witnessed?"

Delray leaned forward. "Detective Cash had noticed that the body tremors Hellyer had in his first interview were no longer present. She knew from his file that this was supposedly a constant physical affliction that he'd suffered ever since the attack. Today, there were no such symptoms. Detective Cash also noticed other changes in his demeanor."

"Like what?"

"In her words, he seemed bored by the interview process. In contrast to the first interview where he presented like a child who was confused by what was happening around him."

Underwood frowned. "So what are you suggesting, that he's been faking it?"

"That was the opinion Detective Cash formed during the interview. It's also supported by an independent medical review we've received, which throws doubt over the severity of his injuries."

"And Hellyer gets released next Monday?"

"Sir, I'm guessing he saw no reason to keep up the charade any longer."

Underwood nodded. "So how did Detective Frost get so involved?"

Delray said, "Detective Cash asked the doctor if Hellyer's tremors were persistent or not. The doctor indicated they were, which is when Detective Frost entered the questioning. Frost challenged Hellyer directly to explain why he didn't have the tremors anymore."

"And what did he say?"

"Nothing at first. Apparently Frost goaded him with a couple more questions to see if he would get a reaction."

"What questions?"

"It's fair to say that Detective Frost mocked Hellyer — a tactic we often use to elicit a response."

Underwood said, "I will need to know those questions, Chief Inspector."

"Sir, Detective Frost asked Hellyer if it was a miracle from God firstly, and then if he'd been faking the injury the entire time he'd been in prison."

"And what was Hellyer's response?"

"Sir, apparently Hellyer made eye contact for the first time with Frost and winked at him. According to Detective Cash it wasn't so much what he did it was his attitude. He had a smirk on his face and Detective Cash believes the response was designed to stir a reaction…"

Cunningham interrupted, "Our detectives need to be much more professional than that, Chief Inspector. You only have to…"

Underwood glared at Cunningham. "This is my meeting, Leon."

Turning back to Delray, Underwood continued, "So, Detective Cash believes Hellyer has been faking it?"

Delray nodded. Underwood pushed back from the desk. "So we've been operating under the assumption that Hellyer has had diminished mental capacity when it looks likely that nothing could be further from the truth."

Underwood shook his head. "And he's being released on Monday."

"Yes, sir."

Underwood mused, "I can understand a prisoner scamming the system to get better conditions, but this — to be able to pull this off for ten years — that takes enormous acting ability and discipline."

"I couldn't agree more."

Underwood picked up a pen from his desk and began twirling it between his fingers. "There are too many unanswered questions here, Felix."

"I agree. Based on what we've learned now, we are changing our entire focus on the Ringwood investigation. We believe Alex Hellyer may have orchestrated the entire thing from behind bars."

Saturday 2:21 PM

Bridgette and Frost sat in Delray's office. Delray had been with them until a few moments before when he'd received a phone call from the Commissioner's office with a request for an urgent meeting. Their boss hadn't said what the meeting was about, but they both knew it was to discuss Frost's future.

Frost said, "I'm going to be suspended, aren't I?"

"It's possible."

Frost lowered his head. "I've really screwed up this time. Do you think they'll fire me?"

Bridgette chewed on her bottom lip. She didn't want to alarm Frost or worry him any further.

"I hope not. It really depends on whether the chief is in your corner or not."

"What do you mean?"

"I was in a similar position when I was on probation. I was involved in a shooting incident in the basement here which I'm sure you've heard about. Delray had my back and believed in me. If he believes in you, you'll have a chance."

Frost walked to the office window. As he peered out, he murmured, "I can't believe I did that."

After the incident with Hellyer, Bridgette and Frost had been escorted out of the penitentiary by a guard. They'd said very little to each other on the trip back to the office.

"So what really happened back there, Levi?"

Frost said, "I lost it. I just snapped is what happened. Why … I'm not sure." He turned back and added, "Did you see the smirk on Hellyer's face when he winked at me?"

"Yeah, I saw it."

Frost said, "That son of a bitch has played us, and them. All of us!" He raised his left arm and rotated his shoulder.

"Are you in pain?"

Frost put his hand in his pocket. "A little."

They stared at each other for a moment. "What happens if I'm suspended?" asked Frost.

"You won't be able to return to work until after the inquiry."

"That's only if they allow me to keep my job."

"Don't give up hope, Levi, this is complex. You were shot and almost killed two days ago and are clearly in pain."

She studied Frost for a moment. "They probably made an error allowing you to return to work so soon. So there are lots of things in play other than just your actions."

Frost returned to his chair. "It doesn't sound like this will be resolved any time soon."

"Probably not."

They were quiet for a moment before Frost asked, "So how does this change the investigation?"

"Your possible suspension?"

"No, the fact that Hellyer has being playing the system."

"It changes everything. It's clear he could have orchestrated Ringwood's murder from behind bars."

"But how could he do it and keep up the brain-damaged charade?"

Bridgette tugged gently on her left earlobe. "What I want to know is how did he find Ringwood? He spends all his time in the infirmary, masquerading as someone he's not and under constant supervision."

"Maybe he's getting access to a smartphone like you suggested?"

Bridgette nodded. "Maybe. All we have is a bunch of theories right now, and Hellyer will be out of prison before we get a chance to prove any of them."

It was a long afternoon for Bridgette. She and Levi had returned to their desks to work for a while until Frost was called into Delray's office just before four. She had tried to busy herself but found it hard to concentrate. She tried to rationalize that it was simply because she was tired, but deep down she knew it was more to do with Levi.

Just after five, she heard footsteps approaching her cubicle and expected to see Frost returning. She was surprised to see Delray. "Where's Levi?"

"He's gone. You got a minute?"

"Sure." She followed Delray back to his office.

As he walked into his office, Delray said, "Close the door behind you if you don't mind. I don't think anyone else is here this late on a Saturday, but you never know."

After closing the door, Bridgette sat down in a chair opposite her boss.

Delray said in a weary voice, "I've had to suspend Levi. In the end, we had no choice."

Bridgette nodded. "How did he take it?"

"Not great, but I think he understands."

"What happens from here?"

Delray pulled off his glasses. "There will be an inquiry, of course. The meeting with the Commissioner was helpful. Cunningham wanted Frost sacked immediately, but after hearing about the extenuating circumstances, the Commissioner wants to widen the scope of the inquiry. While he didn't say as much, I think he feels the doctor slipped up letting Levi come back to work so soon after being shot by Avery."

"Can't say I'm surprised."

"We'll both be called to give statements along with a host of others — it'll take a while."

"If I can ask, what do you think his chances are of being exonerated?"

Delray scratched his chin. "To be honest — and this doesn't leave the room — it could go either way. I think the Commissioner wants to give him another chance, but it will depend on how Internal Affairs interpret the evidence. Being traumatized by the shooting, and in pain, and being cleared to come back to work so soon all have to count in his favor. But, that said, he shouldn't have done what he did."

Bridgette nodded. "I agree," and then added, "I assume it's okay to contact him?"

"I'd encourage that, Bridgette. Right now, Frost can do with all the friends he can get."

They were quiet for a moment before Delray said, "So tell me about Hellyer. You really think he's been faking it all these years?"

"I can't say for sure, but the tremors and mannerisms he displayed in the first interview definitely weren't there in the last one."

Delray frowned. "How come the doctors didn't pick up on this earlier?"

"I read the medical file again this afternoon. He definitely has scar tissue on the brain associated with the beating, and I don't think you can fake a coma. I guess it's hard to tell how much of a recovery you can make after that. Some of it would have to be based on observation. Perhaps as he healed, he started faking the symptoms so he could keep his cushy room."

Delray shook his head. "This guy is next level if he can fake something like that for all those years."

"I agree."

Delray chewed on the arm of his glasses. "With Hellyer now our number one suspect, we've gotta figure out where he was getting help from. If it really is him, he can't have been doing it on his own."

Bridgette nodded again. "While it's possible it's someone in the prison we don't know about, Francine Turello and his mother remain the prime suspects. Turello has to be involved. She's on the inside and has regular contact … and we already know she's taking money."

Delray thought for a moment and added, "What about Shriver? We can't rule him out either. Maybe it's worthwhile you and I interviewing him as soon as possible?"

"Maybe?"

Delray frowned. "Maybe? You're not convinced?"

"If he gets a lawyer like Turello and Hellyer's mother have, we may not learn much more than his address and date of birth."

"So what are you thinking?"

"After the incident today, we had to go back to the infirmary for a few minutes to wait for a guard to escort us out. When I looked through the window at all the sick inmates, I noticed they were all different from the first time we visited … all except one."

"So there's another inmate who's in the infirmary permanently?"

Bridgette chewed on her bottom lip. "Possibly. I asked one of the nurses about him. His name is Larry and he suffers from Leukemia and spends most of his time in the infirmary. I think it might be worthwhile interviewing him. He may be able to tell us things no one else can."

"Do you think he'll talk?"

"He might. Hellyer has been moved out of the infirmary now. Until he gets out on Monday the warden's not taking any chances with anything else happening to him and he's been given a cell in solitary. So once he leaves, he'll no longer be a threat."

"Okay, let's see what Larry's got to say."

Bridgette grimaced. "I'll probably need another court order. I can't imagine Shriver letting us talk to anyone else after what happened today."

"Leave that with me. Just set up the interview for Monday."

"Thanks, Chief."

Delray looked at his watch. "The Commissioner also asked me how the rest of the team are doing. I told him okay, but he didn't seem convinced."

"I guess he doesn't want another incident."

Delray nodded. "Which brings me to my next question. How many days straight have you worked, now?"

"Eleven."

"Well, you're not working tomorrow and neither am I. Commissioner's orders."

Bridgette was secretly relieved. She felt worn out by the case and a day off would do her good. "I'm not sure I'll be able to think about anything else right now, but I'll give it a try."

"Getting your mind off it for a day will do you good. Me, I'm gonna play golf." Delray gave a wry smile. "Chasing that little white ball around a golf course for four hours is very distracting, and I rarely think about work. But come Monday morning, we'll refocus and move forward."

Delray studied Bridgette for a moment. "You don't look convinced?"

Bridgette shook her head. "Sorry, Chief, something you said distracted me."

"What'd I say?"

"Monday. Alex Hellyer gets out of prison on Monday."

"That he does."

"If I'm right, he's killed or had a hand in killing, three people. His father, Carl Stockton and Paul Ringwood."

Delray grimaced. "A murderer is walking free and there's not a damn thing we can do about it."

"It makes you wonder…"

"Wonder what?"

"If there's anyone else on his list?"

Monday 9:54 AM

It took Bridgette and Delray less than ten minutes to go through the security screening at Vancouver's maximum-security prison.

As they sat in the waiting room, Delray verbalized what Bridgette was thinking. "How long are they going to keep us waiting?"

"I'm not sure. Shriver isn't rostered on today, so maybe not as long as we've normally had to wait."

Delray made a face. "I want to interview Shriver myself."

Bridgette smiled to herself. An interview involving Shriver and her boss would be interesting. Something you could almost sell tickets for, she thought. As she was about to comment, she noticed a group of people milling around the elevators.

Delray frowned. "What's that all about?"

Bridgette glanced at her watch. "Given the number of reporters gathering outside, I'd say it could be the entourage who'll be escorting Hellyer off the premises."

"What time's he due to leave?"

"Ten o'clock. Apparently, he's doing a press conference with his lawyer out front."

"What a circus that will be. If only they knew what kind of scumbag they were letting out."

A moment later, the elevator doors opened. Two guards emerged, followed by two men in suits and a man in casual clothes. Bridgette discreetly pointed at the man in casual clothes and said to Delray, "You've seen him on video. Now you get to see him in person. That's Hellyer."

They both watched as Hellyer, the warden and the other man in a suit conferred.

Bridgette said, "I would give anything to know what they're talking about."

Delray grinned. "By the look of the warden's tense body language, I'd say he's hoping Hellyer goes easy on him at his press conference."

They watched as the huddle broke up and the guards led the group towards the main exit. Hellyer kept his head down as they walked forward. She could see no sign of the tremors and she wondered whether he would put on a show in front of the cameras outside. As they walked forward, Hellyer looked up and around, as if he were taking one last look before he tasted freedom for the first time in ten years. As his gaze swept by Bridgette and her boss, he did a double take. Bridgette held Hellyer's gaze. Then he grinned and winked at her before dropping his head again.

Five minutes later a guard came to escort them to the infirmary. They were shown into the same conference room where the incident between Frost and Hellyer had taken

The Cold Light of Day

place. A minute later, the door opened and Larry Pocock was wheeled in.

Pocock was in his early sixties. He had wispy gray hair and was extremely overweight. His pale complexion and washed-out eyes suggested to Bridgette that Leukemia would claim another victim soon.

The nurse positioned Pocock's wheelchair next to the conference table and said, "There's a guard outside if you need anything."

Pocock watched the nurse leave the room and then asked, "Do I need a lawyer?"

Bridgette assured him he didn't as she introduced herself. Pocock didn't look convinced and she knew she would need to be careful how she approached the questions if she wanted his cooperation. After providing Pocock with some background to the Ringwood murder case, she said, "The reason for meeting with you today, Larry, is to learn as much as we can about Alex Hellyer. We know your condition has forced you to spend a lot of time in the infirmary, so we figured you'd probably know as much about him as anyone else."

Pocock looked blankly at them for a moment. "Why don't you ask the nurses?"

"We will in time, Larry, but we thought it would be worthwhile getting a patient's perspective as well."

Pocock looked stunned. "You're trusting the word of a con?"

Bridgette replied patiently, "You have no reason to lie. Hellyer was released this morning. He can't hurt you."

Pocock still didn't look convinced. "I'm not sure I can really tell you anything."

"Let's start with some background. How long have you known him?"

"I've been in this time for six years, but my Leukemia only flared up about five years ago. So, five years."

"So I take it you've gotten to know him pretty well?"

"Not really. We were in the infirmary together, but he was hard to talk to."

"How would you describe him as a patient?"

Frowning, Pocock said, "What do you mean?"

"Was he a good patient or did he cause trouble?"

"He didn't cause trouble, but he was different to everyone else in here."

"In what way?"

"He was needy and hard to understand. So we all avoided him."

"Did he ever do anything that was out of character?"

"Like what?"

"Did he ever behave like a normal adult? For example, did the tremors come and go, or were they constant?"

"They were constant, from what I could see." Pocock paused, and then added, "There was this one time though…"

"What happened?"

"There were only three of us in the infirmary. Me and one other guy were in our beds sleeping and Alex was having his lunch. The nurse had set him up to feed himself like she normally did. I remember she left the room for a minute and he dropped a spoon which woke me up…"

"And what happened?"

"He bent down and picked it up with his right hand."

Bridgette raised her eyebrows as she responded, "He used his paralyzed arm?"

Pocock nodded. "I didn't realize it was his right hand at first, because I'd just woken up. But later, I thought about it

— where he was sitting, and where I was lying — it made me wonder how bad his injuries really were."

"Did you ever notice anything else like that?"

"No. But I don't make a point of staring at other people in here either. Even in the infirmary that can get you into a lot of trouble."

"So did you think he was faking his injuries?"

"I wasn't sure. If you want to survive in here, you mind my own business."

Bridgette wanted to keep the conversation moving and asked, "What was his relationship with the medical staff like?"

Pocock shook his head and said flatly, "I'm not talking about any of the medical staff."

"If you're worried about Francine Turello, they fired her yesterday."

Pocock raised his eyebrows. "I didn't know that."

Bridgette nodded. "She's admitted to taking money from Alex Hellyer's mother in return for giving him favorable treatment. Can you tell us anything about their relationship?"

"When she was on night shift, he got most of her attention. And he almost always got a private room as well."

"Was there anything else unusual about their relationship?"

Pocock's eyes got wide. "She's been fired, right?"

Bridgette nodded.

"And she's not coming back?"

"No, she's not coming back?"

Pocock shifted his enormous frame in the chair. When he seemed comfortable, he said, "She worked four nights a week. When she was on shift and out here in the general ward, she talked to him just like everyone else did — like he was a child. But when they were in a room together with the door closed…"

Pocock stared off into space. "I really couldn't ever hear anything more than whispers, but it was different. There was something strange about it."

"Were the lights on or off when she was in the room with him?"

"Mostly on, but when the lights were off, there was almost always a faint glow coming from under the door."

"Like a nightlight or a piece of medical equipment was on?"

Pocock nodded. "Yeah, only Hellyer didn't need any medical equipment. He only needed help feeding and going to the bathroom."

Bridgette thought about the possibility of the glow coming from a smartphone as she asked, "So this only happened when Nurse Turello was on night shift?"

Pocock nodded. "If he got a room when she wasn't on shift it would stay dark just like everywhere else."

Bridgette looked at Delray who was busy scribbling notes on a scratch pad.

Pocock frowned and then added, "Huh. I've just figured it out."

"The glow coming from the room?"

"No. The whispered conversations. It all makes sense now…"

"What makes sense?"

"While I couldn't make out what they were saying, Hellyer was doing most of the talking."

"What do you mean?"

"He wasn't speaking in short sentences. It was just like two normal people talking."

The Cold Light of Day

The interview with Pocock turned out to be brief. Bridgette could see he was tiring after just twenty minutes. Fearing he would pass out and not wishing Vancouver Metro to be embroiled in any more controversy, she reluctantly cut the interview short.

She and Delray said very little to each other on the way out because neither of them wanted their conversation overheard. As they exited the building, Bridgette noticed the media crews packing up and dispersing.

Hellyer and his lawyer were nowhere to be seen. "It looks like the press conference is well and truly over."

Delray nodded but said no more until they were halfway across the car park and well out of earshot. "So what do you make of that?"

Bridgette reflected on what Pocock had said about the conversations between Hellyer and Turello. "It adds weight to what we already know."

"This business about Hellyer spending so much time in a private room. I'm positive you're on the money with Turello supplying him with a smartphone."

"After we saw him leaving this morning, there's no doubt he's made a full recovery."

Delray stopped walking. "What I still don't get is how he tracked Ringwood down. Even if he had access to the internet, how did he find a story about Ringwood that was only online for two weeks?"

"Sometimes the data persists in search engines long after the article itself is taken down. And if you're tech savvy, you can set up specific alerts and still find what you're after."

"So Turello gives him a smartphone each night she's on shift."

"And takes it back at the end of her shift before she leaves to go home."

Delray shook his head as he added, "Hellyer never had to worry about hiding it."

As they started walking again, Bridgette said, "Of course, unless we get proof, this is just a theory."

"Let's hope the search at Turello's house turns up something."

Bridgette nodded but said no more. She thought it was a long shot that the search of Avery's property would turn up the smartphone and even if it did, it wasn't enough to build a murder case on.

Tuesday 9:17 AM

Bridgette glanced up at the sky as she stepped out of her car in front of Ron Burns' house. With Frost suspended for the foreseeable future and without enough evidence to make any arrests, the dark clouds matched her mood. Her decision to visit Burns had been an easy one. Concerned for his safety now that Hellyer had been released, she'd tried repeatedly to call the retired detective after her meeting with Delray, but only got as far as leaving a message. She could see that all the curtains were drawn as she walked up the footpath. She knocked on his front door, hoping he was home.

Between failed calls to Burns, she'd contacted Stanwyck Police to set up another meeting. With her fear mounting that Hellyer would be out for revenge, she'd hoped to get more information on what he had been doing prior to his arrest ten years earlier. If there were other targets out there, she needed to know who they were.

Bridgette knew there could be many reasons Burns hadn't called her back. But she had a nagging feeling something was wrong as she knocked a second time. Nothing. She tried peering through a window but couldn't see anything through the heavy brocade curtains. She dialed Burns' number again with her ear hard up against the window listening for the sound of a phone ringing. Nothing, just eerie silence.

Bridgette scanned the street. It was quiet, almost too quiet. Perhaps he was in the garden and hadn't heard her, she thought, as she walked round to the back of the house.

Nothing looked out of place in the small paved area at the back of Burns' house. She peered through the glazed sliding door, but more drawn curtains made it impossible to see anything inside.

She rapped hard on the glass. "Ron, are you in there? It's Detective Cash. I need to talk to you urgently."

She waited a few seconds, but the house remained quiet. She tried the glass sliding door… it slid open. The curtain blew slightly on a breeze that swirled in the courtyard behind her.

Technically, it was trespass if she didn't have a search warrant. But if she thought someone might be injured, in danger, or worse, it wouldn't be a problem. Bridgette took a deep breath, withdrew her Glock, pushed the curtain out of the way and stepped inside.

A small kitchen area with modern stainless-steel appliances greeted her. It was separated from the rest of the living space by an island bench with a breakfast bar. Although the kitchen was clean and tidy with no dishes in the sink or dirty cups on the breakfast bar, three timber stools had been overturned. Cupboards and drawers had been opened and the contents thrown around the living and dining room. On the large mirror facing the kitchen a message had been left in red Sharpie. YOU'RE NEXT! Beside the message, the author had drawn a circle and inside it were two crosses. Beneath the crosses was a crude slash. She'd seen similar artwork before and knew what is signified.

Bridgette tightened her grip on the Glock, took a shaky breath and headed into the hallway where two doors on either side beckoned and the silence was only broken by her tentative footsteps.

The first door on the left led into a bathroom — clean, tidy — and empty. A sliding door connected the bathroom to a master bedroom, but that wasn't what caught her attention. Bridgette's heart galloped at the sight of another dead-eye face on the bathroom mirror.

She backed out and opened the door on the opposite side of the hallway; the laundry, undisturbed. She closed the door then moved to the next one. Her heart was still pounding as she snatched open the door. An office; the chair tipped over and drawers pulled out but nothing else. Bridgette stood stock still in the hallway, listening. But only silence filled the air. The last door had to lead to the master bedroom. As she touched the handle her heart raced again. The door was partially ajar but not open enough that she could see in. With her two hands firmly wrapped around her Glock, she gently pushed the door open with her foot. She lowered the gun and took a steadying breath. The room was empty; no Burns, no body, nothing except another warning: SOON with the 'Os' filled with crosses and slashes.

She looked past the bed that was perfectly made, and her heart sank when she looked at the mirror above Burns' dressing table. She let out a long breath as she read the words.

Bridgette pulled her phone from her pocket and called Delray.

"Hey Bridgette, what's up?"

"I'm at Ron Burns' place."

"And?"

"The rear door wasn't locked, so I went inside."

Bridgette described the scene inside the house.

Delray said, "Any signs of a struggle?"

"No. Not really. But it looks staged, like someone was there just to leave a message."

"It's got to be Hellyer."

"I agree. Although I am surprised he's started so soon."

"We can't touch him, Bridgette. I have express instructions from Cunningham that we can't go near him unless we have solid evidence. What's next?"

"I'm going to call the local police and then knock on some doors. Maybe the neighbors saw something?"

"Let's hope."

Bridgette thought about Ron Burns and what she'd just seen inside. She knew the best-case scenario was that he'd gone into hiding.

"Let's hope we can find him before it's too late."

Tuesday 6:11 PM

Bridgette pushed open the heavy metal and glass door that led into the Grapevine Bar & Grill. To her left was a thirty-foot timber bar with matching stools. Behind the bar, two barmen stood in front of a mirrored wall that appeared to double the number of bottles on each shelf. There were only seven patrons in the bar — all men, and none of them were Frost.

She checked the dining area where about forty tables were set up. Half of them were occupied. Bridgette spotted Frost at a small table for two on the far wall. His head was bent over the menu and he didn't hear her approach.

"Hi, Levi."

Frost looked up. "Hey. Sorry, didn't see you come in."

"No problem, it's me who should be sorry. You said six and I'm late."

Frost looked at his watch and shrugged. "Only a few minutes. Have a seat."

Frost said, "I hope you don't mind, but I need more than a drink. I haven't eaten all day and I'm starved."

Bridgette suddenly realized, she too, was hungry. "Suits me, I've only had one protein bar all day, so this is good." She studied Frost for a moment. "How are you?"

Frost shrugged. "I don't like the waiting. I'd rather know if I have a job or not, but that's not the way it works."

"The longer it takes, the better your chances are of being exonerated."

Frost answered, "I guess," and then returned his gaze to the menu. "How goes the case? I hear Hellyer is a free man now."

Bridgette knew she shouldn't be discussing the case with an officer who was suspended, but she also wanted to bounce a couple of ideas off him. She told him everything about her visit to Ron Burns' house.

Frost was dumbfounded. "Hellyer?"

"I'm almost certain of it. He would have only needed five minutes to do what he did."

Frost shook his head. "Seriously? He's just been released from prison."

"He's had ten years to think about it. I guess he doesn't want to wait a second longer than he has to."

"He has to be stopped."

Bridgette grimaced. "We're not allowed go anywhere near him. He's a protected species unless we have concrete evidence of his involvement in a felony. We're hoping we'll turn up his DNA at Burns' house, but I think that's a long shot."

"So where's Burns?"

A waiter approached them before Bridgette could answer. She ordered a salmon salad and a Club soda while Frost ordered ribs and a light beer. After the waiter left, Bridgette answered, "Nobody knows."

"He could be dead already? Maybe Hellyer…"

Bridgette shook her head. "I think he's come home, found the messages and gone into hiding again, back to his secret cabin, which I think is exactly what Hellyer wants."

"Why?"

"It's the way I found his house. The messages were drawn on mirrors in the living room, bathroom and bedroom. They could be easily rubbed off. The overturned chairs were not damaged, and the cupboards and drawers hadn't been rifled through. I got the feeling Hellyer did enough to make Burns panic and then planned to come back and tidy up after he'd run."

"To hide the fact that he'd been there."

Bridgette nodded. "I think whatever he has in store for Burns, it's too risky to pull off in a retirement village where so many people are home most of the time."

"If he's spooked Burns into running, we may not have much time."

"You remember last time we thought he was missing?"

"Sure. We triangulated the signal from his phone. You thought he was somewhere out past Tangmere Falls near the state forest, but he wouldn't tell you where."

"Correct. All I got out of him was that he'd rented a cabin for three months. I think that's where he plans on dying."

"You think that's where he is now?"

"It's as good a place as any if you don't think anyone else knows your whereabouts."

"So what are you suggesting?"

Bridgette pulled her phone from her pocket and opened Google maps. She pinched the screen to zoom in and said, "This is Tangmere Falls. From what I've been able to gather there are about sixty cabins in the area for rent, but they're very spread out."

Frost studied the map for a moment. "It looks like we've got about thirty square miles to cover."

Bridgette liked Frost's use of the word 'we.' "There are two main roads leading up there. It's fairly dense forest area and I can't possibly get to every cabin in one day."

Frost raised an eyebrow. "You want me to help?"

Bridgette nodded. "Alex Hellyer found Paul Ringwood with a smart phone while he was locked up in a prison hospital. I can't see Burns being safe out there for very long. I was hoping you might help me?"

"But I'm suspended."

"You wouldn't be doing any police work. You don't need a gun or a badge to help look for someone who's missing."

Frost didn't look convinced.

Bridgette added, "You can go in your own car and enjoy the sites and the drive. If you check all the cabins off Franklin Road, I'll do the same on Heeney Road."

"And what if I find him?"

"You call me and let me take it from there."

Frost scrunched up his nose; his thinking pose. "The doctor told me to go for some walks or a drive in the country to clear my head, so … I guess I'm just following her orders."

Bridgette grinned. "Thank you. I wouldn't be asking except I'm really concerned for Ron. I've asked the chief, and he's put out a general alert to all police to be on the lookout, but he's not prepared to instigate a search."

"I guess it doesn't help that Burns is facing corruption charges."

"No."

"When do we start?"

"It's over an hour's drive out there. I want to be knocking on doors by eight tomorrow. We'll leave at six-thirty."

Wednesday 8:14 AM

Bridgette pulled off the road and onto a stretch of gravel just before a T-junction. A faded wooden signpost marked Franklin Road pointed to an unsurfaced road on her right. She sat enjoying the morning sun as it streamed through the forest while she watched the road behind her in her review mirror. A minute later, Frost's green Ford came into view. They had traveled from Vancouver in convoy, but this was where they would separate. Bridgette waited until Frost pulled up on the gravel behind her before she got out of her car. He wound down his window as she approached and said, "So this is it?"

"Yeah," she said, opening up a map on her phone.

Frost pointed to Franklin Road. "I didn't realize they were all going to be gravel roads. Your car will get dirty."

Bridgette looked at her car. It was a fully restored midnight-blue 1966 Mustang Fastback, and she liked to drive it every chance she could. Frost got out of his car and she shrugged. "It will get a little dirty, but I've got a nice car wash close to home."

Frost pulled up the same map on his cell phone. They swiped and enlarged their screens so they could both see all the cabins available for lease.

Bridgette pointed. "Almost all of them are either on Franklin or Heeney roads."

Frost studied his screen for a moment. "Both roads circle back on each other."

"That's right. They both trail up into the mountain before looping back again. This is the only road in or out."

Frost raised his eyebrows. "There are a lot of cabins up there."

"Thirty-eight on Franklin and the rest on Heeney."

"And I'm taking Heeney Road?"

"Yes, if that's okay with you?"

"You've got a lot more to cover than I have."

Bridgette pointed to Heeney Road on the map. "Heeney Road is almost twice as long as Franklin. You've got a circuit of over ten miles to cover. I figure it will take us about the same amount of time to cover each road."

"And Burns drives a late-model Mazda, right?"

"Yes, a white Mazda 3. Of course, there's a possibility he's driving a different vehicle, so we'll need to physically check every property."

Frost nodded. "I can't imagine signal reception being great in some of these higher areas."

"I agree. I think we should check in at least every hour by text message and only call if we have coverage."

"Okay, got it." Frost paused and frowned. "And what happens if I find him? Do you want me to approach him or contact you?"

"Probably best to wait for me if you can. I've built a relationship with him. I think he trusts me now. The whole idea is to convince him to come back to Vancouver where we can protect him."

Bridgette looked up at the dense forest that covered the mountain. "Because we sure can't protect him up here."

After only six-hundred yards Bridgette came to the first cabin on her list. Nestled on the right about ninety yards back from the road and surrounded by fir trees, the cabin could only be accessed by a narrow gravel track with deep ruts from soil erosion. She wasn't about to risk leaving the Mustang's undercarriage in a pothole and parked her car by the roadside.

The walk up the drive took her less than a minute. She stopped and admired the log cabin in front of her. The two-storey building included a carport underneath. While there was easily enough room for three cars, Bridgette was disappointed to find it empty.

It wasn't what she had expected this far from the city. It looked more like a luxury snow chalet than a cabin in the woods. She knew at least one resident was home when she heard a dog barking out back.

There were two windows on the ground floor, all with their curtains drawn, but no door. After climbing the stairs, Bridgette reached a large landing which could easily have served as an outdoor sitting area with views of the picturesque valley below had it not been devoid of furniture. Knowing she had a lot more houses to check, she ignored the view and knocked twice on the heavy pine front door. The sound sent the dog's barking into overdrive, but nobody seemed to be home. She knocked again and then waited a moment before descending the stairs. She walked through the carport to a rear timber door which she assumed lead to the property's backyard.

There she heard the dog scratching at the door. Bridgette decided it wasn't wise to go any further but glanced around the carport for any other clue as to who might own or rent the residence. The area was empty except for a small oil drum and a coiled hosepipe.

She noticed the gravel driveway didn't make it all the way into the carport, which had been finished with light brown soil that had been compacted to a hard surface. She could just make out some tire prints that looked recent. They were almost a foot wide. Bridgette wasn't much of an expert on car tires but knew enough to know the car that left those tracks was much bigger than a Mazda 3.

With nothing more to see she set off back to her car making a mental note that the house might be worth checking again later if she had time. She started the Mustang and took another look at her Google map. The next cabin was two miles ahead, but this time on the left side of the road. With the houses set back from the road amongst the trees, they were easy to miss. She put her car into gear and moved off.

The next cabin was clearly visible about sixty feet from the road. Bridgette parked in front of the single-story dwelling. The small log cabin had been built in keeping with the traditions of the area. There was a Toyota Corolla parked in the driveway and Bridgette hoped she would have better luck this time finding someone home. A crazy-paved stone footpath led to the front door which was opened by a small woman in her early sixties. The woman had a messy shock of gray hair and a pleasant face. She smiled at her visitor and said, "Good morning. Can I help you?"

Bridgette pulled out her badge and introduced herself. The woman's face fell when she focused on the badge causing Bridgette to add quickly, "This is just routine, ma'am. I'm here looking for a retired police officer who we believe can help us with a current case. We believe he's staying up here somewhere, but the cell phone coverage out here isn't great and I'm having trouble contacting him."

The woman's smile was back again. "Yes, I know what you mean. The reception is quite patchy. My husband is out fishing at present and I always worry in case he has a fall when he's on his own because I know his phone may not work."

Bridgette nodded politely. "Are you from around here?"

The woman shook her head. "No, we come up twice a year. My husband is retired now, and this is a great place to get away from it all. Some of his favorite fishing spots are close by."

"The man we're looking for goes by the name of Ron Burns. He is in his mid-sixties and drives a white Mazda 3."

She gave the woman a physical description of Ron Burns and then added, "Have you seen anyone around here that might be him?"

The woman thought for a moment. "We've only been here two days this time. I haven't seen any cars like the one you describe, and we've hardly said hello to a soul, so I don't think I can help you."

Bridgette smiled and passed across her business card. "That's okay, ma'am. Here's my card. If you see a vehicle you think might be Ron's or anyone who looks like him, please call me as soon as you can."

The woman took the card and promised she would. "I hope you find him soon."

Bridgette thanked the woman for her time and then returned to her car. She looked at her map again. The next cabin was a further half mile up the road. She murmured, *This is going to be a long day*, as she started the Mustang.

Bridgette's heart raced as she pulled up in front of log cabin number thirty-three on her list. The cabin looked no different to most others she had visited that morning. It was single storey, compact and set back from the road among the trees. What made this cabin different was the car parked out front. A white Mazda 3. She pressed speed dial on her cell to call Frost. When her call wasn't answered she left a voicemail. "Hi, Levi, it's me. I'm outside house number thirty-three on the list and I think I've found Ron Burns' Mazda parked in the driveway. Call me as soon as you can."

After disconnecting, she sent a text to him as well urging him to call her as soon possible, then she studied the house. The front curtains were drawn. It was impossible to tell if anyone was home. She figured given the car was in the driveway and Ron Burns had late-stage lung cancer, he wasn't likely to be venturing far from home on foot.

Convinced she was right she strode optimistically up the short path to the front door. The giant fir trees that framed the back of the house were already hiding the early afternoon sun, leaving the house in shadow. After stepping onto the cabin's front porch, she stood for a moment listening for any signs of life coming from inside. She hoped to hear music, or television, or someone moving around, but everything remained quiet.

She knocked on the front door three times. When no-one came, she knocked again, and this time called out, "Ron, are you home? It's Detective Cash."

The house remained silent. Bridgette knocked on the door once more but got no response. She tried peering in through a window next to the front door but couldn't see much as the curtains were almost fully drawn. After her eyes adjusted to the darkness inside, she could see a small section of the sitting-room and the kitchen beyond, but not much more.

As she studied the scene inside the cabin, she thought she saw something move on the floor. She frowned. Why wasn't there a light on, it seemed very dark even though there was daylight coming through the kitchen window. Rapping on the window, she called out again, "Ron, can you hear me? Are you all right?"

When she didn't get an answer, Bridgette walked around the side of the house, zipping up her jacket as an icy breeze blew through the fir trees growing less than fifty feet from the back of the cabin. Bridgette felt the hairs on the back of her neck rise. She cocked her head, listened, but heard nothing but the tree branches rustling in the wind. It was too quiet. Her heart banged in her chest as she withdrew her Glock.

Cautiously, she stepped up onto the rear porch then approached the back door. The bottom half of the door was solid wood, but the top half held a glass pane. She peered inside but the house was in darkness. She rapped on the glass with her Glock and called out, "Ron, are you in there?"

She tried the handle. The door opened without a sound and Bridgette slipped into the kitchen. No dirty dishes, no messy bench tops. Almost as if no one was living there. An open doorway led into the living room. She was about to head in that direction when a scuffling sound pulled her up short. "Ron, is that you? Are you OK?"

"Aaagh!"

Bridgette gripped her gun and moved to the doorway. She was startled by a light that came on inside the living room and a voice which said, "Drop the gun, Detective."

Bridgette gasped as she stared into the fully lit sitting room.

She focused on the two figures standing just inside the front door, both of whom she recognized instantly. A very thin and sickly-looking Ron Burns was shaking uncontrollably. The terror in his eyes and the anguish on his face were not lost on her, but she couldn't take her eyes off the man who stood behind him. Alex Hellyer's left arm was wrapped around Burns' chest, and a scalpel was pressed against Burns' jugular.

Wednesday 1:33 PM

Unsure what to do next, Bridgette stood in the doorway and brought her Glock up into the firing position as she held Hellyer's stare. She wondered if Frost had received her message, but the tiny trickle of blood she now saw dripping down Burns' neck told her it would all be over long before he arrived.

She held her Glock steady and shifted her position slightly to get a better shot at Hellyer. But he shifted, too. With his left arm wrapped tightly around Burn's chest and his right hand continuing to press the scalpel against his neck, she could only see a small portion of her adversary's face. Subtly, she shifted her aim until she had Hellyer's right eye lined up in her gun sights. She cursed silently as she did the calculations in her head. With less than three inches of Hellyer's head mass to work with, she knew she could easily hit Burns instead.

She stared back at Hellyer, realizing her weapon was almost useless and he was in control. In an attempt to buy time, she said, "I underestimated you."

What she could see of Hellyer's face turned into a sneer. "How so?"

Bridgette stole a glance at Burns who'd turned ashen. She locked eyes with Hellyer again. "I knew you'd find him. I just thought it would take longer."

"I've waited ten years for this. Once I knew Ringwood was dead, I got Avery to fit a tracking device to his car. I've known every move he's made ever since."

Bridgette gave a slight nod of acknowledgment. A tracking device made perfect sense. "You realize you won't get away with this…"

Hellyer laughed. He seemed to be growing bolder by the second as he retorted, "I wouldn't be so sure about that, Detective. Paul Ringwood disappeared for ten years and he wasn't overly bright."

"But he didn't have the full force of the law after him."

"I rotted in that prison for ten years and thought about little else other than revenge … nobody is taking this away from me."

Bridgette barely heard the last part of Hellyer's response as she saw Burns' eyes roll back in his head. She sensed this could be her opportunity if Burns passed out.

Through gritted teeth, Hellyer said, "Don't collapse on me now, old man. I'm not done with you yet."

The standoff continued for a more few seconds until Burns' eyes fluttered open again. Nobody spoke. Bridgette felt it was like a prize fight with the combatants glaring at each other while they looked for an opening. She was surprised by Hellyer's wiry strength despite his slight build.

It was Hellyer who broke the silence. "I don't have time for any more games, Detective. Drop the gun now — I won't ask you again."

It had been drilled into Bridgette throughout her police

training that a police officer should never relinquish their weapon. Rather than defying Hellyer outright she tried to stall for time. "How do I know you don't have a gun hidden somewhere?"

A cruel sneer spread across Hellyer's face. "You don't."

Bridgette made fleeting eye contact with Burns again. He seemed to have regained consciousness and despite his terror, he shook his head slightly as if to say, 'Don't give up your gun.'

"Last chance," said Hellyer.

Bridgette kept her eyes on Burns and shook her head as she tightened the grip on her Glock.

Suddenly, Hellyer twisted Burns' body and grabbed at his left arm. She gaped in horror as Hellyer brought the scalpel down in a single slicing action across Burns' wrist just above his palm. Burns' whimper as blood spurted from his radial artery was drowned out by Hellyer who screamed into his ear, "Shut up, old man. I'm just getting started!"

After regaining his grip on Burns, Hellyer looked up at Bridgette and said defiantly, "I warned you. Now drop it!"

Bridgette felt her heart race. She faked moving her Glock from left to right, hoping to get Hellyer to move enough to give her a clean shot, but Hellyer wasn't buying it and remained still.

She glanced down at the growing pool of blood on the floor at Burns' feet and then at his chinos, which were quickly turning red. She knew enough about human anatomy to know Burns would bleed out in less than ten minutes without treatment.

Shifting her Glock less than an inch to her left, Bridgette pulled the trigger. The enormous boom of the weapon almost completely drowned out the sound of an etched glass mirror shattering on the wall next to the front door.

For a moment Hellyer look stunned as glass shards peppered his face. Even though the bullet had missed him by at least a foot, he clearly hadn't expected her to fire.

Bridgette stole another look at Burns. His eyes rolled back into his head a second time and he went completely limp. Now faced with holding Burns' full body weight, Hellyer crouched even lower and used his unconscious victim as a shield as he inched backward towards the front door. With her feet separated and her body weight leaning slightly forward, she followed Hellyer's progress looking for a clean shot. But it never came. Even though the distance between them was less than twenty feet, she wasn't prepared to risk killing Burns to stop Hellyer. She watched helplessly as Hellyer kept Burns propped up in front of him while he reached back and opened the front door. She debated rushing forward, but without backup and not knowing if Hellyer had a gun or not, she realized it could be suicide.

With growing frustration, she watched as Hellyer shuffled out through the open doorway. Keeping Burns' body in front of him, Hellyer said, "I promise you there will be another day for both of you."

The words were lost on Bridgette as Hellyer wielded the scalpel a second time. She screamed "No!" as Hellyer slashed Burns' forearm. The retired detective barely flinched. Shocked by what she was witnessing, Bridgette stood motionless as Hellyer dropped the scalpel. The next few seconds were a blur as her nemesis produced a gun.

Bridgette recoiled as Hellyer brought the gun up and fired. She heard the gunshot ringing in her ears as the bullet lodged in the wooden door frame only inches to her right. She heard a muffled thud and the front door slam as she fell backward and landed heavily on the kitchen floor. Everything went quiet again except for the ringing in her ears.

Bridgette half expected Hellyer to appear in the doorway to take a second shot at her, but the sound of running footsteps outside told her he was gone. She crept back to the doorway and peered into the living room and saw Burns slumped face-down on the floor. Instinct took over as she pulled two dishtowels off a rack and rushed to Burns' side. Ignoring the pool of blood, she knelt down and turned Burns over to check his pulse. Relieved to feel a faint but steady pulse, she said, "Stay with me, Ron," as she frantically tried to stem the blood.

Wednesday 6:27 PM

Bridgette looked up from her magazine when she heard a murmur from Ron Burns. His eyelids fluttered for a moment before they opened. Burns blinked several times as he stared up at the ceiling before peering around the room. When his eyes locked on Bridgette, he stared at her for a moment before saying, "Where am I?"

"You're in Stanwyck Base hospital, but everything's okay, Ron."

Burns twisted his head to look around the room. "What happened?"

"You're safe, just relax for now."

Burns let his head rest back on the pillow, "It's all coming back to me now."

"Try not to think about it. You've been through a lot."

Burns closed his eyes for a moment. "I remember now. He…" Burns opened his eyes again. "Did you catch him?"

"We can talk about that later, Ron. Right now, you need to get some rest."

Burns seemed fully awake and even in his weakened

condition, the last thing he seemed interested in was rest. He persisted "Did he get away?"

Bridgette nodded. "I'm not sure how much you remember Ron, but he cut your wrist — you were going to bleed out. I…"

"But I have cancer, Bridgette. I only have a couple of months to live at best. You should have left me and gone after him."

"I wasn't going to let him take another victim, Ron. His day will come, you can be sure of that."

Burns let out a long breath. "Sorry if that came out ungrateful. Thank you for saving me."

"I understand how you feel, but I know I made the right call."

"How did I get here?"

"You don't remember?"

Burns shook his head. "My last memory is of him slashing my wrist and shoving me onto the floor. What happened then?"

Bridgette didn't think now was the time for Burns to be reliving the ordeal in detail. "I called an ambulance then bandaged your arm as best I could. But they were at least twenty minutes away. Fortunately my partner arrived just as I got you stable, so we got you in my car to drive you here ourselves. You don't remember any of that?"

Burns shook his head. "So then what happened?"

Bridgette recalled the ordeal of driving back from Tangmere Falls to Stanwyck. At times she'd reached speeds over eighty miles an hour. She figured it was probably just as well the former detective had no memory of the trip or his arrival at the hospital where he was met by a team of emergency doctors and nurses. After a blood transfusion and surgery to repair his severed artery, the chief surgeon had praised Bridgette for her quick thinking. He conceded if Burns' arrival had been just a few minutes later, he probably wouldn't have survived.

Now wasn't the time to be conveying that much information, so she settled for a simple answer. "When we got you to the hospital, they gave you a blood transfusion and stabilized you. The doctor has been in several times since your surgery to check on you and she's happy with your progress. I think with a couple of days of monitoring you'll be well enough to be released."

"I'm not sure where I'll go," said Burns. "I know he'll come after me again."

"You don't need to worry about that, Ron. We have a police guard posted outside your room around the clock. And, we're organizing a safe place for you after you get out until they capture Hellyer."

Bridgette could see the relief on Burns' face. "I can't get him out of my mind. If I close my eyes he's there staring at me."

Bridgette would have preferred Burns try to rest. But it was clear he needed to talk. She said, "Do you want to talk about what happened, Ron? Maybe it will help."

"I went to see my doctor for a checkup. He said the cancer had spread and I don't have much time. I asked him how long, but he wouldn't give me a number. Afterwards, I drove home and when I got inside, I saw…"

Bridgette interrupted. "I went to your house and saw what he'd done. That's when I suspected you'd gone into hiding."

"I panicked. I packed a few things and went up there straight away. I thought I'd be safe."

"He had a tracking device fitted to your car. He knew

every move you were making. He may have even followed you out there."

Burns shook his head. "I get very tired these days and need a lot of sleep. I was having a nap in the chair in the sitting room, and when I woke up he was there. I'm a light sleeper but I didn't hear a thing. Normally I'd at least hear a car pull up."

"There was no car parked out front. But as you know, criminals rarely park out front of where they intend to commit a crime."

"He must have let himself in through the back door which I forgot to lock. He was just standing there staring at me, holding that knife at his side. I tried to get up, but he pushed me down."

Burns was quiet for a moment. Bridgette wondered if it had been a good idea to encourage him to talk about his ordeal, until he added, "I said to him, just get it over with, but he just laughed."

"And then what happened?"

Burns turned his head towards Bridgette. "He told me I had to pay for his ten years of suffering — and that it would take a while — I've never felt so scared in all my life. And then he started rambling on about all the injustices he'd suffered, right back to his father. I just sat there praying for a miracle and then we heard a car pull up outside … I'm guessing that was you?"

Bridgette nodded.

"He pulled me out of the chair and held the scalpel against my neck and told me to be quiet or he'd cut me. When you knocked on the front door, he marched me out of view from the front window. And then you came around back…"

Burns held a hand to his chest and breathed deeply.

Bridgette didn't want to push him for too much information knowing any more stress could hinder his recovery. "I think that's enough for now, Ron. You need to get some rest."

Burns didn't see it that way. "How did you find me? How did you know where to look?"

Bridgette explained how they had triangulated his cell phone location to the three towers beyond Tangmere Falls when they'd thought he'd gone missing the first time. "And when you told me you'd hired a cabin, I thought it was the logical place to start looking."

Burns frowned. "But I never gave anyone my address. Not even my daughter knows the location."

"We got lucky finding you when we did. Speaking of your daughter, she's on her way. She was interstate at a conference. We had trouble tracking her down."

"She must be beside herself."

They were quiet for a moment before Burns asked, "Do you have any idea where he is now?"

Bridgette shook her head. "Every law enforcement agency in the country has been notified and is on the lookout for him. But right now, it appears he's gone to ground."

"I've never been so frightened in my life. That look in his eyes ... it will haunt me forever."

"Does he have any other enemies that you know of? It seems he's hellbent on revenge at any cost."

"No one that I know of. It may be worthwhile re-interviewing his mother. She won't give anything away, but you may learn something."

"I was thinking along the same lines. We've got a team working on this and we're going back over all the information we have on file to see if there's anyone else."

Burns sniffed and wiped his eyes. "This isn't how I

wanted it all to end. I had a hard time coming to terms with the fact I'm dying from cancer … but the thought of being cut up into little pieces by him terrified me."

Bridgette touched his heavily bandaged arm. "There's no need to worry Ron. I promise you we'll keep you safe."

"How are you going to find him?"

"I'm not sure yet, but I'm developing a plan."

Thursday 7:04 AM

Bridgette was glad her boss had requested an early morning meeting because it gave her a chance to pitch him her plan. After she had settled into her chair, Delray asked, "How's Burns?"

"He's stable and the doctors are happy with his progress. But, because of the cancer, they don't think he'll make a full recovery."

Delray grimaced. "How much longer has he got?"

"They aren't giving him a specific timeline, but I think it's weeks rather than months."

Delray nodded. "Well, I guess that's better than bleeding to death at the hands of a psychopath. That was impressive work you did up there yesterday, Bridgette. I've given the Commissioner a briefing and he wants to thank you personally."

Bridgette was taken aback. "I was only doing my job."

"Maybe so, but Burns wouldn't be alive today if it wasn't for you."

"Hellyer did get away though."

"You made the right call and Hellyer's days of freedom are numbered. With every law enforcement agency on the lookout for him, he'll slip up at some point." Delray shook his head. "I gotta say, it makes you wonder."

"Wonder what?"

"Hellyer. He could have had it all. He was a free man and everything we had against him for Ringwood's murder was circumstantial. Unless new evidence came to light, there's no way we could have convicted him."

"I agree."

Delray took his glasses off. "So why go after Burns? He was going to die anyway. If he waited three months, both the men who put him in jail would be dead. I just don't get it."

As part of her criminology degree, Bridgette had taken several psychology subjects. She knew Hellyer fit the category of psychopath and was suffering from one or more disorders, but didn't think Delray was interested in any clinical analysis. "We know he's always had a problem with people that cross him, even as far back as high school. After seeing him up close yesterday, revenge is a single-minded obsession for him. He needs to be the one meting out the punishment."

"Well, I'm glad he didn't kill Burns, but not too unhappy that it happened. Once we catch him, it will be far easier to put him back behind bars where he belongs."

They were quiet for a moment before Bridgette said, "When I was in the cabin, he said two things to me while he had a scalpel at Burns' neck."

"What?"

"The first was that he plans to disappear, just like Ringwood did. Only, he thinks he's a lot smarter than Ringwood and I get the impression he plans to disappear forever."

"Okay, we'll see how that plays out. It's very hard to disappear forever, unless you're dead."

"I agree."

"What's the second thing?"

"He promised me there would be another day for both of us."

Delray frowned. "Both of us?"

Bridgette nodded. "I think I'm on his radar too." Not wanting to dwell on it, she added, "Any progress on finding him yet?"

"Not yet, but as soon as I hear anything you'll be the first to know."

"Thanks. Hopefully it's just an idle threat."

"We can't be too careful. He…"

Delray paused mid-sentence as his mobile phone buzzed on his desk. Reaching down, he mumbled, "Let me check this …" Without looking up he added, "The commissioner's asked to see me and Cunningham at nine."

"The Hellyer case?"

Delray nodded. "Now that Hellyer's on the run and we're confident he and Avery killed Ringwood, Cunningham wants to disband the task force. I don't think the commissioner sees it quite that way. At least not yet."

"There are still a lot of loose ends to tie up."

"For starters, we still need to find out how involved Francine Turello, Shriver and his mother are in all of this."

"It sounds like you're in for an interesting meeting."

Delray frowned. "They're always interesting when Cunningham's involved. Thankfully, the commissioner's more concerned with solving crime than he is with the budget."

Delray held Bridgette's gaze. "Before we move on, I want to talk about Levi Frost for a moment."

After finding Burns, word had got out quickly that Frost had been part of the search. She figured a conversation about his involvement would come up eventually, but she didn't think it would be quite so soon.

"Okay."

Delray lent his elbows on his desk and steepled his hands. "Technically, he shouldn't have been involved yesterday. It was police business and he is suspended."

Bridgette found it hard to meet Delray's gaze as she responded, "And I accept responsibility for that, Chief. I should have told you."

"I don't expect any blowback from higher up now that Burns has been found alive."

"I'm sorry I overstepped the line."

"Next time give me a heads up. God knows I crossed the line often enough in my early career to get things done, so I will rarely say no." Delray held her gaze for long enough to make her uncomfortable before he added, "I can't cover for you if I don't know."

Bridgette nodded and repeated her apology.

"No harm no foul, but I'm glad we've talked. If I get asked by Cunningham, and I'm sure I will, I can say we've discussed it and you've apologized and that will be the end of it."

It was rare for her to receive a reprimand from Delray, but Bridgette understood why. She appreciated him always having her back and this was no different. She wasn't sure whether now was an appropriate time to ask about Levi Frost's future, but she couldn't help herself. "Speaking of Levi, has there been any progress with his review?"

"There's a meeting scheduled for tomorrow. I've got Levi coming in later today to brief him and get him ready.

We've got the Police Support unit working with him and I'm hopeful he'll be exonerated."

"Will yesterday count against him?"

"I doubt it. We got a good outcome, and he wasn't pretending to be on duty or anything, so I'm hoping it won't be a factor."

"What are his chances of being cleared?"

Delray grimaced. "Hard to say. If he's not forced out, there's a good chance he'll be assessed as mentally traumatized and no longer be suitable for fieldwork."

"I don't think he'd survive a desk job."

"Me neither, so let's hope it doesn't come to that."

"If it helps, I'm more than prepared to speak on his behalf."

"I appreciate that, Bridgette, and I'm sure he will as well. Let's see how the meeting plays out, then I'll let you know. Now, getting back to Burns. Do you know how long he's likely to be in hospital?"

"I talked to the doctor just before I left last night. They want to keep him in hospital for another forty-eight hours at least and they're adamant he can't be released unless he has someone to care for him when he comes out."

"Well, that won't be a problem. I've got all the paperwork done and as soon as he's ready to go, we'll put him in a safe house with around-the-clock police presence and nursing care."

"So, what's next for the investigation?"

"I'll know more after my meeting with the commissioner and Cunningham about how many detectives stay on the task force, but you're certainly not going to be reassigned. I think I'd like you to focus on Hellyer's mother. If anyone knows where he is, it will be her."

"I plan to go and see her today."

"You realize we have a squad car parked out front of her house, just in case her son shows up?"

Bridgette nodded. "As I got close to Burns' cabin yesterday, I saw a light blue Subaru parked off the road. I didn't think anything of it at the time."

Delray frowned. "So what of it?"

"It's the same make, model and color as Hellyer's mother's car. It gives me a reason to interview her again."

"We need to go after her hard. I'm free after ten. Let's do it then."

"Okay. That will give me time to plan out the questions."

"If we can get her to break, we may even find out where he's hiding."

"Perhaps."

Delray raised an eyebrow. "You're not convinced?"

"I've been giving it a lot of thought. Unless the mother is up to her neck in this, she probably has no idea where he is. I think we need a different approach entirely to find him."

"What do you have in mind?"

Bridgette spent the next ten minutes outlining her plan. Delray didn't interrupt once, which was unusual for him. At the end, he sat in silence for a moment, chewing on one arm of his glasses.

Eventually he put them down on the table. "I like it. So much so I want you to come to my meeting with the commissioner and Cunningham. I think it just might work and I want you to pitch it to them as they're the ones who'll need to sign off on it."

Thursday 10:57 AM

Bridgette pulled up behind the squad car that was parked out front of Lauren Hellyer's house. She cast an eye toward the sky as they got out of the car. The morning was overcast and repeated attempts by the sun to warm the town of Stanwyck had been thwarted by thick grey clouds that refused to dissipate.

Bridgette waited by the front gate while Delray spoke to the two uniformed officers who were sitting in the squad car. She could hear their conversation and listened intently to the exchange. Nobody had seen Alex Hellyer since he left prison. She had called Michael Grayson, Hellyer's lawyer, the previous evening after she'd left the hospital and had briefed him about the attack on Burns' life, and that his client was now wanted for attempted murder. Grayson had been vague in his response and only after Bridgette persisted did he begrudgingly promise to notify the police if his client contacted him.

She doubted Hellyer would call Grayson or anyone else

for that matter. He was now out and operating as a lone wolf and that wouldn't change until he was stopped.

She and Delray walked up the footpath. "So nobody's seen him?"

Delray shook his head. "There's been a car here since about seven o'clock last night. No sign of either him or his mother's car."

As they stepped up onto the front porch, Delray said, "Let's hope she doesn't clam up and insist on a lawyer."

They waited for close to a minute after knocking before the door was finally opened. Lauren Hellyer looked haggard. Her red eyes and blotchy complexion suggested she had been crying and hadn't had much sleep.

She glared at them both and demanded, "What do you want?"

"We would like to talk to you for a moment, Mrs. Hellyer."

The woman stood in the half-open doorway and made no move to let them in. "I have nothing to say to you. If you want to interview me you'll need to contact my lawyer."

Delray weighed in, "Where's your car, Mrs. Hellyer?"

"What do you mean?"

"It's a simple question," said Bridgette.

Hellyer look from Bridgette to Delray. "It's not here."

Bridgette locked eyes on Hellyer. "Did you lend it to your son?"

"I'm not sure I should answer that."

"It's a simple question, Mrs. Hellyer. Either you did or didn't lend him your car."

"Alex borrowed it yesterday."

"So where is he now?"

Hellyer hissed, "I don't know, and even if I did, there is not a chance in hell I'd be telling you."

Delray said, "You're aware your son tried to murder a retired police officer, yesterday, Mrs. Hellyer?"

Hellyer shook her head. "Alex isn't capable of doing such a thing."

"I was there in the cabin," Bridgette snapped, "I saw your son use Ron Burns as a shield before slashing his wrist. If we hadn't got him to hospital when we did he would be dead now."

"I haven't seen him, or spoken to him. So I can't help you."

Bridgette tried a different tack. "It's only a matter of time before we find him Mrs. Hellyer. The best thing you can do for him is cooperate with us. If he kills anyone else it will only make things worse."

"Alex hasn't killed anybody."

"What about your husband? Surely you don't believe the fire was an accident?"

Hellyer bellowed, "This has nothing to do with my husband! That was an eternity ago, and I'm not discussing it."

"Do you regret paying all that money to Francine Turello, Mrs. Hellyer? Your son wasn't anywhere near as sick as he made out, but you knew that, didn't you?"

Hellyer remained silent.

Bridgette continued, "All that money. It wasn't to keep him safe was it?"

"My son should never have been in prison in the first place."

"It must be disappointing."

"What?"

"You spend all that money, and this is the way he repays you. Barely out of jail a day and you're abandoned."

"My relationship with my son is none of your business."

Hellyer went to close the door. "If you want to talk to me further, you're going to need to contact my…"

Bridgette put her foot in the door. "If he calls, you are to notify us immediately."

Hellyer shouted, "I'll do no such thing!"

Bridgette pushed the door open and leaned in. "We've almost got enough to charge you with bribery and perjury. Don't add aiding and abetting a murderer to it as well."

Bridgette let the door go but held Hellyer's glare. "Do you love your son, Mrs. Hellyer?"

"What kind of fool question is that. Of course I do."

"Do you want him to stay alive?"

Hellyer held Bridgette's gaze but said nothing.

"Your son is psychotic. Unless he is stopped and gets treatment he will keep on killing. Eventually, someone will kill him."

The glare was as strong as ever, but the voice faltered as Hellyer responded "I've got nothing to say to you," before slamming the door.

Friday 9:02 AM

Bridgette glanced at the digital readout of her desk phone as it rang. She recognized the number and smiled to herself as she picked up the handset.

"Hi, Chief."

Her boss was succinct and simply said, "He's here," before disconnecting.

She thought about her partner as she walked towards Delray's office. Although not totally surprised that Levi Frost had been exonerated at his hearing, she was surprised when he had challenged the ruling that he be confined to desk duties until a further psychological assessment could be made.

Frost had insisted on the assessment straight away, and while it had delayed his start by two days, he'd been cleared of any ongoing trauma from the Avery shooting, and was returning to full active service.

The door to Delray's office was shut. After knocking once, she opened it after hearing Delray's familiar low bellow, "Come in."

Frost was seated in one of the two visitors' chairs in front of her boss' desk. When he turned to face Bridgette, she smiled and said, "Welcome back, stranger."

She detected a hint of awkwardness as he mumbled a thank you in response.

Eager not to waste time, Delray said, "I need to keep this short," before Bridgette was even seated. He then added. "So firstly, Levi, I'm glad you're back with the team." He paused and looked at Bridgette who added, "Me, too."

Delray continued, "There's been quite a few developments since you went on leave, not the least of which was the incident at the cabin where Burns was almost killed."

Frost asked, "How is he now?"

"He's recovering," said Delray. "But it's taking longer than it otherwise would on account of the cancer. Since then, we've split the investigation in two. I've got one team still working on the investigation itself, but it's the other angle that I want to talk to you about … the one I've got Bridgette leading."

Frost looked attentive, which Bridgette took as a good sign.

Delray continued, "We've spoken about it and we think with your background in undercover work, you're ideally suited to help."

Frost turned to Bridgette and asked, "So what part of the investigation are you handling?"

Before she could respond, Delray said, "Surveillance."

Frost frowned. "Surveillance?"

Delray nodded. "I'll let Bridgette explain, but we're very hopeful something will come of it soon."

Bridgette said, "After the incident at Burns' cabin, it occurred to me that one of Hellyer's strongest personality traits is his need for revenge. We've seen that back as far as high school when he was hanging the family pets of anyone who crossed him."

Frost agreed, "Which we believe then escalated into the murders of his father and Carl Stockton."

"Exactly," said Bridgette. "I got to thinking about what Hellyer would do now … where would he go."

"And what did you come up with?"

"I think he's close by. With revenge being such a single-minded obsession, I don't think he'll disappear for good just yet. I think he aims to finish what he started."

"You mean killing Burns?"

Bridgette nodded. "He made it quite clear to me in the cabin that he wouldn't rest until both the men responsible for his imprisonment were dead."

"Okay, that makes sense," said Frost. "Only, how do you do surveillance when you don't know where he is?"

"We don't need to know exactly where he is."

Frost shook his head. "I'm confused?"

"Two days after Burns was admitted to the Stanwyck Hospital, he'd recovered enough to be moved. We moved him late that evening for his safety and in secret. He's now in a safe house with around-the-clock care and protection."

Delray added, "But only a handful of people know. As far as the general hospital staff are concerned, Burns is still there in a private room on the third floor."

Bridgette added, "Because of his advanced cancer, the hospital has been advising the media and anyone else who calls that he's receiving palliative care in the hospital and won't be moved for some time."

Frost said, "But how do we know Hellyer will fall for it? Maybe he saw Burns being moved, or maybe…"

Bridgette interrupted, "We set up a recording system at

the hospital and are tracking all incoming calls through their switchboard. Any inquiries about Burns are automatically reviewed. Last night we got a call from a man inquiring about Burns' condition. He said he was Burns' nephew and wanted to know about visiting hours."

"And you think that was Hellyer?"

"We're certain of it. We have a sample of his voice from an interview tape with his doctor during his time in the infirmary and created a digital voice print. It was a hundred percent match to the caller."

"So you think Hellyer will try and take him out while he's still in hospital?"

Delray and Bridgette nodded in unison. Delray said, "We're hopeful he'll try. Nothing has happened yet, but we've got around-the-clock surveillance. It's just a small team so we don't arouse suspicion."

Bridgette added, "Burns is officially listed as being cared for in the psychiatric ward on the third floor."

"Psychiatric ward? I didn't think he had mental problems?"

"He doesn't. The psychiatric ward has a secure six-bed facility that's divided off from the rest of the wing by a floor-to-ceiling safety glass partition. You need a security pass to get in or out."

Delray added, "It saves us having to have a guard stationed outside the door and also means it's far less likely that any of the general hospital staff will discover the only thing in Burns' room is a mannequin."

Bridgette continued, "The door to Burns' room is kept closed and only a handful of the senior hospital staff know what's going on. We have two officers in a room near the nurse's station on the floor monitoring the security cameras for any sign of Hellyer."

Delray said, "And we have a further two officers stationed in the general hospital. We'd like to have more of an undercover presence, but it's a trade-off. The more police, the more likely…"

Frost finished the sentence. "Hellyer will realize it's a setup."

"Exactly," replied Delray.

Bridgette said, "If you're up for it, Levi, we'd like you to join the surveillance team."

"When do we start?"

"Your first shift is with me tonight. We start at seven."

Friday 11:07 AM

Bridgette had planned for Delray to accompany her for the interview with Scott Shriver. But now that Frost was back on duty, Delray had insisted that Frost resume his role as her partner. The three had worked out a plan for the interview before leaving Delray's office.

Now as they knocked on the door of Shriver's upmarket inner-city apartment, Delray's words echoed in her hears. "Go hard on him, Bridgette, you've got nothing to lose."

While they waited, Frost said, "Are we sure he's home?"

"No, but he's not on duty today, so I figure we'd try here first. This is our best chance of an interview without a lawyer."

Before Frost could respond they heard the sound of a latch being unlocked inside.

The door was opened by Shriver. He was unshaven and looked like he'd just gotten out of bed.

Shriver blinked and then snarled, "What are you two doing here? You haven't made an appointment."

Bridgette responded, "Good morning, Doctor Shriver. We were hoping you'd have a few minutes to talk to us in light of what has happened."

"In light of what?"

"Surely you watch the news?"

"I try to avoid the news. It's full of misery and fiction."

Frost said, "Your patient tried to kill Ron Burns. If it hadn't been for Detective Cash's intervention he would have succeeded."

Shriver snarled, "I'm surprised they've let you back out on the street, Detective Frost. Am I safe?"

Frost returned the snarl. "For now."

Bridgette said, "Alex Hellyer tried to murder Ron Burns. I witnessed the attack myself."

"I've got nothing to say to you."

"We were hoping to talk to you about where he might go and who he might be staying with. It's important that we find him before he tries to kill anyone else."

"And why would I know where he is?"

"You're his doctor, remember?" said Frost.

"He's not my patient anymore. I have no idea where he went after he left prison."

Bridgette said, "May we come in? This isn't the kind of conversation we should be having out here."

Shiver glared at them for a moment and then said, "Give me a minute."

After he had closed the door, Frost murmured, "I didn't think we'd get inside."

"It may be a short interview. When he figures out why we're really here, he will probably demand a lawyer."

"Let's hope not."

A moment later Shriver opened the door and let them inside. The apartment was not what Bridgette had expected. The furniture looked old and worn and not in keeping with a building that was only two or three years old. There were only a few photos on display, all of Shriver as a boy or as a young man with an older couple, whom Bridgette assumed were his parents.

Shriver's lounge was covered in books, blankets and empty food containers. He led them past it to his dining table. He glared at them both as he sat down. "This needs to be quick. I've got a lot to do today."

"As we mentioned," Bridgette began, "Alex Hellyer is now a fugitive. He's wanted in connection with an attempted murder and we have reason to believe several other crimes as well."

"I can't help you."

"Would he try to make contact with you? You were his doctor after all."

Shriver shook his head. "I have no idea where he is. In the unlikely event that he calls me, I'll be sure to let you know."

"When did you figure out he was faking his injuries?" said Frost.

Shriver opened his mouth, but then paused. "What do you mean?"

"It's a simple question," responded Bridgette. "I witnessed him attempting to murder a retired police detective. He is as able-bodied as you or I and was clearly faking his condition while in prison."

"I can't help you. I'm a medical doctor, not a psychiatrist."

"So what does that say about you as a medical professional, Doctor Shriver? Surely you knew. Or were you just incompetent?"

"How dare you!"

Bridgette said, "Lauren Hellyer has admitted to paying Francine Turello five hundred dollars a fortnight in cash to give her son special treatment in the infirmary. You started at the hospital at roughly the same time as her, didn't you?"

Shriver bristled. "What are you insinuating?"

"Right now we're gathering evidence. We know her partner was involved in the murder of Paul Ringwood. It's only a matter of time before we join the dots, and we're not buying your line that you knew nothing about Hellyer's condition."

"I want a lawyer."

Bridgette pushed back from the table and stared at Shriver for a moment. The doctor fidgeted under Bridgette's gaze and avoided eye contact. "It's like a house of cards, Doctor Shriver. You only have to pull out one or two before the whole thing comes crashing down, and there's not a thing you or anybody else can do about it."

Shiver stammered, "You've got nothing on me."

Frost leaned in close to Shriver. "We will find the truth. We'll pull your phone records and your bank statements. We'll question your superiors and…"

Shriver's eyes flashed. "You can't do that!"

Bridgette responded, "Watch us. Right now, we have all the power and you have none. Everything we do will be legal and there's not a thing you can do to stop us."

Shriver's mouth opened. "I…I…"

"If you want any control over what happens to you, come clean with us now."

"Like hell, I'll lose my job."

"There's a lot more than your job on the line," said Frost.

Bridgette said, "If you're smart you'll resign before they sack you for misconduct. Because if they sack you, you'll probably lose your license to practice as well. If you resign and admit you made a mistake, you may only be fined or suspended if you're not implicated in a murder."

Frost weighed in again. "The problem is, Shriver, there are too many people involved in this. Eventually someone's going to lose their nerve and talk. It's only a matter of time and then it's going to get really ugly, and quickly ... for everyone."

Bridgette added, "Right now, you're in a position to negotiate. We don't have a full confession from Turello yet, but when we do, my guess is she'll throw you and everyone else under the bus."

Shriver eyes widened. "I'm innocent. I haven't done anything wrong!"

"How much did you know? You had to have known that Hellyer was faking it."

Shriver shook his head. "No, I..."

His furrowed brow wasn't fooling Bridgette. "How long can you hold out, Doctor? A month or maybe two? This isn't going away and we won't stop until we get the truth."

Frost also sensed Shriver was close to caving and added, "You must have known about the payments?"

Bridgette and Frost watched Shriver's shoulders slump. Bridgette added, "If you're not involved in the murder of Paul Ringwood, you need to tell us what you know, now. Turello has hired one of the best lawyers in town and he'll implicate you and anyone else he can to save his client's skin. By the time he's done spinning this, it will be almost impossible to separate fact from fiction and you could be facing a charge of accessory to murder."

Shriver's head dropped. Bridgette and Frost could see him weighing up whether he should say anything or not.

They looked at each other as if to say let's give him the time he needs.

Eventually Shriver looked up at Bridgette. "Can I cut a deal?"

Bridgette placed her phone on the dining room table and pressed record. "That depends on what you tell us. We'll record this now and I'll speak with my boss. When you come in to make a formal statement, you'll need to bring a lawyer. He or she can do the negotiating with my boss."

The room went quiet for a moment. Shriver put his head in his hands and said, "Mrs. Hellyer approached me not long after I started working at the prison. She offered me a thousand dollars a month to get her son a room each night and to make sure he wasn't raped. I said no to her at first even though I thought her son was seriously disabled. She asked me a second time and I felt sorry for her. I didn't see any harm in it. I don't work the night shift as a rule and I worked out a deal with Francine where we would split the money and she would make sure Alex always got a room."

"When did you realize he was faking his condition?"

"It was some month's later before I had my first suspicions."

"Why didn't you report it?"

"Are you kidding? If they found out about the money, I would've lost my job."

"What else do you know?"

"Nothing, I swear."

"What about the thirty thousand?"

Shriver's mouth fell open. "Thirty thousand?"

"We believe Turello's partner, John Avery, was given thirty-thousand dollars to kill Ringwood. The money was found in a plastic bag in a safe belonging to him."

Shriver held up his hands with his palms facing out. "I know nothing about that, I swear."

"Turello never mentioned it?"

Shriver paused for a moment. "I remember her talking on the phone once to someone. I think it was her partner, but I never asked. I was already uncomfortable with taking money for a prisoner who wasn't really disabled."

"What did she say?"

"I heard her use the term '30 K but I swear, I had no idea what it was in connection to."

"You have no idea where the money came from?"

Shriver's faced turned red. "I can't believe this is happening. We were splitting a thousand dollars a month to make one prisoner's life a bit more comfortable. I didn't see anything really wrong with that, and then it all got out of hand."

Bridgette persisted. "Doctor, with all due respect, that's not an answer."

Shriver shook his head in disbelief. "It was probably Lauren Hellyer, but I've got no proof. I remember Francine coming to me one day and saying Lauren had a lot of money in a safe deposit box and she wanted to figure out a way to get it off her."

"And what did you say?"

"I told her she was crazy. That's the only time we ever spoke about it."

"Did she say how much money?"

Shriver shook his head. "After that, I kept my distance. I would have fired her if I could have, but that would have blown back on me, so I was stuck with her."

"How long ago was this?"

"About six months ago, I guess."

"Lauren Hellyer never mentioned anything to you?"

"No. I told her never to talk to me about money. That was Francine's department."

"What about Alex Hellyer?"

"What about him?"

"Did he ever say anything?"

Shriver paused a moment. "It's complicated. I think he knew that I knew, but we never said anything. I treated him like a severely disabled patient and he played the role."

"Did you ever see him talking to Turello?"

"She talked to him every day, just like any other patient."

"No, I mean, did they ever have a normal adult conversation that you observed?"

"Not that I heard, but Francine told me in recent months he'd started making additional demands."

Bridgette frowned. "What kind of demands."

"She wouldn't tell me."

"Sexual?"

"Maybe, but not that I ever saw."

"Then what?"

"She would give him a phone at night, a smartphone to search the internet, but he also made some calls with it."

"Who did he call?"

"Apparently he used to talk to John Avery a lot."

"What about?"

"I never asked. I realized this was all getting out of hand and I was in way over my head. I even went to a lawyer to get some advice."

"And what did the lawyer say?" said Frost.

"Stop taking the money and get a new job."

"Sounds like reasonable advice," said Bridgette.

"I'll give you his number. You can call him to verify what I'm saying is true."

"Where did Turello keep the phone she was loaning to Hellyer?"

"She kept it in a locker. Not hers, but a spare one that she'd found a key to. That way the phone couldn't be traced back to her if they found it. But I don't think you'll find it at the prison. If she was smart she would have removed it when she cleaned out her stuff when the warden fired her after that interview with you."

"Have you talked to her since then?"

Shriver paused. "Once, but I've stopped taking her calls."

"What did you talk about?"

"She called me when she was told you were going to interview her the first time. I told her not to tell you anything about the money. It was all cash and there was no proof." Hellyer stood up and started pacing. "This is all so unfair. I don't make much more than a normal public servant, even though I've spent seven years in med school. That's not right. I should be paid better. If I was paid properly, this never would've happened."

Bridgette decided they had enough for now. "I think we'll continue this downtown, but first we need to call your lawyer to verify your story."

Shriver pulled out his smartphone and showed Bridgette the number. "When can we talk about a deal?"

"I'll talk to my boss after I've talked to your lawyer. If you're story checks out, you'll need to have him present when we continue the interview back at our office."

Saturday 12:47 AM

Alex Hellyer strolled into the Emergency Department of Vancouver Metro Base Hospital and stood for a moment surveying the scene in front of him. Even in the early hours of the morning, the hospital was busy. He glanced around the waiting room. There were two couples with crying babies, an old man with a gash on his head being comforted by his wife, a very pregnant woman on her own, and a meth addict who looked fifty but was probably closer to thirty.

Lost in their own misery, no one paid him any attention which suited him fine. Although there had been a brief news report on him after his attack on Burns at the cabin, he wasn't too concerned about being recognized. Now with a shaven head, he was confident he could move about incognito.

He pretended to read the instructions on a sign just inside the entrance while he scanned the facility. The two staff working the reception counter behind security glass were oblivious to his presence, both on phones and tapping away at computer keyboards. He noted three doors. Two that led to public toilets for those in the waiting room and one double door that led back to the emergency treatment rooms. Hellyer focused on the double door. He was debating whether to push on them to see if they opened until he noticed the swipe card access and figured they were probably locked. He sat down three seats away from the pregnant woman. She looked to be close to term and in a lot of distress. Had he been a praying sort of man, he would have prayed that she'd go into labor there and then. But he had no need of a deity and decided to sit and wait. After all, he had all night.

Ten minutes went by before the next patient was called. Hellyer watched as the old man with a gash on his head was led by his wife to a nurse who was waiting at the double doors. Hellyer suppressed a smile as he watched the nurse hold the door open. She made no attempt to come and help the man and if she repeated that pattern, getting into the ward would be easy.

Five minutes later, the next patient was called; this time it was the pregnant woman who struggled to her feet. Hellyer was immediately beside her, wearing a concerned look. "Can I help you?"

The woman shook her head. "I think I'll be fine. It's probably just Braxton Hicks."

All of a sudden she winced and clutched her belly in pain. Hellyer reached out and touched her back. "Are you sure you're okay?"

"The pain just catches me sometimes," she said.

Hellyer took the woman's arm. "I'll help you to the door. You can't be too careful in your condition."

He continued to make a fuss over the woman until he handed her over to the nurse. While the nurse took the woman by the hand, Hellyer held the door open for them.

He watched for a moment until they disappeared into an examination cubicle and then stepped forward, letting the door close behind him. He was in.

Following a Google search earlier that day, Hellyer had located online plans for the hospital and had spent some time studying the layout. Armed with a rough idea of where everything was, Hellyer headed east along the main corridor. Within two minutes he had located the laundry room.

Hellyer opened the door and stepped into a large rectangular room that was eerily quiet and dimly lit by the control panels on a row of commercial washers and dryers that stood against the rear wall. He stood still for a moment to allow his eyes to adjust to the dim light. In front of him were six large laundry trolleys, about four feet long and three feet wide. He grinned to himself as he focused on two of the hampers which were overflowing with soiled linen. They would serve his purpose well, but for now he needed a uniform of some sort. Moving across to the right wall, he studied the rows of neatly pressed linen stacked in shelves that stretched from floor to ceiling. His eye tracked along a row of green surgical gowns. He picked one up and unfolded it. It wasn't quite what he was looking for so he threw it back and continued his search. After scanning several more shelves he found more garments that interested him. He pulled one down and inspected it — a white lab coat. He grinned as he tried the coat on for size.

Satisfied the coat was a good enough fit, he transferred the gun he had tucked away in his cargo pants to the coat's right pocket. From another pocket in his pants he pulled out a small bottle of lighter fluid and a cigarette lighter.

Murmuring to himself, *now the fun begins*, Hellyer walked back to the hampers and spread a liberal amount of fluid over the two which were overflowing with dirty laundry. After rummaging around in one of the other hampers, he pulled out a laundry bag that was about half full and flung it across the floor towards the door he had come through minutes earlier. Hellyer moved back to the two hampers he had selected. Using his thumb, he spun the spark wheel of the lighter and was momentarily mesmerized by the small blue flame it emitted. A grin spread from ear to ear as he imagined the chaos this innocuous flame would cause in just a few minutes.

Hellyer touched the lighter to the linen then watched the fire take hold. He kicked the hamper into the center of the room. He would have loved to watch the conflagration develop as he'd done when he'd set fire to his family home all those years ago. But he was conscious that the fire alarms would soon be wailing.

Flames from the first hamper were now leaping four feet into the air and spreading fast. He marveled at the grotesque shadows the fire projected on the walls as the linen in the racks started to burn. Savoring the experience, he opened the door and backed into the corridor. With the sound of fire alarms now ringing in his ears, he strode down the hallway back to the Emergency Department to execute the next part of his plan.

By the time Hellyer reached the treatment rooms, chaos had taken hold. Doctors, nurses and patients were all panicking. Nobody seemed to be following any fire evacuation procedure, which was exactly what he wanted. He positioned himself in the center of the corridor about ten feet back from the double doors that lead to the Emergency reception area and waited. In less than a minute a young nurse burst through the door. Hellyer strode forward. The collision was heavy. The nurse fell backwards and landed flat on her back. Hellyer bent down, apologizing profusely as he helped her to her feet. After admonishing him to be more careful, the nurse continued down the corridor at a run. Hellyer smiled as he held up the clip-on security pass he had just stolen. The photo ID was of no use to him, but the white plastic swipe card would allow him to go where he needed. He mumbled, *child's play*, and headed for the fire stairs on the west side of the building.

Saturday 1:11 AM

Alex Hellyer ascended the fire stairs in the concrete stairwell two at a time until he came to the third floor. The sound of the fire alarm echoing off the concrete walls was deafening, but Hellyer barely heard it such was his resolve and focus. He paused with his left hand on the handle of the fire door. The door was painted a dark gray and looked no different to any of the other security doors he'd passed on his way up. But to Hellyer, this door was different and he felt his excitement growing at the possibility of what lay beyond.

He had dreamt of this moment for ten years. A moment he would savor as he decided exactly when to the end the life of the other man responsible for his incarceration. The rage following his first foiled attempt turned to excitement as he swiped the security pass and stepped into the psychiatric ward.

With his pistol in his right hand he opened the door enough to be able to look up and down the short corridor. Three doors to his left and three to his right, all closed and laid out just like the plan he'd studied earlier. He grinned for

The Cold Light of Day

a moment as he eyed the nurse's station just beyond the glass security doors at the end of the corridor. It was empty; his fire diversion seemed to be working.

Hellyer moved into the corridor and grabbed the patient's chart out of its holder just outside the first door on the right and held it up to the light. Someone named Kowalski. Not who he was looking for. He moved on to the next door and peered at the patient's chart and felt a fresh tingle of excitement as he read the name Ronald Burns. He let out a satisfied sigh despite the incessant noise of the fire alarm. He quickly entered the room where a man was sleeping. After turning on a tiny red laser sight he had fitted to his pistol, he played it over Burns' body. The man was facing the wall, hidden beneath a sea of blankets. He was surprised that someone even as sick as Burns could sleep through the fire alarm. Perhaps they had sedated him. It would be a pity if he couldn't be aroused to experience the terror of being burned alive. But Hellyer consoled himself — watching his victim burn for a minute or two before he made his escape would be a memory he would treasure for the rest of his life.

Hellyer up ended the laundry bag on the bed. As the dirty linen fell out in a pile, Hellyer noticed the color of Burns hair for the first time and let out a roar. Burns' hair was gray, but the person in the bed had light brown hair. He grabbed hold of the blankets and ripped them back before letting out another roar as he stared down at the body of a mannequin. Realizing he'd been duped, Hellyer exploded. Teeth clenched, Hellyer thought about the bitch detective who was no doubt behind this interference. He breathed in and out deeply to bring his rage under control before moving to the door. Hellyer cracked the door open and peered into the corridor. No sign of police or hospital staff. Time to go.

He headed back to the fire door but was cut short by the sound of his name. "Hellyer!"

At the other end of the corridor the bitch detective and Frost were standing on the other side of the glass security door. Without bothering to aim he fired three times and sprinted for the fire door.

Saturday 1:17 AM

Bridgette's plan specified that two detectives would be stationed on the ground floor behind the hospital's main reception area in the security room. They had access to a bank of monitors running the video feed from every security camera in the facility. Another two detectives were stationed on the third floor in a room close to Burns' hospital room, monitoring video feeds from the psychiatric ward only.

Because it was Bridgette's plan, Delray allowed her to choose which location she would cover. She'd figured if Hellyer was disguised, it would be easy enough to get into the building but getting into the secure six-bed psychiatric ward would be another matter entirely. The ward was closed off from the rest of the floor by a thick glass partition and was only accessible by security doors with an electronic pass.

Bridgette would have preferred to be inside the ward itself, but the hospital insisted that the five spare rooms needed to be available for patients, so they were forced to settle for a small office behind the nurse's station just outside the ward.

Frost and Bridgette sat at a long table that had been brought in specifically for their surveillance. The table housed three monitors that were connected to security cameras on the ward. The camera on the left showed a view of the main corridor leading up to the nurses' station. The middle camera gave them a view of the short corridor inside the ward, and the camera on the right was setup inside Burns' room. The feed on the monitor from Burns' room was dark, almost black. Lit only by the panel lights on the monitoring equipment in the room, they could just make out the image of the mannequin lying in the bed.

This was Bridgette's second night on the surveillance detail. The challenge with her plan was staying awake in a small stuffy room in the middle of the night when she had worked most of the day as well. She had taken to swapping her daily peppermint tea intake for coffee, but that only went so far; she was happy there was a restroom next door. As her eyelids grew heavy, she murmured, "How are you doing, Levi?"

"I'm awake, but only just. These monitors get mesmerizing after a while, particularly when nothing's happening."

"I guess this is not the kind of surveillance you're used to?"

Frost chuckled. "Surveillance inside a hospital is definitely a first for me."

The stillness returned. As Bridgette debated stepping out of the room to get a can of Coke, Frost asked, "Do you think he'll show tonight?"

"I have no idea. I actually thought it might have been last night."

"How long have we got? There must be a time limit on this."

"The operation gets formally reviewed at the end of the week. Given he made the call to hospital a couple of days ago, I think we'll get an extension if we need one."

"Good to know," said Frost as he stretched and yawned. She was close enough to smell his aftershave.

Keeping her voice low so that she couldn't be heard outside the room, she said, "This is probably not what you expected when you returned to active duty."

"Staring at monitors for eight hours is not exactly how I imagined I'd be catching bad guys."

Bridgette smiled to herself. She found comfort in his humor, which she thought was a good sign he was returning to normal. Shifting in her chair to keep comfortable, she kept switching her gaze between the three monitors. "I never really understood how tedious surveillance work could be until now."

"It takes a special sort of person to do this. There's a lot of surveillance work in undercover. Not every cop who starts in undercover stays. Most don't give up because of the stress, but the boredom can take its toll. With surveillance you need to be patient, that's for sure."

About to respond, she was interrupted by the sound of a fire alarm.

Frost frowned. "Could this be him? This is just the kind of distraction he would pull."

Bridgette hadn't taken her eyes off the monitors. "Let's hope it's just a false alarm, but I wouldn't put it past Hellyer to pull a stunt like this."

"Should we go check with the duty nurse?"

"No. Let's just keep watching the monitors for a minute

and see what happens. It's probably just a false alarm and they'll turn it off in a minute."

"Do you really believe that?"

Bridgette looked at Frost. "No. But right now we can't panic. Let's just…"

Before Bridgette could finish, the duty nurse burst into the room. "The fire alarm is sounding. You need to evacuate."

Bridgette stayed in her chair. "How do we know it's not just a false alarm?"

"The laundry on the ground floor is on fire. There are no patients in the psychiatric ward tonight, so I'm going over to the general ward to help, but you need to leave now."

"I want to stay here for a couple more minutes. I have a feeling the man who we're after might have started this."

The nurse flushed. "I don't have time to argue with you, but if you stay it's on your own head," and hurried out.

Frost said, "Be back in a moment. I'm just going to check what it's like out on the ward."

Bridgette kept her eyes glued to the monitors. She saw the nurse running down the main corridor, but she was more concerned about the feed from the psychiatric unit and Burns' room. She could see no movement on either screen, but her gut tightened; a sure omen.

Frost appeared a moment later. "We don't have long. I can smell smoke out in the corridor."

Bridgette kept her eyes fixed on the screens and over the sound of the alarm said, "He's here. This is definitely his doing."

Frost stared at the screens. "No sign of him?"

"No. I'm just trying to think which way he'd come."

"If it were me, I wouldn't be coming along the main corridor. Too much chance of being spotted."

"I agree. Which leaves the fire stairs."

Frost sat down next to Bridgette and pointed to the middle screen. "The door at the end of the psychiatric ward, that's the fire stairs, right?"

"Yes. The stairwell leads down to the ground floor and also up to the roof."

"Does it unlock if there's a fire?"

"Not from the outside. I checked it when we looked for the best place to set this up. The doors allow you to get out not in. Even in an emergency, if you're in the stairwell, you're locked out of each floor except the ground floor or the roof."

"So he can get in through there?"

"Only with a security pass."

"We need to keep an eye on that door. I can't imagine he'll find it too hard to steal a pass."

They watched the screens for a few more seconds before Frost said, "We probably can't stay here too much longer."

"I agree. If we have to leave, I was thinking one of us could head down via the main corridor and the other can take…"

Before she could finish her sentence a guard burst through the door. "You two have to leave now. The fire brigade is on its way and we've been ordered to evacuate everyone."

Bridgette glared at the burly guard. "You're aware we're running a surveillance detail here?"

"Not any more. You both need to leave now. I've got orders to clear this floor as soon as I can, and I don't have time to argue with a couple of cops who won't follow instructions."

Frost said, "We believe he's set this up. We need to stay at least a few more minutes…"

"No, you don't!" shot back the guard. "Every minute I stay here arguing with you is a minute I waste not helping others."

Bridgette sighed. "We'll get our stuff."

The guard bristled. "No packing of any equipment. Just grab your coats."

The guard waited while they put their coats on. Bridgette turned when she got to the door and took one last look at the monitors. She frowned then ran back to the table ignoring the guard's protest.

She studied the screen on the right oblivious of the fire alarm and the guard yelling at her. She felt the hair stand up on the back of her neck as she saw movement inside the darkened room. "He's here."

In a moment, Frost was back by her side. "Where."

She pointed to Burns' room. "There's a light inside that wasn't there before."

"We need to go after him."

Over the protests of the guard, Bridgette and Frost pushed past him and raced around the corner to the nurses' station, just as Hellyer emerged from Burns' room.

Frost drew his gun and yelled, "Hellyer!"

Hellyer fired three shots and then sprinted for the fire door and didn't look back.

Frost yelled again, "Stop or I'll shoot!" but Hellyer ignored him as he leaned on the panic latch to open the door. Frost fired at the fleeing man. The security glass had already crazed from Hellyer's shots and it was impossible to tell whether he had hit his target.

Frost pushed through the door and yelled, "He's getting away."

Bridgette raced after Frost, but her partner was already bounding down the stairs three at a time when she reached the fire exit.

The noise of the fire alarm echoed throughout the confined concrete space, making it impossible for her to hear anything as she watched Frost round a corner below and disappear out of sight.

Bridgette noticed fresh blood on the landing and realized Hellyer had been hit. She peered down the stairwell but could see no further signs of bleeding.

Bridgette swung left and noticed more drops of blood on the stairs leading to the roof. She shouted to Frost, "He's heading for the roof!" but was unsure if he would have heard her above the fire alarm.

Resisting the urge to sprint knowing Hellyer could have set himself up to shoot as they rounded the corner, she climbed the stairs one at a time. Bridgette held her gun up but saw no sign of Hellyer as she reached the landing that led to the roof.

Although desperate to escape the noise that had become a screeching pain in her head, Bridgette stopped abruptly. The fire door to the roof was partially open and there were two bloody palm prints on the door's handle.

Saturday 1:25 AM

Bridgette stared at the bloody prints on the door handle. Conscious that Hellyer could be just outside waiting to shoot anyone who walked through the door, she considered her options. If he wasn't badly wounded, logic said he would try to escape. But if he was badly injured, he could be preparing for a last stand, and that was what she feared the most.

The smart play would be to wait for Frost or the two other detectives who had been on the stakeout. But she also knew that Hellyer could have sprinted across the rooftop and already be descending the fire stairs on the other side of the building. Mindful that every second counted, she pushed the door a crack and peered out. She could see a small sliver of the roof in the moonlight. It was flat, as she expected, and had a four-foot concrete wall running around its perimeter. From her position, she could see one vent two feet high and three feet wide which was barely big enough to hide behind. She twisted around to get a fresh angle, but still couldn't see any sign of Hellyer.

Glock in hand, Bridgette opened the door fully, constantly scanning for any sign of her adversary.

She breathed in and out slowly as she studied the layout of the roof. From her position, she could see twelve vents spread out across the rooftop about thirty feet apart. She barely paid them any attention as she focused on the large air conditioning unit in the center. About the size of a shipping container, the structure offered plenty of room to hide behind. Conscious that her silhouette presented an easy target, she crept to her left and crouched in the shadow of one of the vents.

The air conditioning unit stood about fifty feet in front of her. Even sprinting to it would take several seconds and leave her vulnerable. While she pondered her next move, she heard a siren and expected the fire brigade to be on site within minutes. The chaos they would cause downstairs would make it easy for Hellyer to escape.

Bridgette focused on the AC unit and crept forward. She could hear her heart thumping, the beats pounding in her head above the sound of the alarm and the sirens.

Sweeping her gun from left to right, she tiptoed forward until she was in line with the second row of ventilator shafts and then concentrated on the AC unit again.

After taking a deep breath and telling herself to stay calm, she moved forward again until she was about twenty feet from the structure. She wondered which side she should approach on — left or right? She'd always been more accurate with her Glock swinging in a left-to-right arc rather than the reverse. She veered left.

As she moved forward, she could hear the fire truck's siren growing louder by the second and figured they would be on site within a minute.

Pushing the sound to the back of her mind, Bridgette

focused on the task in front of her. Her mouth went dry at the possibility that Hellyer could be waiting to ambush her. Her steps were slow and deliberate and her concentration intense. She took two more steps and then stopped as a red laser dot from a gun sight appeared on the wall of the AC unit in front of her. Her heart sank as she realized Hellyer was behind her.

Before she could turn, Hellyer shouted above the noise of the alarms and sirens, "Don't move, Detective. If you do, I'll shoot."

Bridgette lowered her Glock but kept her grip firm as Hellyer added, "You should have checked behind you. There was a gap behind the exit that was just wide enough for me to squeeze into."

She was conscious of Hellyer's voice growing louder and pictured him walking toward her. She went to turn again, but Hellyer said, "Don't give me an excuse!"

She sensed him stopping a few feet behind her. The laser dot was still visible on the wall of the AC unit. It was now in line with her head and just to her right.

Hellyer demanded, "Drop the gun!"

After closing her eyes and taking a deep breath, she responded, "You're going to have to shoot me. I'm not giving up my gun."

He laughed. "You're a stubborn bitch. It looks like…"

Hellyer never finished his sentence … the door to the roof swing open. Instinct took over as she saw the laser from Hellyer's gun sight swing rapidly to the right. Bridgette pivoted, knowing that he was turning to fire at whoever was coming through the door.

She caught sight of Levi Frost as her gun swung through a 180° arc and zoned in on her target. Hellyer was about ten feet in front of her, but she only had a narrow side view of his torso. Glocks were extremely accurate provided they were fired with a steady hand and aimed correctly at their target.

In stressful situations and with the gun needing to move rapidly to lock onto a target, a distance of ten feet may as well have been a hundred.

Bridgette had no time to think about the computations required to make a clean shot so fired three rounds in quick succession, hoping at least one of them would hit Hellyer without hitting Frost.

In a moment in time she would never forget, she heard Hellyer's gun discharge once just as the fire alarm stopped. She watched Hellyer collapse to the concrete in front of her then looked over at Frost. Barely daring to breathe, she held Frost's gaze expecting him to also fall.

The moment in time passed as a stunned Frost stammered, "You okay?"

She wanted to respond, 'Yes,' but no words came out of her mouth. Instead, she nodded once and stood in silence as she watched Frost walk towards fallen man.

Keeping his gun trained on Hellyer who hadn't moved since his collapse, Frost knelt down and placed two fingers on his carotid artery. After a moment he looked up and said, "We need to get a doctor… he's still alive."

Saturday 10:46 AM

Bridgette followed Frost into Delray's office. As they settled into his visitors' chairs, Delray looked at each of them and then said, "If you don't mind me saying, you both look like crap."

Frost managed a tired grin. "We've been awake for about forty hours — I guess this is what it looks like."

"Well, let's get this over with quickly and get you home for some sleep."

Bridgette slid their signed statements across the desk. "I think we've covered everything."

Delray thanked her as he placed the documents on top of a pile. Leaning forward, he asked, "Any word from the hospital?"

"He's out of surgery," replied Bridgette. "It looks like he'll pull through."

"I never thought I'd say this but that's a relief." Holding Bridgette's gaze, her boss added, "You don't need the death of another person, not even someone like Hellyer on your conscience, Bridgette."

Bridgette nodded. "He's lucky to be alive. One of my rounds hit him in the chest. If he hadn't already been at the hospital, the doctors don't think he would have survived."

Delray shook his head. "He went to extraordinary lengths to kill Burns."

After pulling his glasses off, he added, "Tell me … if he'd found Burns in that room, what had he been planning?"

Frost said, "Bridgette and I both think he was going set him on fire. There was a bag of dirty laundry spread over his bed and we found lighter fluid and a lighter on him."

Bridgette added, "In our statements we make note of the fact we found a fire fighter's suit on the roof behind the AC unit. We think he'd planned on changing into it and using it as a disguise to escape once the fire brigade arrived."

"That makes sense." Delray shook his head. "What kind of scumbag wants to burn a sick old man to death?"

Bridgette had no answer for that. "The doctors have told us it will be at least a week before Hellyer will be well enough to interview. He's currently in ICU and likely to need further surgery."

"Our taxpayer dollars hard at work keeping a low-life like that alive," said Delray.

"So what happens now?" asked Bridgette.

Her boss looked at his watch. "I've got a briefing with the commissioner and Cunningham at eleven. It's not often you see them in here on a Saturday, but they're holding a press conference at noon and they want a final briefing before they step in front of the cameras."

Delray paused and looked soberly at each of them before he added, "You've done some outstanding work here … both of you."

Bridgette looked at Frost as she answered, "It's good to get some closure."

Frost nodded. "I agree, and no one has any doubt now that it was Hellyer who orchestrated Ringwood's murder."

"But we've still got work to do on his accomplices."

Delray nodded. "Shriver is coming in with his lawyer at eleven-thirty to make a full statement. I've got McCartin and Watts running that interview, but I'm going to sit in on it to make sure we get all we can out of him. I'm hopeful we'll get enough evidence to nail both Turello and Hellyer's mother too."

"Do you want Levi and me to hang around for that?" asked Bridgette.

"No. I want you guys to take two days leave. I think that's the least we can do for you after what you've achieved."

When there were no objections, Delray raised an eyebrow and said, "I know I should ask you this question separately, but I think I know the answer anyway. Are you two happy to keep working together?"

Bridgette looked at Frost. Her first thought was to say something light-hearted with typical cop bravado, but then decided her answer needed to be genuine given what Frost had been through. "I think we make a good team."

Frost managed a sleepy grin. "Despite being shot at twice on my first case, strangely I'm enjoying it here."

"Well, that's settled. I'll let the commissioner know," said Delray, putting his glasses back on. He glanced at his watch again and raised an eyebrow. "I don't have much time before my meeting, so unless there's something else, I need to keep moving."

Bridgette said, "Sorry, there is just one thing."

"Okay."

"Now that Hellyer's in custody and no longer a threat to Ron Burns, will he need to stay in the safe house?"

"Maybe for a couple more days until they get his clearance sorted. Why do you ask?"

"I know his time is short, and if I've got a couple of days off, I'd like to go and see him. I think hearing what happened from me would help give him closure."

"That's very thoughtful of you, Bridgette. I'm sure I can arrange something."

Delray looked at his watch again, a less than subtle hint that he wanted to keep moving. Frost and Bridgette took the cue and got up from their chairs and walked to the door. Bridgette lingered in the doorway and waited until Frost was down the hallway and out of earshot before she turned back and said to Delray, "Thanks, Chief."

Delray looked puzzled. "For what?"

"For giving Levi a chance. Working as a cop is important to him. If you hadn't have given him a chance, and he'd left the force, I'm not sure…"

"I'm always happy to help someone who wants to help themselves. And clearly he wanted to help himself."

They were silent for a moment before Delray said, "I have high hopes for you two as a team."

Bridgette nodded. "When we were on the roof, Hellyer got off a shot at Levi before he went down. For a horrible moment, I thought, not again…"

Delray shook his head. "You can't think like that, Bridgette. In time you'll learn that most cops survive when they work as a team, just like you two did on the roof. That's how it goes. I'm only sitting in this chair and alive today, because twenty years ago, one of my partners had my back in a similar situation."

"I never knew that."

"I'll tell you about it sometime, but not today. Anything else?"

"I can't think straight, so nothing right now."

"You've done some great work, now go home and get some sleep."

Bridgette stifled a yawn as she responded, "I'll see you on Tuesday."

Epilogue
8 DAYS LATER

Bridgette paused in front of apartment number sixty-four. With her hand poised to knock, she still wasn't sure this was a good idea and murmured to herself, You need to check.

After knocking gently on the door, she took a step back to wait. She relaxed a little when she heard footsteps inside and then felt instant relief when the front door opened.

She looked up at Levi Frost who, apart from not having shaved for several days, looked normal. No bloodshot eyes, no signs he was strung out on drugs or alcohol; a good sign.

Frost looked surprised to see her as he said, "Hi, Bridgette."

"Hi, Levi. Sorry for stopping by like this, I…"

"Hey, no problem. Do you want to come in?" He opened the door wide and motioned her inside.

Feeling slightly embarrassed, Bridgette had had no intention of entering his apartment. Although she tried not to look, she was surprised when she saw several moving boxes stacked inside the door.

"You're moving?"

Frost looked back at his apartment. "Yeah. Tomorrow as a matter of fact."

Bridgette nodded. "This is starting to make sense. When the chief told me you had to take some emergency leave, I ... I guess I assumed the worst."

"Come in. I could do with a break from the packing."

"I shouldn't be interrupting you. I feel bad now."

Frost smiled as he motioned her inside. As she walked into the living room, she explained, "I got a message from the chief that you'd taken leave and wouldn't be back until next week. I tried calling you a couple of times yesterday and then again today to see if you were okay."

"Sorry, my bad. My phone's on the fritz. The battery only lasts about half an hour before it needs recharging. I've been so distracted, I forgot to charge it."

She sat on the couch as Frost settled into an easy chair opposite her, and said, "I won't stay long. I can see you've got a lot to do."

Frost glanced around his apartment. "Sorry the place is a mess. Normally I'm a neat freak but moving makes that impossible."

Bridgette smiled as she glanced around the apartment. Apart from a few picture hooks on the walls, the couch and the easy chair, the rest of the living area was now just packing boxes. "You look very organized."

"I've had practice."

"I detest moving and try and avoid it wherever possible. No matter how much I try, stuff always seems to go missing."

Frost laughed. "Let's hope my phone goes missing. I could do with an excuse to buy a new one." He paused for a moment and then added, "I appreciate your concern and sorry about not returning your calls."

"Don't worry about it, I'm just glad you're okay."

"Can I get you a coffee? The machine's still plugged in."

Bridgette glanced at her watch. "Thanks, but I need to go in a minute. I'm meeting some girlfriends for dinner."

"Well, I won't keep you then."

As Bridgette looked around the apartment again, she said, "Tell me to mind my own business if I'm out of line, but this all seems kind of sudden. I don't remember you mentioning you were moving?"

Frost grimaced. "The lease on the apartment was in my wife's name and she conveniently forgot to tell me about the renewal when she moved out. I had the landlord knocking on my door at eight o'clock the other night because my wife hadn't been returning his calls. He told me I had five days to decide whether I wanted to renew the lease or move on." He looked around. "I can't afford this on my own so, I asked the chief for a couple of days off to look for somewhere new to live."

"That would explain why you suddenly took personal leave."

Frost nodded. "Yeah, I meant to talk to you, but you weren't around when I saw the chief. He was understanding and told me to take whatever time I needed. I thought he'd have explained that to you."

"I got the message you were on leave, but not the details. He was out of the office today and will probably remember to tell me sometime next week."

Frost chuckled. "That sounds about right."

"Do you need a hand packing?"

"No, I'm mostly done, but thanks for the offer. Tomorrow's move day, and I'll use Sunday to unpack. The plan is to be back at work bright and early on Monday."

"So you've found somewhere else to live?"

"Yeah, a little studio about ten minutes from our office. I'm pretty happy with it."

"Well, that's a relief."

"You can say that again. For half a day there, I thought I might be homeless."

Bridgette grimaced. "So I take it there's no chance of a reconciliation for you and your wife?"

Frost stared at the floor for a moment then shook his head. "It's all turning very ugly. Some years ago, my grandma left me a sixty-thousand-dollar inheritance as a deposit for my first house. She died a long time before I ever met my wife, but somehow Jasmine thinks she's entitled to half of it…"

"I'm sorry to hear that."

"I've hired a lawyer. Something I hoped I'd never have to do, but what can you do? Anyways, I'm looking forward to it all being over, and starting a new chapter."

Bridgette was feeling uncomfortably warm. There were several questions she still needed to ask Frost and said, "Do you mind if I take my coat off? It's quite warm in here."

"Sorry," said Frost. "The heater hasn't worked properly in about three weeks. It's either on full or not at all."

After removing her coat and sitting down again, she said, "I got a call from Vancouver Base Hospital this afternoon. They said Hellyer will make a full recovery."

"That's a relief. Better for him to rot in prison than die and get off easy."

"I agree. It's a weight off my shoulders. No cop likes being responsible for the death of another human being, even if it's a scumbag like him."

"I couldn't agree more." Frost paused and pointed at her left arm and then added, "I didn't know you had tattoos?"

Bridgette stared down at the small concentric ring tattoo on her inner left forearm as she realized this was the first time Frost had seen her in a short sleeve shirt.

"Just one actually."

"I can't read the words inside the rings from here. What do they say?"

"Family, friendship, peace and faith."

"And I guess they all have a special meaning?"

Bridgette nodded. "Yes."

"One of them seems new?"

Bridgette looked down at her arm again. "I had the word 'Faith' added just a week ago."

"So what, you just found God?" Frost's eyes widened as he realized he may have gone too far. Holding a hand up he quickly added, "Sorry, I'm getting too personal."

Bridgette laughed. "No big deal. While I have a faith in God, this is more about faith in myself."

Frost frowned. "I'm not sure I follow?"

"Not long after I became a detective, I started having doubts about myself."

"Well, I never would've picked that."

"When two cops you work with die on your first three murder cases, you wonder if it's you…"

"Delray told me about your rough start."

Bridgette nodded. As tears welled in her eyes, she said, "My partner on my first case was three months from retirement. If he hadn't … well … I wouldn't be alive today."

"I'm beginning to understand."

Staring at her tattoo, Bridgette said absently, "The chief told me to have faith in myself … but it's hard when people you work with die." She looked up at Frost. "The Ringwood case has helped."

Frost managed half a grin. "I got shot at multiple times and I'm still here so you're definitely not bad luck."

"I guess it's taken a while for me to believe that." She checked her watch again. "I really need to be going, but there is one more thing I need to ask you."

"Okay."

"The chief came to me yesterday and told me about a new cold case the team has just picked up. A mother and daughter were murdered in their home about ten years ago. There were no witnesses and no apparent motive and the case has remained unsolved. However, they collected DNA evidence from a recent robbery crime scene…"

"Let me guess — they got a match for the cold case?"

Bridgette nodded. "The chief has offered us the case. It would mean stepping away from the final part of the Ringwood murder."

Frost mused, "We've already charged Francine Turello as an accessory to murder and I think by the end of next week we'll having enough evidence to charge Lauren Hellyer as well."

"McCartin and Watts can finish up the Ringwood case if you want to try your hand at a cold case?"

Frost thought for a moment. "I'm easy either way, but we've put a lot of time into this one… I guess it would be nice to see it through to completion."

"I was hoping you'd say that."

"You feel the same way?"

"Hellyer didn't do this entirely on his own. His mother, Turello, and John Avery all played their parts in Paul Ringwood's murder. If nothing else, I'd like to see it through for Ringwood's widow's sake."

Frost nodded once. "Well, I guess that's settled."

Bridgette rose to her feet. As she put her coat on, Frost added, "Thanks for asking, Bridgette. I appreciate it."

"No problem."

Frost stood and then said, "Out of curiosity, what would you have done if I'd wanted to move on to the cold case?"

"I guess we'd have talked about it some more. Like you, I don't have to stay with the Ringwood case."

"Good to know," said Frost, opening the front door. He waited until Bridgette was out in the hallway before adding, "And again, sorry about not answering the calls."

Bridgette smiled. "Don't worry about it, Levi. I'm just glad you're okay."

"I'll see you Monday."

"Good luck with the move."

"Thanks, I'm going to need it."

Bridgette walked to the elevator and two minutes later was out of the building. Her phone rang as she was getting into her car. It was Renée Filipucci.

"Hi, Renée."

"Hi, BC. You haven't forgotten about us have you?"

Bridgette put her phone on speaker and started the engine. "I'm on my way, but I had to stop and check on a colleague. I'll be there in fifteen minutes."

"Okay, that'll work. Samantha has just arrived, and I just got a text from Jade to say she'll be here in five, so we'll wait for you at the bar."

"Sounds good. I'm really hungry."

Filipucci laughed and said, "You're always hungry," before disconnecting.

Bridgette put her smartphone in its car cradle and hit random play on her Spotify collection.

After putting her Mustang in gear and checking for traffic, she pulled a U-turn to head back into the city. Tapping her hand on the steering wheel in time to the beat of *It's My Life*, by the group No Doubt, she relaxed for the first time in weeks as the music filled her car. The call from the hospital earlier about Hellyer had eased weeks of anxiety and seeing Frost getting on with his life was a bonus.

After checking the rearview mirror, she changed lanes and shifted into top gear. Smiling to herself she said, "Bridgette, you deserve a night out."

Next in The Bridgette Cash Mystery Thriller Series

vinci-books.com/out-cold

A secluded cabin. A vengeful killer. Detective Bridgette Cash's ultimate test of survival.

Detective Bridgette Cash's much-needed vacation takes a chilling turn when psychopath Alex Hellyer escapes prison, determined to settle old scores. He has a vengeful obsession and is headed straight for her. Cut off from the world, Bridgette must rely on her wits and training to survive a deadly game of cat and mouse.

Turn the page for a free preview…

Out in the Cold: Chapter One

THURSDAY 2:02 A.M.

Detective Bridgette Cash felt her heart race as the silhouette of the man came into view. She tried adjusting the focus of her binoculars to get a sharper image of the man's face, but the steady stream of misty rain made it impossible for her to recognize any of his facial features.

A voice to her left said, "Do you think that's Anderson?"

Keeping her binoculars steady on the man, she responded, "I'm not sure. He's about the right height and build. But he's got the hood up on his jacket and I can't get a good look at his face."

"He's staying in the shadows and away from street lights. I think it's him."

Bridgette lowered the binoculars and studied the man as he continued his journey. She too, had noticed he was staying close to the buildings, but she was not about to jump to any conclusions.

"He might be just trying to avoid getting wet."

"If he wanted to avoid getting wet, he'd be walking a lot quicker than that."

The voice reached out a hand.

"You mind if I take a look?"

Without taking her eyes off the man, Bridgette handed the binoculars to her partner, Levi Frost.

At just over six foot three, Frost found it hard to stay comfortable for long periods in a car, and shifted in the driver's seat as he raised the binoculars. After attempting to adjust the focus for several seconds he lowered them and growled, "You can't see squat with these."

Bridgette smiled to herself as she glanced at her partner. They had gotten off to a rocky start but eventually found a way to work as a team. Now on their second murder case together, they weren't exactly friends, but they'd worked out each other's strengths and weaknesses and settled into a routine. While she was reserved and considered, Frost was the exact opposite, a trait which caused some within the Vancouver police department to label him as reckless.

She turned back and followed the man's progress as he walked along the inner-suburban street.

Frost rubbed his hand across the interior of the windscreen.

"Bad enough that it's raining but now we're fogging up as well."

Bridgette estimated the man had closed to within about thirty yards of the apartment block.

Parked on the opposite side of the street between two delivery vans, they had a good view of the front of the building without being too conspicuous. She was reasonably confident they wouldn't be spotted as they slumped lower in their seats to follow the man's approach. Bridgette knew they would have their answer soon enough as the man slowed his step to a cautious walk.

Frost remarked, "He's definitely checking out the place. It has to be Anderson."

Bridgette held her breath. If the man stopped in front of the building, there was a high probability Frost was right.

As if reading her mind, Frost said, "It's just after two in the morning. Nobody in their right mind would be out walking around in this unless they had to be."

Bridgette murmured, "I agree," as the man she now believed to be Gerrit Anderson slowed his step and glanced into the dimly lit lobby of the apartment block. Until recently, Anderson had run a successful business importing air compressors for the construction industry. But the relationship with his business partner had soured in recent months when he had accused Anderson of embezzling company funds.

She watched as the man quickened his step again and walked on.

"He's not stopping," said Frost.

"I think he's just being cautious."

Bridgette frowned as the man stopped in the shadows of the next apartment block on Haro Street and pulled out his phone.

Frost asked, "What's he up to?"

"Maybe he's calling the girlfriend. If he doesn't have a pass to the building, she'll need to buzz him in."

The man abruptly turned and started walking back.

"He still on the phone?"

Bridgette nodded. "I think she's going to let him in."

Keeping low in their seats, they watched the man retrace his steps to the front of the apartment block. He paused with his hand on the front-door handle and glanced back up the street to see if he had been followed. Bridgette got her first good look at the man face.

"Bingo," she said. "That's definitely Anderson."

Frost asked, "So, do we call this in?"

Bridgette barely heard the question as she watched Anderson push on the front door and slip inside. She was already thinking ahead. Gerrit Anderson was a prime suspect in the murder of his business partner, John Goldsack, who had been reported missing three weeks earlier. The case had been upgraded to murder when his body had been discovered in a shallow grave in parklands outside the city. Bridgette and Frost were assigned to the case at the beginning of the week. Anderson had been cooperative in his first interview, but had come across as cold and calculating. Their suspicions were further heightened when Anderson went to ground and did not show up for a second interview or return any of their calls. Unlike his business partner, whose accounts had not been touched, Anderson was still withdrawing cash and shifting large sums of money from business to personal accounts.

Afraid that he was getting ready to disappear for good, they had interviewed Anderson's girlfriend in her West End apartment. She swore she hadn't seen him in more than a week but told them little else. After an hour of questioning she finally conceded that her boyfriend's business had some cash flow problems, then she requested a bathroom break. While the woman was in the bathroom, Bridgette noticed two laptops on a side table in the living room. One was a slimline Mac Book in a pink case and the other was a high-end Dell laptop in a black ruggedized case designed for outdoor use. It was the case on the Dell that caught her attention. It was almost identical to the case on Goldsack's laptop that the Vancouver police had seized shortly after they had found his body. Bridgette was suspicious and wondered if the laptop belonged to Anderson.

She quickly powered up the device and while the prompt for a password prevented her from exploring any further, the background picture of Anderson holding up a marlin on a large fishing boat was all she needed to confirm her suspicions.

Bridgette had wondered if Anderson was deliberately hiding it at his girlfriend's place. Rather than getting a search warrant for the girlfriend's apartment, Bridgette had convinced her boss to establish a stakeout team to watch the apartment and a second team to follow her. Two days in, her hunch that Anderson would return had proven right.

Frost repeated his question, "Are we going to call this in?"

"Yes, we…" Bridgette paused and focused on the front of the apartment block. "Can you lower your window, Levi?"

"Why?"

"I think he still in the foyer. It looks like there are two people in back near the stairs, but I can't be sure."

Frost held down a button on the console until his side window was almost fully open.

Now with a clear line of sight to the front of the building, Bridgette focused the binoculars on the shadows and two figures came into view.

"There are definitely two people. It looks like they're just talking."

"The girlfriend?"

"I think so but it's hard to… wait… one of them is going back upstairs."

Bridgette dropped the binoculars. "We need to move now, I think he's going to leave through the back exit."

Out in the Cold: Chapter Two

THURSDAY 2:08 A.M.

Bridgette signaled Frost to head to the right side of the apartment block as she sprinted across the street. With her SIG Sauer pistol drawn, she cursed herself for allowing Anderson a way to escape as she raced down a walkway to the left of the building.

She had discussed the rear entrance to the apartment building with Frost when they had first set up surveillance. The door was always locked and only accessible from the outside by a key. Her boss had offered her an extra team to stake out the rear lane as well, but Bridgette declined. Extra cops increased the risk that Anderson would realize he was walking into a trap and no one wanted to scare him off. Besides, the rear door led directly into the foyer, making it impossible to get to the elevator or stairs without being seen through the building's front windows. Now, as she sprinted down the paved walkway, her decision looked flawed. She hadn't counted on Anderson coming in through the front entrance and then leaving by the back.

Bridgette paused at the rear of the building and looked

into the lane behind the apartment block. The access way was dimly lit and barely wide enough to allow cars to pass. As the light rain continued to fall, she scanned for any sign of Anderson. Her view of the rear entrance was partially blocked by two parked cars and a dumpster. She couldn't see any sign of her quarry, and wondered where Frost was.

Bridgette glanced to her left. The lane opened onto Jervis Street and provided Anderson with multiple directions for escape. But he only had a few seconds' head start on her. The lane was quiet. No telltale sound of footsteps of someone fleeing the scene. She frowned—surely he couldn't have got out that quickly? Was he still here? Hiding close by? And where was Frost? They had arranged for him to come around the right side of the building and he should have been at the other end of the lane by now.

Bridgette looked past the two parked cars and the dumpster and focused on the rear door that led into the building. It was possible Anderson was already out of the lane and escaping down a side street. But it was also possible he was still inside—hiding in a rear corner of the building that couldn't be seen from the front. Using a double-handed grip, Bridgette brought her SIG up into the combat firing position and took two steps forward. She barely noticed the light rain falling as a lump formed in her throat. It was quiet —too quiet. She moved three steps forward and stopped between the two cars. The poor light made it hard for her to distinguish shapes from shadows.

Bridgette sensed movement in the shadows behind her as she turned to check the dumpster. She pivoted in time to see a dark figure rushing forward. The stillness of the night was broken by a low whooshing sound as the man swung a two-by-four length of timber at her.

She had no time to react as the two-by-four struck her

pistol. Bridgette felt the force of the blow jolt through her hands and wrists as her weapon discharged. The subsonic boom shattered the night as it echoed across the lane, drowning out the clattering sound of her SIG as it skidded across the pavement.

Now defenseless, she kept her focus on the two-by-four as Anderson feigned a second swing. Once a junior champion in Taekwondo, Bridgette still took at least one night a week off from CrossFit workouts to practice the martial art. It had been drilled into her that observation was one of her primary defenses. Being able to discern your opponent shifting their weight forward or backward, or from left to right, invariably gave you an advantage as they telegraphed how they were going to attack. But in the lane's gloom it was impossible for her to see the almost indiscernible shifts in Anderson's body weight as he readied himself to strike again.

Bridgette stepped back on her right foot to balance her weight as Anderson moved out of the shadows. He feigned another swing, which Bridgette flinched at but stood her ground. The standoff lasted three seconds before Anderson lost his patience and swung the two-by-four again, this time using a baseball swing. Bridgette was better prepared. She bent her knees and ducked forward in one motion without taking her eyes off her opponent. As the weapon fizzed harmlessly above her head, she knew Anderson was off balance. That fraction of a second it took for him to regain his footing was all she needed.

Pivoting on her right foot, Bridgette turned her hips and swung her left foot around in an arc parallel to the ground. The roundhouse was her favorite kick and a move she had practiced thousands of times and executed regularly in competitions. At five-feet-ten, Bridgette's long legs gave her a reach advantage over many of her female opponents. Although Anderson was close to six feet tall, his forward stumble had placed him well inside her range and she caught him flush on his rib cage. It was not quite a perfect execution, but good enough to see him drop to the ground in agony. Bridgette turned him onto his stomach and, with little sympathy for his discomfort, handcuffed him.

Frost appeared a moment later.

Bridgette looked up and asked, "Where were you?"

"Sorry, I saw somebody take off when I got to the other side of the building so I gave chase—turned about to be some homeless guy."

Feigning disappointment with a shake of her head, she responded, "Some help would've been nice."

Frost repeated his contrite apology before asking, "Where did you find him?"

"He was hiding behind the dumpster," replied Bridgette. As she rose to her feet, she added, "I haven't questioned him yet, but I'm wondering if he spotted us across the road?"

Frost looked down at Anderson, who was still writhing in agony on the ground, and asked, "Does he need to go the hospital?"

"Probably. I think I broke some ribs."

Grab your copy…
vinci-books.com/out-cold

About the Author

Trevor Douglas is a multi-award winning author and the recipient of the gold medal for best crime fiction novel, and the gold medal for the best overall novel in the 2024 Global Book Awards.

Trevor is married with two adult sons and when he is not writing, enjoys bushwalking, watching AFL and discovering the best coffee shops in Brisbane with his wife.

After a long and successful career as an IT consultant, Trevor now writes full time.